THE HEADHUNTER'S DAUGHTER

By Tamar Myers

THE HEADHUNTER'S DAUGHTER
THE WITCH DOCTOR'S WIFE

Den of Antiquity Mysteries
THE GLASS IS ALWAYS GREENER
POISON IVORY
DEATH OF A RUG LORD
THE CANE MUTINY
MONET TALKS
STATUE OF LIMITATIONS
TILES AND TRIBULATIONS
SPLENDOR IN THE GLASS
NIGHTMARE IN SHINING ARMOR
A PENNY URNED
ESTATE OF MIND
BAROQUE AND DESPERATE
SO FAUX, SO GOOD
THE MING AND I
GILT BY ASSOCIATION
LARCENY AND OLD LACE

THE HEADHUNTER'S DAUGHTER

Tamar Myers

WILLIAM MORROW
An Imprint of HarperCollins*Publishers*

THE HEADHUNTER'S DAUGHTER. Copyright © 2011 by Tamar Myers. All rights reserved. Printed in the United States of America. No part of this book may be used or reproduced in any manner whatsoever without written permission except in the case of brief quotations embodied in critical articles and reviews. For information address HarperCollins Publishers, 10 East 53rd Street, New York, NY 10022.

HarperCollins books may be purchased for educational, business, or sales promotional use. For information please write: Special Markets Department, HarperCollins Publishers, 10 East 53rd Street, New York, NY 10022.

FIRST EDITION

Designed by Rhea Braunstein

Library of Congress Cataloging-in-Publication Data

Myers, Tamar.
  The headhunter's daughter : a novel / by Tamar Myers. — 1st ed.
    p. cm.
   ISBN 978-0-06-199764-8 (pbk.)
    1. Congo (Democratic Republic)—Fiction. I. Title.
PS3563.Y475H43   2011
813'.54—dc22
                                                    2010040998

11 12 13 14 15   OV/RRD   10 9 8 7 6 5 4 3 2 1

For Tessa Woodward

NOTES TO THE READER

Unlike in Indo-European languages, the plural forms of words in Bantu languages rely on changing prefixes. Thus the words for the name of a tribe, a single member of the tribe, and the tribe's language, will all have different prefixes, although the suffixes will remain constant.

Baluba—name of Cripple's tribe
Muluba—a member of the Baluba tribe, e.g., Cripple
Tshiluba—the language spoken by the Baluba tribe (Note: "Tshiluba" was the spelling in 1958; it is sometimes spelled "Chiluba" today.)
Bashilele—name of the headhunter's tribe
Mushilele—a member of the Bashilele tribe
Bushilele—the language spoken by the Bashilele tribe

This is a work of fiction and, as such, none of the characters are real people. However, many of the incidents are based on childhood memories. I did, in fact, live amongst the Bashilele people for ten years (from age two to age twelve). Both the elephant scenes and the driver-ant scenes had to be tweaked, but very little, to make them adapt.

THE HEADHUNTER'S
DAUGHTER

ONE

◈

The gravel pits had been haunted for the past six years, ever since the first white woman drowned. During those intervening years the lives of eight other people were claimed by the pits—or else by the ghost of this white woman, one may pick her truth.

For those who believed the latter, it was important to know that the white woman's hungry spirit preyed upon anyone, traveler or hunter—always a stranger—who dared to pass near the pits by themselves, or at the dark edges of the day. The victims were first drowned, and then their bodies were stashed between the roots of the great trees that grew on stilts. When the bodies were soft and ripe, and without eyes, they rose to the surface as the white woman's body had done. At this point a victim's soul, which had lingered near the pit, was transformed into a demon. Such was the truth of those who believed.

The pits had not always been evil; that was only a recent invention. When the white man came, he found clear streams that emptied into the muddy brown Kasai River and the black tannic waters of the Tshikapa River. The streambeds contained gravel that yielded an extraordinarily high percentage of diamonds, some of them even gem grade. Unlike the famous mines in South

Africa where miners had to burrow into the earth, all one had to do here was scoop up the gravel and slough off the waste material.

That is exactly what happened here. The white man scooped great quantities of gravel out of the streams and trucked them just a few kilometers into Belle Vue, but he left behind huge pits, some deeper than a standing man. These pits filled with water, much to the delight of the Europeans, who would bathe in them together, men and women, while still remaining clothed—scantily clothed, to be sure. The nannies and chauffeurs looked away, embarrassed by the sight of a white woman's knees, but at the same time curious, for it was said that the European was not white all over.

After the white woman drowned, the Europeans ceased to hold their picnics along the banks of the many ponds, and the jungle took over. Therefore it was highly unlikely that a much-respected nanny—a *baba*—should visit the largest pit early one August morning in 1945. That's what made it the perfect plan.

Last Born Child had no children of her own, yet surely she had a mother's heart. For nearly two generations she had raised the children of Whites—both Europeans and Americans. As it would have been with her own flesh and blood, not all of them survived their first few years, and often as soon as they were weaned, their real mothers would whisk them off to Belgium. However, there were a few who had returned as adults and had greeted her warmly, and with the respect due a proper mother.

Last Born Child had always put the children first; that fact could not be debated. Now it was time to think of Last Born Child. She carried, wrapped within her headpiece, enough franc notes to buy her own manioc plot back in her home village. The infant in the carriage would be well cared for—of that she had the Mastermind's assurance. Last Born Child trusted Mastermind with her life.

Still, as she pushed the baby carriage past the building where her employer worked, she could not help but feel some moments of extreme anxiety. Were he to spot her, he would run out and perhaps demand to know what she was doing so far from home. Then she would have to lie and say that she had brought the child for a visit.

Nzambi must have been with her, for she was not spotted. Her heart pounding wildly, Last Born Child wheeled the carriage the two kilometers down the hard-packed dirt road in the direction of Luluaburg. When she reached the acacia tree with the L-shaped trunk, she took a right turn down a sandy lane that led just fifty meters farther, to the largest gravel pit. Here the going got tough, and Last Born Child would have been sorely tempted to abandon the carriage, had not her orders been so precise. When at last she got to the clearing, her forehead was glistening with sweat and her breathing was shallow. What's more, there was the urgent need to relieve herself.

Last Born Child regarded her surroundings for the first time. The big gravel pit was really a pond. There were trees growing along the far bank now, as well as some in the water. The morning mist had yet to rise in its entirety, or was that, perhaps, the spirit of the hungry white woman? Last Born Child was well acquainted with the stories of ghosts and demons that were said to haunt this place, but she would have no truck with them, for she was a Christian. Still, it was one thing to only hear of a place, and quite another to see it with one's eyes.

Now the urge to relieve herself was compelling.

"Think clearly," Last Born Child said aloud. "It is the hasty move that results in trouble."

The baby mewed as if in response.

"I am early," Last Born Child said to the baby. "I will hear the approaching truck well in advance. All will go well for us."

Satisfied that she'd solved her problem, Last Born Child backed into some nearby bushes and undid the colorful cloth that wrapped around her thickening waist. But in her haste she did not see the mamba that coiled on an overhanging branch. The deadly poisonous snake struck, attaching itself to Last Born Child's neck just above her left clavicle. Last Born Child jerked, her body becoming momentarily rigid with pain. Within seconds her eyes began to glaze over, even before the serpent detached itself and fell to the jungle floor. The last thoughts that went through Last Born Child's conscious mind were not of the infant in her care, nor were they of her precious Jesus; they were of the *mukishi*—the ghost of the drowned Belgian.

For the ghost of the white woman had come out of the water and taken Last Born Child's hand in hers. Together they walked down to the pond's edge. Last Born Child was not afraid; she was merely curious. There were those who would say that she was even eager to see her new home.

When Born-With-Cord-Around-His-Neck stepped into the clearing to retrieve his arrow, he was but a boy, despite the hair that had recently begun to grow in the damp parts of his body like a tangle of black moss. This was as far as he could come on his mission—too far, actually; his father would not approve were he to find out. Not that he ever would. For who was there to tell on him?

This path along the pits, along the man-made ponds that were off the main road, but yet where there was fairly regular foot traffic, this was the perfect place for Born-With-Cord-Around-His-Neck to perform his task: that of taking a human life—a man's life—so that he himself could become a man. Only then could he return to the tribe as worthy of taking his place on the council.

Of course there were rules one had to follow. In order to prove that he had taken a human life, Born-With-Cord-Around-His-Neck had to return with a part of that man's body, ideally one that could henceforth be worn around his waist as a sign of his manhood. In this case, the boy decided on an ear. When dried it would resemble a fig, nothing more, and should the Belgians raid the village, he might escape a lashing from the infamous hippo-hide whip.

Kah! His people were not cannibals; they would not eat human flesh, no matter how loud their stomachs growled. Leave that to the Bapende people and some of those river tribes up north. However, the skull of the unfortunate individual would forever be the personal property of Born-With-Cord-Around-His-Neck. The skull would have to be cleaned, of course—stripped of all flesh, then boiled—after which as a newly elevated man he would drink his palm wine from it, using it as a mug, as his father had done, and his father before him.

These ponds—dug for the removal of diamonds—were said to be haunted by the spirit of a white woman. A Belgian. Born-With-Cord-Around-His-Neck was not worried about this ghost; around his neck now hung a monkey-skin bag containing a potion especially created to protect him on this quest.

These ponds were a good place for they drew game, and game drew hunters of other tribes. Born-With-Cord-Around-His-Neck was allowed to kill a man only from another tribe; for to kill a man from his own tribe was taboo. Murder.

But the boy was hungry, for he had come a great distance on his quest. In the clearing was a strange beast that, despite having been shot with his finest arrow, did not move. What manner of beast was this, for it appeared not to have a head, and although it had four legs, they were round, and thus totally useless?

Born-With-Cord-Around-His-Neck advanced slowly on the strange animal, his hunting knife drawn from its antelope-hide sheath. Suddenly the beast began to cry out in pain. The boy had been taught by his father never to let any creature suffer. Summoning all the courage available to him, the young hunter leaped in the air, before landing with a startled cry of his own in the sand at the beast's feet.

"*Kah!* There's a child inside! The beast is eating a child."

His words echoed with ominous clarity across the large pond, which was now clear of its fog. But his words returned to mock him, for a fog was lifting in his brain as well. Although he had never in his short life seen such a beast, he did recognize some of its individual parts. What a strange species of animal this was!

Was this part not metal? And here, surely this was metal as well. Ah, and the body of the beast, did it not comprise a substance very much like cloth, only stiffer—like palm-fiber cloth, but of the color known as dark. This, then, was not truly an animal, but a white man's invention.

What, then, about the child? Born-With-Cord-Around-His-Neck had seen many albino infants, and they had appeared similar, but at the same time not so similar. The difference was hard to explain. Of course there was always the possibility that this was not even a child, but a trick devised by the white woman's ghost— or it could be the ghost herself—the possibilities were endless. If it had not been for the fact that the boy's best hand-smelted iron arrowhead seemed to be inextricably embedded in the bunched fabric, where a head might have been positioned, Born-With-Cord-Around-His-Neck would have simply turned on his heels and retraced his steps. As long as he did not mention the incident to anyone, it was the same as if it had never happened.

But then he heard the sound of the truck. It too was something new, although in this case, there was nothing with which his brain could compare the sound to—except perhaps to the rumble of an elephant cow, one whose calf had been threatened. Judging by the sound this enraged elephant was making, it was headed directly this way.

Perhaps it was because he was still just a boy—and not yet a man worthy of his skull—that Born-With-Cord-Around-His-Neck did what he did next without even thinking about it. Or perhaps it was because there had been many other children born after him to the same mother, all of them with their cords wrapped snuggly around their necks, and not one of them surviving. Even now their mother sat grieving, her breasts full of milk and aching. Whatever the reason, the boy—still not a man—scooped up the strangely hued infant and slipped back into the surrounding bushes.

He did not see the body of Last Born Child for she was hidden by other bushes some yards away. And anyway, had he seen her, he would not have stopped. Something inside the youth—perhaps something called destiny—compelled him to run all the way back to his village. It was a journey of many kilometers across savannahs and the occasional riverine forest. It was a journey to a world left behind by modern times.

It was supposed to have been the perfect crime because it followed a foolproof plan. Last Born Child—known to Driver as Baba—was supposed to have delivered the infant to the largest gravel pit at precisely eight o'clock in the morning. Driver knew that Baba already kept a cheap tin clock, manufactured in Japan, in the cubicle in which she lived at the rear of her master's villa. However, just to make sure that she was on time, he purchased a second clock for her.

When Driver first spotted the perambulator parked prominently in the middle of the clearing, he whooped with relief—arguably even joy. But where the hell was that damn woman? And what the Flemish was an arrow doing sticking out of the pushed-back hood? What the hell was that supposed to mean? Because in Africa, *everything* meant something. Driver left the truck idling, with the door open, as he approached the slain buggy cautiously.

The Africans were full of rhetoric these days. Angry stuff about retribution, getting back at the whites for all the misery that they'd caused the natives ever since they'd first set foot in sub-Saharan Africa centuries ago. *Mai oui*, it was true, but Driver was a native as well. He'd been born in Luluaburg, not more than one hundred kilometers away. The only difference was that—oh hell, there were a thousand differences, he'd grant you that. He was white, for starters. But that wasn't his fault. And it certainly wasn't Driver who'd caused the Africans all this misery, which they couldn't let go of; Driver had been far too busy making his fellow whites miserable.

But that was water over the falls, was it not? What mattered now was—

"*Mon Dieu! Mon Dieu!*" Driver's screams rang out across the string of placid ponds, returning to him as distorted echoes courtesy of the forest along the opposing side. His anguished cries enraged a troop of baboons that had been resting in the limbs of a dead ebony tree a football field's length away. The baboons barked like dogs and ran up and down the tree's bare branches as they vied for a better look at their new enemy.

Driver realized that the only smart thing to do now was to get back on the main road and drive south as fast as possible to the neighboring colony of Angola. Once across the border, Driver could look into the possibility of taking a train to the port city of Luanda and ditching the truck. *Oui*, a train! The Portuguese were so much more civilized in the way that they ran their colony; then again, hundreds of thousands of them had actually made their permanent homes in Angola. To them it was not just a game of take, take, take.

As for notifying Mastermind that something had gone wrong with the foolproof plan—now that would be really stupid. Mastermind would find out soon enough, although hopefully not until Driver was safely on a freighter headed for Rio de Janeiro, Brazil. Driver had heard it said that a person could live quite well there—servants, even a gardener—without turning in a decent day's work. Ah, now *that* was a goal worth perusing!

It was not Mastermind's intention that harm should come to the infant, Danielle. Mastermind merely wished to relieve the Consortium of the responsibility of having so many diamonds in their vaults. Ha, you see? One could even joke about it. But all joking aside, it was supposed to have been a foolproof way to redistribute the colony's resources, with a greater goal in mind. Yet somehow it wasn't foolproof. When Driver didn't show up as planned, Mastermind grew very agitated—*very* agitated indeed. Then a runner arrived at the house with a message stating that the O.P.'s little daughter was missing, along with her African governess.

Mastermind had been planning to drive to the gravel pits that same afternoon, but now it was too late. There would be search parties out and one of them was sure to check out the gravel pits. If the child was there, then it would be discovered. At best, the Mastermind's presence would be redundant, and it might well be suspicious. From this point on the most advantageous course for Mastermind would be that of observer, not active participant. Let the Consortium keep their jewels. God help the child.

The boy—and from that point on he must remain a boy until the tribal council declared him otherwise—ran like an antelope that smells the savannah burning at its back. He did not stop to drink, he did not stop to urinate, nor did he stop to rest at any time. Had he stopped, he would not have been able to feel his feet despite the many cuts and bruises he had suffered. When he finally burst into the great compound of his village, he was swallowed by a swarm of curious dogs and children, all of which he left in his wake, so fast did he run.

Mother's special friend, Iron Sliver, recognized the lad first. "Your son has returned! And so soon!"

The boy's mother stood. She'd been pulling apart the fibers of a palm leaflet, using her toes as pegs to keep the threads separate.

"But look," she cried, discarding her work. "He has been successful; he cradles the thing in his arms."

"It is not what you think," Iron Sliver said.

"*Kah,*" Mother said sharply. "Must you always be so negative?"

"Negative? I am not negative," Iron Sliver said angrily. She too had been making thread and this she threw on the ground at Mother's feet. "I think it is a pig's head your son cradles in his arms. Will you be changing his name to Pig Killer?" She stomped off, muttering angrily over her bare shoulder.

Mother braced herself for her son's arrival. He fell on his knees in front of her, panting so hard that she feared he might go into convulsions. In the meantime he managed to lay at her feet a very strange bundle. The pig's head—but it most certainly was nothing of the sort—was wrapped in a white man's cloth. Mother had never seen anything in her life that remotely resembled this strange cloth.

For one thing, it was fuzzy—like the stems of some highly irritating vines, ones that were capable of raising instant welts, should one be so unfortunate as to brush up against them. Another very odd characteristic of this fabric was the color; like a tincture of blood and water. What a thing to marvel at!

"*Aiyee*," Mother said, jumping back from the strange bundle. "What is that? A monkey?"

By then a crowd had gathered, and amidst the laughter there was pushing and shoving amongst the neighbors so that this one or that one might get a better view. Then Father appeared, having walked calmly over from the palaver hut.

"Stand back, everyone," he said. "This is a family matter."

"Yes, maybe," said the chief, who was a neighbor from two huts over as the sun sets. "But as I am your chief, anything that affects this village affects me as well."

"Not everything," Father said. "Remember, Chief, that you are also a slave—and do not even belong to this tribe. You were captured as a boy so that we might present you before the Belgians, should we misbehave in their eyes. If they should say, 'Give us your chief so that we might beat him on account of such and such a crime,' then we can do so, and we will not be hurting one of our own. Yes, you are our chief when it comes to ceremonial purposes as well, but the real power in this tribe belongs to the men of the council who sit in the palaver hut."

There was a chorus of "eh," and the chief, who hung his head in apparent contrition, stumbled off to his hut as the crowd parted to let him through. Mother anxiously tore her eyes away from the bundle before her. Although the chief was indeed a slave, he was not without some power. As a boy the chief had lived in the outside world and observed its ways; who among the villagers could claim the same thing?

"Look," Father said, bringing Mother's attention back to her son and his strange gift. "Now it moves. You can see that it is not a monkey, but the child of a *Bula Matadi*. My son, what have you *done*?"

These words *Bula Matadi* were used all over the Congo to refer to the white man, and literally mean "breaker of rocks," but they were words that struck disbelief, followed by terror, in the hearts of those who heard them. Older people reflexively stepped back. Children began to cry.

Born-With-Cord-Around-His-Neck tried to speak, but after running for so many miles his voice refused to make an appearance. His mouth opened and closed repeatedly, his chest heaved dramatically, but still he remained crouched before his mother on one knee, unable to say a word. Then, while his parents looked on helplessly, the boy's eyes bulged as he clutched the left side of his chest with both hands.

When Mother perceived what was happening, she let out a scream that could be heard as far away as the manioc patch. Custom dictated that when she had caught her breath she should scream again and then commence rolling in the dirt to symbolize the depth of her despair. Instead Mother picked up the bundle and examined its contents closely. The *Bula Matadi*'s baby had not reacted negatively to her keening. To the contrary; the infant was gurgling happily, its tiny fists beating the air with excitement.

Pick me up, it seemed to be saying. *Pick me up, Mother, and put me to your breast, for finally I have come home, and I am hungry.*

TWO

◈

1958

Police captain Pierre Jardin was a man on the verge of falling in love. It was an electrifying, yet terrifying, place to be in. All his senses were heightened; never had he felt this much alive since the death of his parents almost eleven years ago in an automobile accident over in Kikwit. At the same time, his brain—at least that little part of it that wasn't being controlled by his hormones— was warning him that the natural consequence of great heights was the presence of abysmal depths. Then too—more often than not—women expected something called "commitment."

He'd been cogitating on this the night before, when a woman came to see him at his house after dinner. This was highly ir- regular, especially since she came unannounced. Even someone as open-minded as the handsome Pierre Jardin might have been scandalized had it been anyone other than seventy-nine-year-old Dorcas Middleton. Pierre had known Dorcas his entire life. She'd known his parents, and since Pierre had been born in the Belgian Congo, and Dorcas was an "old-timer," the two of them felt a special connection. He even called her Auntie Dorcas, a fact that thrilled her maiden heart to the utmost.

"Auntie, come in," he'd said and kissed her on both cheeks, and then immediately he'd wagged a finger in her face. "It isn't safe for you to be driving alone at night. Please tell me there's a chauffeur waiting outside."

The missionary's eyes twinkled as she spoke. "That very nice woman who runs the guesthouse gave me a lift. She assured me that you would be kind enough to drive me back."

"Hmm," Pierre said, feeling his cheeks flush. "We shall see about that."

"Besides, Pierre, would it be so bad if I had driven? Who's going to harm an old woman like me?"

He took her arm and led her to the chair he'd been sitting in. It was the only comfortable chair he had at the moment. *Merde*, if he was going to have a relationship, he really needed to get on top of things; maybe learn to run a proper household.

"Auntie, would you like some tea?" He knew better than to ask her about spirits. Protestant Americans eschewed anything alcoholic to the point that even their communion "wine" was Grenadine-flavored water.

"I'm fine, dear, and you haven't answered my question."

"Surely you've heard the rumors, Auntie."

"Rumors—yes, well, I thought maybe you might know something more specific, given that law enforcement is your field. As for these rumors: I've heard many of them before over the years. I'm not afraid, Pierre. When it's my time, the Lord will take me."

Pierre smacked his fist into the palm of his hand. "Is that what you will call it when some native—perhaps drunk on *maluvu*— with an authentic gripe against us Belgians decides to take a swipe at you with his machete? A white is a white, you know! No one is going to ask for your passport when the retributions begin."

"Yes, I know," Dorcas said softly. "That's why I'm here."

Pierre fell to one knee and put his arm around the old woman's thin shoulders. Over the years he'd taught the reserved American not to recoil from physical contact.

"What is it, Auntie?"

"Pierre, what I tell you must remain a secret—well, at least as few people as possible should know."

"Of course, Auntie; you have my word."

She took a deep breath. "This year we have some new students in the secondary school from up north. Two of them—a pair of brothers—are Bashilele."

"They are your first Bashilele students?"

"No, we've had some in the past, but they didn't stay long. It was our fault though; we didn't take a strong enough stand on tribal discrimination. But with these two, I think we have a chance. They're living in the student village, and seem to be getting along with everyone. One of them is a pretty fair soccer player. Excuse me—*football* player."

"What's the problem then?" Pierre immediately regretted sounding so impatient.

"Oh, there's no problem with the students. But the younger brother—Born Crouching—I've decided to train as a table boy. He's a personable lad—"

"Excuse me, Auntie, what is this 'personable'?"

"He's pleasant. And very talkative—we talked in Tshiluba, of course, since I scarcely speak a word of Bushilele. Anyway, we were conversing one day—engaged in what we Americans would call 'small talk'—when he casually mentioned that he knew of a white girl living in a village to the west of his. A *white* girl, I asked, or an albino?"

Pierre nodded vigorously. It was a curious fact that there were many albinos amongst the local people, the Baluba, and they were held in high regard. Perhaps the same phenomenon occurred amongst the Bashilele.

"I know what you're thinking," Dorcas said, "but Born Crouching insisted that this girl was white—a European—and that her parents were Bashilele. When I told him that this was impossible, he got huffy—angry—and said that I was calling him a liar. Then he quit his job!"

"That's it?" Pierre cried. "That is all the information you were able to get?"

Dorcas took Pierre's right hand and held it in both of hers. "My dear boy, you are like a son to me."

"And you are like a mother to me, Auntie Dorcas."

"Good. Then you should know that you have taught me better than that; of *course* I was able to get more information. So on second thought, I'll have that cup of tea now. I'll need it to keep my whistle wet while I tell you everything that Born Crouching told me."

The Headhunter's Daughter poked the fire into life with a new piece of wood before continuing on her way to relieve herself. Three of the family's five dogs roused themselves and trotted dutifully along with her. It was always a relief when they did so without having to be prodded. Although none of the five dogs could bark—this feature had not been bred into their kind— they could, and would, growl ferociously if disturbed while sleeping.

Leaving the safety of the hut at night was always risky, and for that reason Mother kept a gourd inside that was emptied and cleaned every morning. Tonight, however, the Headhunter's Daughter needed fresh air and the perspective that gazing up at a star-filled sky was sure to give her. Since basenji dogs were fear- less creatures, and they considered the girl to be a member of their pack, they would protect her to the death from an attack by hyenas or even a leopard.

With her business complete, the Headhunter's Daughter sat on the log bench next to the family's outdoor hearth. Even though her father's sling-back chair was vacant, she had no desire to upset the rightful order of things and try it out for comfort; she wished only to think. And there was so much to think about that it made her head ache. Her stomach churned as well.

This same afternoon an old man by the name of Gizzard had arrived from the neighboring village of Musoko. He'd come unannounced, heading straight to her father's compound. The old man was disgusting to behold: he had no teeth; no hair except for what was on his back; his limbs were spindly and yet his belly was just as round as that of a woman who is about to give birth. The old man reeked of decay, and when he spoke, spittle flew in all directions.

"I have heard that your daughter is approaching marriageable age," he said.

"She has yet to bleed," Father had said, as he motioned to his wife and daughter to go elsewhere.

Mother had scurried off to visit her friend Iron Sliver in the next hut, but Headhunter's Daughter ducked into the family hut to make sure she could hear what was being said. In truth, the voices were so loud that afternoon that the girl couldn't help but think that she was *supposed* to hear what was being said.

"What is it that you offer, friend?" Father had asked, without as much as ordering refreshments for the visitor.

Gizzard was quick to answer. "I have three female goats and a male. True, one of the females is blind and perhaps sterile as well, one is definitely past the age of bearing, but the third goat has only recently borne her fifth kid."

"How recently?"

"Eiyee, so many questions!"

"And yet I must repeat the question: How recently has this third goat given birth?"

"Please friend, do not be angry with me when I tell you that this third goat is the mother of the second."

As horrified as she was by the conversation, it was all the Headhunter's Daughter could do to suppress a laugh. So far she was worth three sterile female goats and one male goat.

"And what about the male goat?" Father said, as if reading her thoughts. "Does he show interest in the act?"

"Oh yes, friend," Gizzard gushed. "All the time. And it is my firm belief that with some training you will be able to get him to show this interest in a *female* goat."

"Go home you son of a jackal," Father said angrily. "You are wasting my time."

"But friend, I have at least ten healthy chickens and a white man's duck. I will confess right now that the duck has only one leg, and thus cannot walk—but it can swim."

"I suppose that it swims only in circles," Father said.

"*Tch*, friend, now you make jokes at a poor man's expense."

There followed a long silence, one so profound that the Headhunter's Daughter could hear the lizards scurrying up and down inside the walls of the palm thatch hut in pursuit of termites. In the distance the laughter of little children at play suddenly made the girl feel sad.

"Do you have any cloth?" Father had finally asked.

"*Cloth?*"

"European cloth—not our palm-fiber cloth. The kind woven with many colors. My wife is very fond of that. Perhaps if you have some cloth we can come to an agreement. But you must find a replacement for the duck. I know in advance that she will accept only two-legged ducks as dowry payment."

"I will find some cloth," the man named Gizzard said.

"Then off with you," Father said rudely.

The Headhunter's Daughter had thrown herself across the sleeping platform as she'd choked back the tears. But when Father entered the hut a short time later in search of her, the girl presented him with a placid face. To do anything other than that was simply not in her ken.

"You heard?" Father asked.

She nodded.

"And you believed this?"

"Father?"

Father's laugh began as a rumble in his belly and worked its way up. But soon he was laughing so hard that he had to hold his chest or it might explode. And suddenly Mother was in the hut as well, along with Iron Sliver, and the two of them were rolling on the floor at Father's feet. The women shrieked with laughter.

"What is so funny?" Headhunter's Daughter demanded. "Why do you act like hyenas when I am to be married to *that*?"

"That," Father said, as he gasped for breath, "is your mother's oldest brother, and he does not truly seek your hand in marriage. Believe me, daughter, I would have insisted upon a better dowry than this."

"Much better," Mother said, finally coming to her senses.

"Perhaps that male goat and my husband could find happiness together," Iron Sliver said.

That brought gales of laughter from everyone, and even Headhunter's Daughter couldn't help but join in the fun. But after that male goat had been paired up with a number of people in the village, and even the duck had found an unlikely mate, it was time to move on.

"Enough," Father said. "This was but a joke, daughter, but the time is coming very soon when I will pick a real husband for you. When that time comes, you must abide by my decision. You must go to live with him. Do you understand?"

"But Father, I do not want a husband; I want to stay here. I am still just a girl."

Iron Sliver was not able to help herself. "You have breasts!"

"*Kah*, they are but little buds," Mother said. "Still, daughter, it is time."

"Go!" Father said. "Both of you. Let my daughter be."

As the Headhunter's Daughter sat on the log bench and thought about her day, a heavy sadness settled over her. No matter how long it took for Father to choose a husband, her childhood was officially over. Now it was a matter of waiting for the day when she would sleep in another man's hut and let him have her as one dog has another. Then along would come pain, babies, death, more pain, and then more babies.

At her feet one of the dogs snarled and looked pointedly toward the bush, as if it had heard some threatening sound. The Headhunter's Daughter knew exactly what the threatening sound was; it was the dread she felt of having to leave the only home she'd ever known. It was coalescing. It was coming together, taking on the shape of a great beast, coming to carry her off to some distant place.

Amanda Brown preferred to take her breakfasts on the east side of the guesthouse. That way she could hear the sounds from the village as it woke up; the laughter of women, the cries of babies, the thud of heavy wooden pestles in heavy wooden mortars, the bleating of glassy-eyed goats, and the latent crowing of cocks—in fact, Congo cocks never knew when to shut up. Amanda especially enjoyed hearing the call of the solitary francolins, a wild fowl-like bird that lived in the strip of savannah that separated the guesthouse from the village. What tasty birds they were too; much better than chicken.

Then, of course, there was the matter of the falls. As dramatic as the west view was, it came with a price. One simply could not have a decent first conversation with all that distraction, not to mention the noise.

But when she stepped out onto the east terrace that Wednesday morning, in October of 1958, the table was utterly bare and there was no sign of the staff.

"Protruding Navel," she called heading toward the kitchen. Immediately she regretted doing so, for her tone had been a little too sharp. Think twice before you say anything, her mother always said, and Mama was a well-bred Southern belle who never misspoke. Mama certainly would never have raised her voice to the help.

Amanda started to the kitchen at a fast clip, but stopped short when, looking through the large window that faced the mighty Kasai River, she saw a scene that nearly made her blood boil. There, on the western terrace, sitting as comfortably as three big cheeses, were the missionaries she'd checked in the night before. Why, the nerve of those people! And what was Protruding Navel about to do? Not serve them coffee!

The young woman, a new missionary of only a few months' standing, ran for the kitchen and the large bell affixed to the back-door frame. She may as well have taken baby steps and stopped to nap along the way; that's how long it took Protruding Navel to respond to the bell's deep metallic clang—a sound that, by the way, could be heard all the way across the river.

"Eh, what is it, *Mamu*?" he asked with studied casualness, as if she'd caught him reading, and he was looking up from a book. Reading! Ha, now that would be the day.

"Protruding Navel, what are the *bakalenge* doing on the west terrace? Is that where we breakfast?"

"Forgive me, *Mamu*, but I do not recall where it is that we breakfast."

Amanda managed a weak smile. "You are skillful at playing word games, Protruding Navel, but that is not what I am paying you for, is it?"

"No, *Mamu*."

"Please set new breakfast things on the east terrace while I speak to the *bakalenge*."

"*Eyo*," Protruding Navel said.

Amanda watched him saunter off as if he had all the time in the world. Well, that was Protruding Navel for you. He didn't like women; he especially didn't care for women issuing him orders, even if they were his employer. But the two of them had an understanding; at least that was a start.

"That houseboy is too cheeky," Mr. Gorman said. When he spoke, his ears moved and his jowls quivered. "If it were up to me, I'd fire him. Allowing that sort of attitude—especially *now*—is just asking for trouble. And it reflects badly on the rest of us missionaries as well. It makes us come across as weak. Just because we're missionaries, that doesn't mean we have to put up with abuse."

"*Harry*," Mrs. Gorman said, "take it easy on this poor thing; she's only just arrived."

"I've been here two months," Amanda said. She'd foolishly made it sound like she was trying to come across as an "old-timer." What a joke. It only felt like she'd lived in the Belgian Congo for most of her life. It was the Gormans who were the real "old-timers." Twenty-one years in May, they'd said. Tomorrow they were going to catch the plane to Leopoldville, the capital city, and from there another plane back to the United States, where they were due a year's furlough. Every five years one was supposed to get a furlough . . .

"Hey, is there any other kind of jam except marmalade?"

"Hay is for horses," Mrs. Gorman said, with a twinkle in her eye, to their fifteen-year-old daughter. "Now ask Aunt Amanda nicely if she has another kind of jam."

That was another thing! *Aunt* Amanda! In the Belgian Congo the children of missionaries had to call every female missionary "Aunt," and every male missionary "Uncle." It didn't matter if the two parties weren't related, or if they were almost the same age.

Amanda turned to the girl. "I'm awfully sorry; I haven't any other kind of jam. It has to come all the way up from South Africa by ship, then up the Congo River by boat, and I was late getting in my order—"

"I told the home office to send someone more experienced," Mr. Gorman said.

"Leave her alone," the woman named Dorcas said gently. Dorcas was an unmarried woman, a self-proclaimed "old maid" who had already served in the Belgian Congo almost fifty years. In a year she would retire. Now she had come to use the rest house for its primary purpose: as a place of rest. Tomorrow she would drive across the river and visit the Belgian town of Belle Vue, where she had many friends, and where there was limited shopping.

"I was only stating a fact," Mr. Gorman said. He turned his head, an act that set a considerable amount of flesh into motion. "Boy! Boy! I want more coffee!"

Amanda rang a small brass bell next to her cup. The overall shape was a Southern belle. It had been a gift from the previous manager of the rest house.

"*Mamu?*" Protruding Navel seemed to appear out of nowhere.

"Protruding Navel, please get *muambi* some more coffee."

"Yes, *Mamu.*"

"Protruding Navel is it?" Mr. Gorman said. "All these years in the Congo and I still can't get over some of the crazy names."

"It's only that *their* names actually mean something," Dorcas Middleton said, her voice still gentle and calm. "It is a shame that in our culture we seem to have lost that feature—of course there are exceptions. Like in your case."

"What do you mean?" Mr. Gorman demanded.

"Your name means something, doesn't it? Oh, it's not spelled the same way, granted, but nonetheless, to the ear it's the same thing."

The teenager giggled. Amanda was tempted to do likewise. *Harry* Gorman was indeed very *hairy*—just not on top of his head. There he had almost nothing at all. But the rest of him was covered in a pelt of red fur that curled over the back of his shirt collar and burst from the *V* at his neck like the *tshisuku* when the rains finally came.

Mrs. Gorman put a freckled hand on her husband's brown hairy arm. "It's not the same, Dorcas," she said quickly.

Harry shook off his wife's restraining hand. "Does the boy speak English?"

"No, sir," Amanda said. "I was told in orientation class that I was not to teach the Africans any English. Any English at all."

"You were told right, young lady. We need a way to talk

amongst ourselves openly. Because it's fellows like this who are going to give us a hard time come independence. I almost envy Dorcas here. She's not going to have to see all her hard work go down the drain."

"Oh come now, Mr. Gorman," his wife said, "don't be such a pessimist."

"What's a pessimus?" the girl asked.

"It's pronounced pessi*mist*," Dorcas said.

Across the river the Operations Manager of the Belle Vue Mine Consortium—or, OP for short—was taking his breakfast alone. It was a damn shame too, given that his was the best view in town, maybe even in all of the Belgian Congo. The house clung to the side of the cliff like a swallow's nest, with one end of the horseshoe-shaped waterfall directly below him. Across the mist and rainbow-filled chasm was another residence with a spectacular view: the Missionary Rest House.

The OP was eating his freshly baked croissants with mango jam—from the company store—and drinking his coffee out on one of his many garden terraces. Of course had it been raining, he would have been eating inside. Rain was always a possibility now that it was October, the suicide month, so named by denizens of the southern tropics because the intense humidity had been known to drive Europeans from temperate climes to take their own lives. Yet the OP was loathe to spend time inside his new home, for it was still decorated in the taste of its former occupant, his blue-blooded Portuguese mistress.

Ah, what a fine woman Senhora Nunez was! She was far too good for the man she'd called husband—that scum-sucking manager he'd hired to run the company store, and who'd mysteriously disappeared along with all the cash at hand. Unfortunately, this had happened at about the time the OP's wife took a nosedive over the falls in a stolen truck, so he hadn't had time to bring closure to the matter.

Wasn't one supposed to wax sentimental about such things? Maybe shed a few tears into the Johnnie Walker Red that flavored his coffee? Well, remind him to do that tomorrow. The two months he'd just spent in Belgium on leave had taken enough of the edge off the pain so that he could still do his job. That's all that really mattered, wasn't it? Because the measure of a man was what he did, and the purpose of living was to do it right.

In this case doing it right meant starting over with new houseboys that were loyal only to him. Too bad there wasn't a school for such a thing nearby. A cold hire from the village was always such a crapshoot, and as for following someone else's recommendation, those were just as reliable as blind dates.

"Monsieur," said his new houseboy, a tall broad-shouldered fellow with the Christian name of Jacques, "there is someone here to see you."

The OP swallowed a particularly full swig of comfort. "A black somebody, or a white somebody?"

"A person, monsieur; a white somebody."

THREE

◈

Cripple was late to work as usual. But now she had a proper excuse, did she not? After all, she was a heroine, a symbol of freedom for her people. At least she had been for one glorious hour.

Independence! They had cried as one voice, though two thousand souls strong. And they had hoisted Cripple's twisted little body to their strong shoulders and carried her aloft as they chanted and danced their way defiantly back across the river to the workers' village. But then once back on their own turf, on the land reserved for them by their Belgian masters, they set Cripple down—not roughly, but not as befits a heroine either—and resumed their old ways.

"Ah, there she is," Amanda said, upon spying Cripple trying to slip into the house unnoticed. "Cripple," she called in the Tshiluba language, "please come here."

Cripple eyed the scene around the breakfast table warily. This morning her young American mistress had company. Cripple was already well acquainted with the equally young Belgian police chief, but she'd only seen the OP from a distance—when viewed from the top of a gallows he'd seemed ever so much smaller.

The other people were American missionaries. You could tell by the way they were dressed. Americans were always dressed as if it were the coldest July morning: they kept their arms and legs covered at all times. Cripple had asked the young *mamu* the reason for this, and was astounded to hear that it had nothing to do with the temperature, but rather with shame. Their God was ashamed of his creation and wished for them to hide it until their death, at which time he would give them a new body.

"And will you have to cover that new body too?" Cripple had asked.

"Of course," *Mamu* had said. "There will most certainly *not* be naked people running about heaven."

"But will not these new bodies be perfect?"

"Yes, of course they will."

"Will the men have baby-making sticks and the women breasts?"

"No! There will be no need for that in heaven!"

"Then *Mamu*, I think your god must be very new at his craft, for then clearly he wishes to hide his mistakes."

"God does not make mistakes, Cripple!"

Cripple had been unable to suppress her laughter. "*Mamu*, you have but to look at me, and say my name, to know that this is not the case."

"Cripple," *Mamu* had said, her unhealthy white skin turning the color of a ripe boil in need of lancing, "this conversation is over."

"Indeed it is, *Mamu*," Cripple had said, "because I have no intention of discussing this matter further. Let it be known, not one word."

At that the young white woman had fumed and stomped away like a petulant child. But now all was forgiven, for as the saying goes: "Everyone makes mistakes, but it is the old women who are able to forgive."

"Cripple! Did you hear me?"

"Yes, *Mamu*," Cripple said. She hurried to stand just to the right, and slightly behind, her mistress. "Forgive me, *Mamu*, but I am old, and sometimes lost in my thoughts."

"Lazy is more like it," the American man muttered to his wife in English. Although Cripple did not understand his words, she felt them.

"This is my housekeeper, Cripple," *Mamu* said to the others around the patio table. "She speaks Bushilele. Don't you, Cripple?"

Cripple thought fast and hard. What had she told *Mamu*? It had always seemed strange to Cripple that the white man regarded words as if they were stones, and their stories like walls that were built with these stones. Did they really believe that this man Jonah was swallowed by a fish? Cripple had never seen a fish as large as this; but the giant forest rat—no, she had never seen one quite so large either, but what did that matter? Was not the point of the story that here was a man who was unhappy because his God had agreed not to punish the man's enemies if they repented?

"Cripple," *Mamu* said gently, "either you speak this language, or you do not."

"No one speaks that language," the American said, this time in Tshiluba, so that Cripple could understand. "It is just a bunch of gibberish if you ask me."

"I speak it," Cripple said. But in truth, Cripple knew only a few phrases of greeting and departure. There had once lived, next door, a beautiful Mushilele girl the same age as Cripple— nine years or so—with long legs and a slender neck, and skin so black that Cripple longed to touch it for the feel of it. When they weren't helping their mothers in the manioc fields, or tending the babies, or sweeping their family compounds, or weaving thatch, they sat in the shade of an old mango tree, side by side, and swatted at flies in companionable silence. Kahinga—for this was the girl's name—was Cripple's only friend.

Then one morning, when Cripple awoke, she discovered that her friend was gone. During the night Kahinga had started to bleed from the secret place, and thus had been taken to the home of her husband. Her *husband*? Yes, Cripple was finally told through an interpreter. Kahinga had been promised in marriage before birth, as was the custom of the Bashilele tribe.

"Good," Captain Jardin, the police chief said. "Then it is settled, *oui*?"

"Excuse me, Captain," Cripple said boldly, for she was not afraid of any white man, most especially the captain, whom she knew to possess a good heart. "What is settled?"

The captain pursed his lips before speaking. He'd been born in the Congo of Belgian parents and spoke Tshiluba fluently, yet he seemed to take extra care in choosing his words.

"Uh—thirteen years ago a white baby—just three weeks of age—uh, disappeared—"

"I remember, Captain. I was living here at the time."

"Yes, yes, of course. You are a local woman. Very good then. At any rate, as you know, the baby was never found and neither has the *baba* been seen since then. However, there was a Mushilele arrow embedded in the—uh—I am sorry; I do not know the word for this."

"It does not matter," the OP said, waving his hands impatiently. His Tshiluba was heavily accented, like that of a newcomer, although it was known by all that he had lived off the Congo for many years. "Proceed with the situation, Captain."

"*Oui*, Monsieur OP. Madame Cripple, it has come to our attention that a white girl is living with the Bashilele of the Tshitumpampa village."

"*Aiyee!*" Cripple pressed her hand to her cheek.

"What is it?" *Mamu* asked.

"*Tshitumpampa* is actually a Tshiluba word," the captain explained matter-of-factly in English. "It translates as 'corpse with the head cut off.'"

"*Mon Dieu!*" said the OP. "*Quell savage!*"

The captain stiffened. "At any rate, Mademoiselle Amanda

and I have decided to investigate the situation. If this girl is indeed white—and not an indigenous albino—there needs to be a resolution. Do you not agree?"

Cripple took an unconscious step backward. "Monsieur OP is right," she said. "The Bashilele are savages, headhunters. If this girl was a white—like you—her head would now be a drinking cup. A very small one, of course."

A sputtered laugh caused Cripple to turn. In the doorway of the kitchen stood Protruding Navel, the head housekeeper. The only tribe he despised more than Cripple's—she was a Muluba, and he a Lulua—was the Belgian tribe.

"Cripple!" *Mamu* said. "That was very insensitive of you."

"Well, I guess that answers our question," Captain Jardin said.

"What question is that?" Cripple said.

"We need an interpreter."

"But I need my head, monsieur."

There it was again; that wicked laugh. This time the arrogant man dared to speak unbidden in the presence of so many white strangers. "Not only is the little one afraid to go, but she does not speak the babble that some have called a language."

"Enough!" *Mamu* snapped angrily, for indeed at times she did lose her temper. "You will go back to your work in the kitchen."

Protruding Navel smirked. "As you say, *Mamu*."

"Wait," Cripple said loudly. Although her voice was authoritative, her knees were shaking. "I will go with you. I will leave with you now, if that is what you wish."

Amanda felt dazed by the morning's events. It had begun with a normal breakfast, albeit one made slightly unpleasant by the presence of Mr. Gorman, missionary in passing. As a Christian, one is supposed to love one's neighbors, but people like Mr. Gorman made it a challenge. At least his wife and daughter weren't so hard to like, and the other woman, the elderly Dorcas—well, she wasn't exactly cuddly like a grandma, but at least she didn't act like a know-it-all.

The Gormans were scheduled to depart the next morning for Leopoldville, but then the police captain dropped by with a bombshell that changed everything. It was one thing for Dorcas to volunteer to stay on at the rest house by herself—after all, she had *planned* to stay that entire week—but it didn't make a lick of sense for the Gorman family to postpone their furlough. Surely that would cost them rebooking fees, and then they would have to cable their loved ones and tell them—tell them *what* exactly? That they had decided to stay on in Africa indefinitely to see if some rumors panned out to be true?

Well, ultimately, that was their business, wasn't it? As Daddy always said: "It takes all kinds to make the world go around." Daddy—how he would love to be along on an exciting outing like this. Scary, yes, but exciting.

"A centime for your thoughts, mademoiselle."

"What?" Amanda said.

"That is close to your saying, no?"

"Yes, but we say *penny*. As to what I'm thinking—look, Pierre, there's not a fence in sight."

The savannahs rolled out on either side of the dirt track they were driving on, uninterrupted by anything man-made. The grass, which had just begun to grow with the new rains, was lime green and ankle high. Here and there flat-topped acacia trees with twisted trunks, their leaves a dark hunter green, punctuated the landscape like buttons on old-fashioned pillow-top sofas. But the sky—how could the same sky that presided over Rock Hill, South Carolina, seem so many times higher and grander here?

Captain Pierre Jardin laughed. "A fence? There is no need for a fence anywhere, because none of this land is private: it all belongs to Belgium. *Oui*, this tribe or that tribe will claim ownership over a certain area, and maybe they will go to war over the land, but a fence proves nothing."

"No cattle?"

"*Non.* We are too close to the equator, and too low in elevation, so we have tsetse flies. They spread sleeping sickness to both humans and cattle. You have heard of this?"

"Yes. But I didn't know that cattle could be affected."

"Ah—look over there; do you see that ant-red hill as tall as a man?"

"Yes. It's very impressive."

"What do you see just behind it?"

"A giant gray rock."

"It is not a rock, Amanda. It is a bull elephant."

"You're kidding."

"I do not joke about such things." Having said that, the devil-may-care captain turned the steering wheel sharply and gunned the engine of his two-ton pickup. Although it seemed to Amanda that the vehicle came perilously close to tipping over, somehow Pierre managed to coax it up over an earthen embankment and onto the grassy plain.

Meanwhile, from the open bed of the truck came the anxious shouts of two African soldiers and the shrieks of one very terrified housekeeper-in-training. Gripping the back of her seat with one hand and the door handle with another, Amanda turned her head far enough to look through the back window. Poor Cripple: the woman's eyes were shut tightly but her mouth opened wide with each scream. Amanda had seen the expression on the faces of kids who never should have been talked into riding the roller coaster.

"Pierre—"

He stopped and turned off the ignition. "Look, your rock moves."

Not only that, but the giant gray rock had transformed into a massive bull elephant with ears the size of barn doors. The great beast appeared to be scrutinizing them intently, all the while rocking back and forth, placing its weight first on one tree-like forelimb, then the other.

"Do you have your Brownie box camera?" Pierre said.

"I can't believe you're asking that," Amanda said. She could barely speak, her throat felt so tight and dry. "Let's get out of here."

He turned off the ignition and leaned out the window to deliver a message to the Africans in the back.

To her credit, Cripple was no longer screaming, but she was whimpering rather loudly. "*Lekele diyoyo,*" Pierre said to her in a tone he would not have dared use to a white person. Cripple gave him a steely look in return but she shut up.

"There is nothing to fear," Pierre said, turning his attention back to Amanda, "until the elephant starts flapping its ears."

And that's exactly what happened next. The great ears began to move slowly at first, like sails on a sunfish boat on Lake Wylie that had been improperly tethered in a summer storm.

"*Merde,*" Pierre said under his breath.

Then all hell broke loose—like Amanda's daddy was fond of saying. The ears flapped with such force that they all but pushed the behemoth forward. The long, flexible trunk rose high in the air as the elephant trumpeted. Its shrill, angry warning cries were so loud that Amanda covered her ears—or was that a silly way of seeking protection? Because if that bull should charge, and if the truck wasn't fast enough—then you could add a new meaning to the phrase "flatter than a pancake."

"*Aiyee!*" Cripple screamed in the back.

FOUR

The African woman had finally opened her eyes and it was her keen vision that detected the forward movement first; the elephant was charging. Pierre reacted swiftly, but perhaps too swiftly. When he stomped on the accelerator he gave the truck too much gas and flooded the engine. He turned the key uselessly, again and again, and in his panic foolishly continued to supply more fuel to the swamped carburetor.

They say that one's life passes before one's eyes at the moment preceding a violent death, but alas, for Amanda, that was not to be. The words of the *"Now I Lay Me Down To Sleep"* prayer were all she could think of as she listened to Pierre grind the starter repeatedly, and felt the earth beneath the truck shake with each step of the lumbering beast.

Then a shot rang out, quickly followed by another. Then a third. Altogether three very distinct cracks of lightning and the earth shook violently one last time as the magnificent bull fell to its knees not more than twenty feet from the stalled vehicle.

The stench was all but intolerable. It smelled of elephant, dung, death, and Amanda's own sweat. Despite the protective cork helmet she wore, the tropical sun drew the perspiration out of her head in salty streams that stung her eyes and trickled into the corners of her mouth. What on earth was she doing on top of an elephant? It was an insane idea, and it certainly wasn't hers.

"Now put your left hand on your hip," Pierre called from the ground. "Like so!" He formed a fist.

Feeling utterly foolish, for her right hand enclosed the barrel of a heavy-gauge gun; Amanda struggled to maintain her balance. Heaven forfend she should lose it and fall flat on the smelly beast. The thick skin was cracked like worn asphalt and surprisingly hairy. Already flies—and not just sweat flies either—had managed to find it.

"Okay, that's enough," Amanda said, and ordered Pierre to help her to the ground. Without missing a beat Pierre nodded to his soldiers. At once they stripped off their uniforms. The rags they wore underneath their khakis did not qualify as underwear in Amanda's book; they certainly did not keep the soldiers' genitals completely covered. For the next couple of hours they labored under the broiling sun as they butchered the elephant with machetes kept on the truck. More than once a testicle popped out in the open between a soldier's legs, and Amanda averted her head politely until its owner noticed.

Although at first it was exciting to watch from a safe distance, soon the smell of blood and gastric gases became overpowering to the point that Amanda retreated to the shade of the lone acacia that had once served as the elephant's refuge from the sun. Cripple hobbled along with her.

"Does the *mamu* enjoy eating elephant meat?" Cripple asked, smacking her lips loudly. She seemed remarkably cheerful, especially in light of the extreme terror she'd been put through earlier.

"I have never eaten it," Amanda said.

"Are there no elephants in *mputu*?" The word *mputu* was a corruption of the word Portugal and nebulous in its meaning: that place out there somewhere, from whence you came. The white man claimed to have come from beyond a lake so vast that one could not see across it; but the fact that Cripple had never formally been to school did not make her ignorant. No such lake could possibly exist, because all that water would pour off the edge of the earth. Here was yet another lie the white man told, and fully expected the Africans to believe because they were ignorant savages.

"We have a few elephants," Amanda said, "but they are all in cages."

Cripple laughed. "But *Mamu*, elephants do not need to be fattened."

"We do not eat them, Cripple."

"Surely you do, *Mamu*. Did you not say that they are kept in cages?"

"Yes, but they are only to look at."

Cripple shook her head. "Forgive me, *Mamu*, but the ways of your people are very strange, are they not?"

"They are not."

Cripple yelped with laughter.

"What is it?" Amanda said crossly. Perhaps they'd have been better off not bringing the woman along as an interpreter, not if she was going to strike this attitude the entire way.

"*Mamu*," Cripple said, "you are very hot with that horrible thing on your head, are you not?"

"It is a hat, Cripple, and yes, I am hot. But we whites were not created like—like you black people. If I were to remove this hat, I would die." That message had been pounded into the student missionaries back in Brussels more than any other excepting one: boil all water a minimum of twenty minutes.

As recently as twenty years earlier one in four missionaries to the Congo died in the Congo. One sure way to topple over dead from sunstroke—or at the very least go as mad as a dog (or an Englishman)—was to go bareheaded. That explained the thick cork helmet. At least the current generation had given up on wearing long woolen underwear as insulation against heat; apparently it had quite the opposite effect, and was rather like deep-frying a turkey.

"*Tch*," Cripple said, by pushing her tongue up against her lower teeth. Although it wasn't exactly a word, still it meant a lot more than any one word in English that Amanda knew, like: "That's dumb, you're crazy, you guys are nuts, what a bunch of ding-dongs you foreigners are." Amanda hated that sound, particularly because it made her feel even more out of place and increased her feelings of loneliness.

"Cripple," she said, taking the high road, "what will become of all this elephant meat?"

The clever little woman rubbed her stomach as she licked the corners of her mouth. "It is my desire that I will feast on some of it tonight, as it was my husband's magic that sent the elephant to us and begged the soldiers that they should shoot it."

"Is that so?" Cripple's husband was a witch doctor and she regularly made preposterous claims pertaining to his powers.

"*Bulelela.*" Truly.

"But even you—with the appetite of a lactating hyena—could not make a dent in so much meat."

"Eh, what you say is true, *Mamu*. But we will no doubt take much of it to those heathen Bashilele as a peace offering, so that they will not eat us—"

"They are *not* cannibals, Cripple."

Cripple grunted. "And some of the meat will surely be given to those poor wretches so that they will allow us to continue on our way unharmed."

"What poor wretches? Where?"

Cripple clapped her hands in astonishment. "*Aiyee! Mamu*, always I forget how poor the white man's eyes are! Yet this is the name we have given you: *Mamu Mesu Mabi*—Mamu Ugly Eyes."

"Cripple, it was *you* who gave me that name, and then others learned it from you. I do not like it, by the way."

"*Mamu*, there are many things we do not like, but cannot change. If we do not learn to accept such things, then we will be like a dog on a rope in the marketplace. We will pull first this way, then that way, never finding a moment of peace."

Amanda averted her gaze while she rolled her eyes. She was not long out of college, and during that time she'd lived with her parents. Then it had been her father's tedious lectures that had gotten under her skin; now it was her assistant housekeeper who gave her unsolicited bits of advice. When was it going to end? Never?

"Cripple," she said, summoning up every scrap of patience she had, "where are these wretches that you mentioned?"

"There, *Mamu*?" Cripple pointed to the horizon at approximately eleven o'clock.

"But Cripple, those are *bilundu*—low anthills. They are the sort that are crushed and used to smooth the roads."

"*Nasha*—those are not anthills; those are people. Look closer, for they move."

Amanda shaded her eyes against the midday glare. Sure enough, either she was hallucinating, or a large number of anthills had managed to line themselves up and were definitely moving their way.

"Where do they come from?" she asked in utter amazement.

"*Mamu*, they are *basenji*—bush people. Perhaps even, they are Bashilele. It is best that you and I remain here by this tree. If need be we can climb to safety."

"Nonsense, Cripple."

"*Aiyee*. I mean no offense, *Mamu*, but if these people are Bashilele, and if the men are indeed in search of new skulls from which to drink their *maluvu*—well, there is no other way to say it; you have an exceptionally large head."

"I do?" Amanda said. She began by patting her cheeks, then her chin, then her pate.

"*Mamu*, I think your skull might hold two liters of this beer—the maluvu."

"Cripple!" Amanda only feigned indignation because she thought Cripple was joking. Or *was* she? Cripple never joked—at least not with her.

"*Mamu*, if it is some consolation, because of its great size your skull will become the property of the headman—the chief."

What do you know? She *was* serious! *Well, take that, Charlene Ferguson, who lived down the street*, Amanda thought. *All those years when we were growing up in Rock Hill, you thought that you were so much better than me—and all because your family owned a boat. You'll probably die a nobody; but I stand a good chance of ending up as a chief's mug.*

"I am deeply honored," Amanda said and then she started to laugh. And laugh. She laughed so hard that her sides hurt. After a while her knees felt weak, and so, still laughing, she squatted. Then exactly how it happened she couldn't remember, but she was actually on the ground—*rolling* on the ground—in the shade of the acacia tree.

"Mamu Ugly Eyes, you must stop this unseemly behavior and get up!"

Amanda laughed even harder.

"*Lekele kuseke, Mamu*," Cripple said. "*Mpindu!*" Now!

There was something compellingly urgent in Cripple's tone that Amanda thought she should probably heed. *But I refuse to be embarrassed*, she thought to herself. She got up slowly, and brushed herself off without making eye contact with the all-too-serious spoilsport.

"Yes, Cripple, what is it?"

"Ants are coming, *Mamu*."

Ants? Amanda thought she recognized the word, but there were many Tshiluba words for ants. This word did not apply to the ants that created the low anthills. Usually there were just two species of ants to be seen roaming about above ground—a miniscule brown ant and the giant stink ant—but curiously, for once the trampled grass around her, and the ground beneath it, appeared devoid of insect life.

"What ants?" Amanda said. "Where?"

Cripple pointed with her chin, but all Amanda could see was a grass-covered hillside and beyond that a shallow vale where a handful of acacia trees kept company in the baking sun. Beyond that the savannah rolled away for miles; it was only just before the sky blended into the horizon that a thin strip of grayish turquoise hinted at a forest.

"Can you not hear them, *Mamu*?"

"Hear the ants? Cripple, do you joke yet again?"

"*Tch*," Cripple said.

Without saying another word, Cripple began hobbling toward the truck. Amanda thought of chasing after her, but instead ran up to Pierre, who stood just out of range of splattering blood, watching his two soldiers butcher the elephant.

"Having fun?" Pierre said, while only half paying attention to Amanda's sudden arrival.

"Cripple said that the *luhumbe* are on their way."

Amanda had Pierre's full attention now. "Are you sure?" he said.

"Cripple insisted that she could hear them."

"Did she say where they were coming from?"

Amanda nodded and pointed.

Pierre grabbed a chunk of elephant hide that was roughly two inches thick and about two feet square. He'd been planning to make a door mat out of it. Normally it would have been a tedious process, but thanks to the driver ants—if indeed that's what they were—the process was about to be greatly shortened.

"Follow me," he said, "but pay attention to where you step, yes? These ants bite so—how do you say—perhaps *firm*, yes? So firm, that when you try to pull them off, the bodies will remove, but the heads will stay tightly in place. Sometimes even the Africans will use them for surgeries."

"Surgeries?"

"*Oui, mademoiselle*. If, for instance, a person has been cut with a machete, then the ants can close up the wound very tight."

"Ah, like stitches!"

"*Oui, oui*, like stitches. But if, on the other hand, someone is sick, and cannot get out of the way, the ants will gapple them up."

"You mean *gobble*?"

"*Oui.*"

Amanda laughed and Pierre couldn't help but feel annoyed. It was a sensitive story; one that still haunted him. A Belgian hausfrau of Flemish heritage was suddenly widowed when her husband, a Consortium employee, died of a heart attack. The young widow worked through her grief by adopting three African orphans who, sadly, she treated more like servants than family members. But, such were the times, were they not?

At any rate, the eldest, a boy, misbehaved. Because the boy was too old to whip, she locked him in the woodshed while she and the two girls made an overnight visit to the provincial capital of Luluaburg. While they were gone, the *luhumbe*—the driver ants— marched through Belle Vue, cutting directly through the widow's property. No one else knew about the orphan in the woodshed. By the next morning when the widow returned, the ants were long gone, but so was every tiny morsel of soft connective tissue of that helpless lad. For when the widow opened the door to release her intransigent son, all she saw was a gleaming white skeleton.

One of Pierre's first official duties had been to arrest the woman on the charge of manslaughter. Public opinion, however—at least amongst the whites—was almost totally on her side. The ant invasion constituted an act of God; how dare he arrest the poor distraught mother? Even the magistrate took pity on her and threw the case out of court.

"Pierre," Amanda said, bringing him back to the present, "That was very rude of me to laugh. I do so apologize. Believe me; your English is a thousand times better than my French."

He feigned surprise. "Who knew that such a beautiful woman

as you could tell a lie?" But it was true; the American spoke passable Tshiluba, but her French accent grated on his ears. The problem was that she simply refused to turn control of her mouth over
to the learning process.

Over the years Pierre had observed many whites attempt to
master a variety of languages upon their arrival in the Congo.
The only ones who succeeded in mastering an accent were those
who gave in to the notion that making a fool of themselves was all
part of the fun. It was only by surrendering their entire mouth to
the process that they were able to capture the native sound they
so desired.

At any rate, it was thanks to Pierre's sharp hearing that he managed to locate the column of driver ants before he and Amanda got
so close that they risked being bitten by scout ants. These patrol
ants strayed well to the side of the advancing column, informing
the main body of danger, if need be. Should the ants encounter
a roadblock, such as a stream, the lead ants would secure themselves to a branch or root on the bank, and then those next in line
would latch on to the lead ants, etc. Eventually, a living bridge
would form. In short, nothing could stop a driver-ant migration.

"Mademoiselle, please observe," Pierre said. He heaved the
bloody section of elephant hide into the middle of the column.

The American gasped, as Pierre knew she would, for immediately the heavy chunk of flesh-covered hide began to move.
Taking care not to encounter any of the scout ants, Pierre squatted
and cleaned his hands by rubbing them with soil. By the time he
stood, the hide had already traveled several meters.

"I will give the *luhumbe* another five minutes to do their job,"
he said. "By then the skin will be clean enough for tanning."

The American nodded, wide-eyed.

FIVE

◈

The people that Cripple had spotted approaching from a distance were Bapende—a tribe whose members filed their teeth to points and wore mud piled in their hair. They claimed to have smelled the blood of the elephant all the way from their village, which was two miles hence. And since the elephant had been killed on their land—or so they claimed—the meat belonged to them.

Pierre was very glad to share some of the meat with them, and of course, to leave them with the carcass, but that was a moot point since the ants had most definitely smelled the elephant kill as well. It was Pierre's men who had been doing all the hard work of butchering who were loathe to part with any of the meat—especially since they were of the Baluba tribe and found the Bapende particularly backward.

"But Captain Jardin," Private Gaspar said, "these people are savages whose ancestors ate humans just a generation ago. Should they not be taught the value of hard work?"

"You are exactly right," Pierre said in French, for he suspected that the Bapende standing before them probably could not speak French. "But we are vastly outnumbered, no?"

"*Oui, Monsieur le Capitain*, but we have guns, whereas these savages have only bows and arrows."

"Again, you are right. But suppose we should get a flat tire one kilometer up the road? Then what? And remember, we must also return this way. Do you want to risk the possibility of an ambush from behind every hill, from out of every gully?"

Private Gaspar shook his head as he muttered something unintelligible. At the same time his eyes, along with the rest of his body language, let it be known that every kilo of elephant meat taken off the truck and transferred to the outstretched wicker baskets held by the half-naked Bapende women was a kilo of meat not destined for a Muluba mouth.

"Tribal politics," said Pierre, still speaking French. "It's the one thing that will keep this country from ever succeeding."

"*Mukelenge Capitain*," Cripple said in *Tshiluba*, for she knew that Pierre was fluent in her language, "I can no longer be expected to ride in the back of this truck."

"Why is that, *Baba*?"

"Because the stink of this elephant meat is overpowering. Besides, there is no place for me to sit except for on top of the meat, and it is still warm with the pulse of life."

"Ah, but my men have spread some heavy mats over the meat. Look, they are quite content to sit up there, for they have a better view, *nasha*? Perhaps they will even spot another elephant."

Cripple felt the vein on her left temple twitch. "*Mukelenge*, I am not one of your men; I am the first wife of a Muluba witch doctor. And I am Cripple, hero to all the Congolese people."

The white man smiled. "Is that so, *Baba*?"

Now Cripple was thoroughly annoyed. "*Eyoa, Bula Matadi*," she said. *Yes, Rock Breaker*. It was meant as an insult, and thus was taken as such.

The young Belgian ignored the fact that Cripple, along with just about everyone else in the Kasai mispronounced the name *Bula Matari*, because their languages lacked an equivalent for the letter R.

"*Baba*," he said, no longer smiling, "some say that the name *Bula Matadi* was given to us because of our character—we are strong like rocks. Others say it is because we force you to break rocks for us with which to build our roads. What is your opinion?"

Anyone who really knew Cripple knew that she needed no time in which to form an opinion. "It is my opinion that you have forgotten that just *makelela*—yesterday—I was carried on the shoulders of men from many different tribes as they demanded our independence. That is why I am a hero."

The Belgian had the temerity to shake his head. "You are not a hero, Cripple; you are a mascot. Nevertheless, you must ride in back."

"Then I will walk."

Both of the soldiers had been listening intently to this shocking exchange of words between the *Bula Matadi* and a simple tribal woman. Now they laughed nervously, as was the custom. Even the white *mamu* made sounds that indicated surprise and dismay.

"Cripple, you cannot mean that," the white *mamu* said. "It is too far to walk home, and you cannot possibly consider continuing on your own to some strange Bashilele village. Not with that big head of yours."

Cripple regarded her employer gravely. "*Mamu*, do you joke?"

"That depends."

"It is best not to," Cripple said.

"Then I do not joke now," the white *mamu* said. "But I am telling you that walking is out of the question."

As fond as Cripple was of the young American, she could not tolerate being told what she could, or could not, do. "*Mamu*, I am not a child, or a possession," she said. "If I wish to walk, then I will."

"But Cripple," the white *mamu* said, "it will be dark before you get home. It is possible that you will encounter leopards, snakes, maybe even lions—right here in the road." The white *mamu* turned to the Belgian. "Is this not true, *Bula Matadi*?"

The captain laughed. "Not you too, mademoiselle. Although you are quite correct about the animals. Did you mention hyenas?"

"*Aiyee*," Cripple said. "I am especially afraid of hyenas, for they are said to tear one apart piece by piece, and make of one a living death—but yet I prefer to walk."

"You see? She is indeed a hero," Private Gaspar said. There was not a shred of mockery in his voice.

"*Eyo*," his companion said. "She makes me proud to be a Muluba."

"What nonsense," the white *mamu* said. "Captain, why is it that Cripple cannot sit in front, when there is yet room? Look at her. She is no larger than a scrawny Lulua chicken."

Cripple clapped her hands with delight. Now this was the *mamu* that she admired. The captain, however, was not at all pleased with the course that the conversation had taken. One could see it in his face, even if he did not shout as Cripple had hoped he would.

That was the trouble with whites; they were so unpredictable. Just when you were hoping for some good entertainment, they sucked their emotions back in like turtles withdrawing their heads.

"Mademoiselle," Captain Jardin said, "this is quite enough. Apparently you have still not been in the Congo long enough to know the way things are."

"Oh," Amanda said, "I am quite familiar with the way things are, Captain Jardin; they are that way in America as well. But who is to say that they must stay that way?"

Cripple held her breath. Never had she heard such shocking words, and that they should be spoken by a woman, no less! Now that alone was worth the stench of the elephant meat—well, at least from this distance. Surely the captain would lose his temper now!

The captain turned *kunzubile*—which is the color of a baby's gums. "This is not America," he said, but still he did not raise his voice. "We whites are vastly outnumbered here. If I give in and put one African up front in the cab, then another will demand to ride up here, and then another, and then where will it stop?"

Amanda put her hands on her hips, a hostile gesture in Cripple's eyes. "You can explain to them, Captain, that it was a one-time special occasion. You were carrying a load of elephant meat and had a woman passenger with no place else to sit."

It was then that the captain raised his voice. Alas, he switched to another language—possibly the one called English, as Cripple was no longer able to understand him.

Had the nosy, but very clever, Muluba woman been able to understand the conversation, she would have heard the following: "You are ignorant of Congo customs, Mademoiselle Amanda Brown. Here, it is not the women who get special treatment, but the highest-ranking men. Congolese women must make do the best that they can with the scraps of life. If I were to put your assistant housekeeper up front with me and leave both of my soldiers in back, I would risk the possibility of a mutiny."

"Are you *sure*?"

"Amanda, I have lived among these people my entire life—with the exception of my university years, which were spent in Brussels. Please believe me when I tell you that I know these people."

More is the pity that the heroine of her people did not understand this very rational explanation. At least she had made her point, but in the end she really was deathly afraid of hyenas, so she sat in the back of the truck, atop the still warm elephant flesh with its rank smell. The hatred that brewed in her heart was toward some amorphous Belgian who had made the rules many years ago, and not toward Captain Jardin, who deep down she knew to be a good and honorable man.

* * *

It was Iron Sliver who first relayed the terrifying news: *Bula Matadi* were coming with soldiers. Never in the memory-story of any living person had a white man set foot in the village. And not only that, Iron Sliver said, but one of the white men appeared as if he might also be a woman—although that detail had yet to be confirmed. Oh, and they were bringing with them elephant meat.

"Where shall we hide?" asked Mother. "Shall we hide in shadows of the forest by the spring, or submerge ourselves in the swamp where the *shindwah* plants grow?"

"I will not hide," Iron Sliver said. "I am no longer such a young woman; my cycles have dried up and my breasts hang down to my waist cord, yet I have never seen a white man. Although I have heard that they are hideous to look upon, I think that it would be very foolish of me to pass up this opportunity."

"*Tch*, watch what you say, Iron Sliver, for you have indeed seen a white person!"

"Friend, now you waste your own time with this bit of foolishness; you know that I have never been away from this unfortunate village."

"Iron Sliver, have you forgotten that Headhunter's Daughter is a white?"

Iron Sliver froze for a second. Then her eyes widened.

"You are sure of this?"

"It has been confirmed."

"*Aiyee!*"

The two women had been standing in the open, just outside the Headhunter's hut. It should not have surprised either of them then when the Headhunter, who was inside the hut taking his afternoon nap, stepped outside to join them. Nonetheless the women were startled, and they shrieked; predictably, Iron Sliver was the louder of the two. The Headhunter quickly put an end to her theatrics and asked her to repeat what she'd said about some approaching *Bula Matadi*.

Iron Sliver told him everything she knew, which is what she had heard from the arrowsmith's wife, who had learned it from her husband, whose job it was this day to keep watch on the trail. Unfortunately, the arrowsmith had, as of late, been plagued with hemorrhoids. When he went to relieve himself he became the victim of a particularly painful and uncooperative bowl movement, and thus was absent from his post for far longer than he might otherwise have been. But when he spotted the approaching party of foreigners, he did his best to run all the way back.

The Headhunter reached for his bow. "Why has the alarm not been sounded?" he demanded. "And where is our daughter?"

"As you know, all the able-bodied men except for you and the arrowsmith have gone on a hunting trip—now that the grass is short—"

"Shut up, Iron Sliver! Please. Again, Wife, I ask you, where is the girl?"

"They are braiding hair, Husband, in the hut of Broken Jaw. We shall all run into the forest if that is your wish."

What was his wish? With the chief gone, it was the Headhunter's job to make decisions for the village, for he was the elder brother of the chief's senior wife. Over the years many problems had presented themselves in the chief's absence, but never anything as unsettling as this. At the same time, what at first appeared to be a problem could well be a gift from his son in the spirit world, could it not?

With his dying breath Born-With-Cord-Around-His-Neck had brought them a *Bula Matadi* infant. At first there had been much fear in the village, and rightly so, that there would be reprisals for this incomprehensible act. But when none came, and the child flourished, it was easy to pretend—if not believe—that she was a gift from the spirit world. The Headhunter's Daughter—her name was really Ugly Eyes, for they were disgustingly pale—was liked by everyone. Likewise, she astounded everyone in that she was able to learn their difficult tongue—something the neighboring tribes said that they could not.

But as much as the girl acted as a proper Mushilele, and for all the talk of marrying her off for a nice fat dowry, sadly the Headhunter realized that his daughter's path was not going to be an easy one. The call of the blood was not something that could be overcome with incantations and charms.

One could cull eggs from a wild guinea fowl's nest and set them under a hen. The hen would raise the chicks as her own and all would be well until a flock of wild guinea approached too near the village crying "*ca-ca-ca-ca-ca*" and in that moment their brethren, though raised like chickens, would abandon their mother for the forest. The same thing could also be said of slaves— including the chief—who could never truly be trusted to act entirely on their own.

Perhaps it was thus for the young of a *Bula Matadi*. How could it not be so? Sadly, the Headhunter recalled how visiting Bashilele sometimes reacted when encountering Ugly Eyes for the first time. Old women often screamed and reared back, as if they sought to protect themselves from devils, and little children usually screamed and soiled themselves. The worst reactions came from people of intermediate ages, for their response was laughter, and crude comments, which cut Ugly Eyes to the core.

Now after all these years, the sudden appearance of *Bula Matadi*, just before the age of bleeding—well, surely it was proof that Ugly Eyes' time amongst the Bashilele had come to an end. For there was no such thing as a coincidence in Bashilele culture; in fact, the word did not even exist. The Headhunter had heard of this strange concept from another Mushilele who had been to the outside world and had heard about it from a missionary. Apparently, the whites ascribed many things they could not explain to this category rather than try to understand them. It never failed to amaze the Headhunter how such a primitive and ignorant people had managed to subjugate his own.

"Husband," Wife said again, but with a great deal of urgency this time, for she could hear the keening as the visitors reached the outer tier of huts, "what is your wish?"

"We wait here and do nothing. But you, Iron Sliver, will run to the hut of Broken Jaw and fetch my daughter."

Amanda realized that she was experiencing a rare privilege. According to Dorcas's students this was the first time that white people had ever stepped foot in this particular Bashilele village. *Ever*. It was hard to say what impressed her the most.

First, there was the fact that the village was laid out in the shape of a spiral, which radiated out from a pair of trees known as the Trees of Life. These sacred trees had been planted over two skulls—one taken from a man, one from a woman—both harvested from a tribe other than the Bashilele. Their trunks were smooth like that of crape myrtle, and their oval leaves were the color of cooked spinach and roughly the size of a tablespoon. In the branches of the trees lived the spirits that protected the village.

The huts closest to the center were occupied by the chief and his wives—in this case thirteen wives—each with her own hut; then the witch doctor, and senior council members such as the Headhunter; and then so on, until the occupants of the very outer ring might be slaves, or recent arrivals from other Bashilele villages.

All the huts were rectangular, with exactly four walls, and each had a door but no windows. The door was set about a foot above the hard-packed ground as protection against snakes. The roofs were all pitched A-frames. The materials used on both walls and roofs were woven mats tied to pole frames. The mats were woven from the fibers of the raffia palm (*Raphia hookeri*) which grows in the swamps and along the streams that wind among the grassy hills of Bashilele country.

Although the men of hunting age were absent that afternoon,

there were perhaps a hundred women in residence, and maybe four times that many children, and a score of elderly men; and as the small party progressed around the very clean, coiling street, doors slammed, and people either shrieked in fear or hurled angry insults at the passing demons. But not *everyone*.

There were a few sophisticates—folks who had been to the outside: a young blind man who mysteriously spoke three English words, "Call me Charles"; the occasional crone with the gift of second sight; and groups of young boys who, although terrified, refused to act in any way but foolishly brave. The last took turns pushing one another at the foursome, and then squealing in genuine terror while their comrades laughed nervously. It was a boys' game that Amanda recognized as something that could be played in any culture, and in any country, around the world.

"*Waddabushekke*," she said.

The boys fell back, apparently stunned by that one word of greeting in their tongue. But an old crone dressed only in a filthy loincloth of woven palm fibers, and whose shrunken dugs hung flat on her chest, took Amanda's soft hand in hers.

"*Eh, waddabunne.*"

Amanda smiled at the woman, who smiled back. As with every Mushilele individual beyond the age of weaning, she was missing her two front teeth. This was a sign of tribal membership; one which "civilized" Bashilele often came to regret. Already Amanda had heard stories of young Bashilele men who, upon deciding to make their way in the city, had first fashioned for themselves false teeth out of wood. One truly innovative youth with a high tolerance for pain had managed to cut a pair of metal front teeth from the side of a tin can.

The old woman's rough fingers felt like dahlia tubers, and she smelled strongly—perhaps of wood smoke, if one were to put it kindly, but Amanda thrilled at her touch. *Here* was the real Africa. This was what she had come to experience—not the judgmental pronouncements of the corpulent Mr. Gorman, or the relative luxuries of the Missionary Rest House. Only this could redeem her—yes, yes, she knew that only the blood of Jesus Christ could redeem her, but that's not what she meant. Or was it? No one else she knew was guilty of taking eleven innocent lives; *no one*. And until they were—well, let them preach all they wanted then. Funny, but the Bashilele, they were sort of like her, weren't they?

"Amanda? Are you all right?"

"What, Pierre?" If she sounded annoyed, that's because she was. A little.

"You seem a bit—um, stunned."

"Yes, it is somewhat of a culture shock."

"*Oui*, but it is a shock for them as well. A good one, I think. You have attracted quite a follow-group, yes?" As usual, his English was charmingly accented, if not quite perfect.

The young woman glanced over her shoulder and was taken aback by what she saw. "The word is follow*ing*, Pierre."

At any rate, there were perhaps fifty children, women of various ages, old men and infirm, trailing behind her as if she were the pied piper. They'd even been joined by a couple of the beautiful indigenous dogs called basenjis that, like wolves, are incapable of barking, and which have short sleek coats and tails as tightly coiled as cinnamon buns. As for Cripple and the soldiers, they seemed to have dropped out of sight.

"Just think, Amanda, you are more popular even than elephant meat! How many women back in your American city can say that?"

She laughed, which for some reason prompted the old crone to laugh as well. "None, I guess," Amanda said, "except for Lilibet Vass, who was the most popular girl in the entire high school."

"No," Pierre said, "I do not believe that."

They rounded the end of a great coil of huts and found themselves facing the pair of trees with the smooth bark and dark ovoid leaves.

"The famous Trees of Life," Pierre said. "Be careful not to touch them, so that you do not accidentally break any branches off."

"Good idea. Pierre, look. It's the girl!"

"*Mon dieu!* She *is* a *blanc*—like you!"

Amanda couldn't help but stare; it was the strangest sight she had ever seen.

SIX

Mastermind took a deep breath before proceeding. All would be well. It was all downhill from here. Still, if only there had been a sign—even just one—during those thirteen long years of silence. Well, never mind. What mattered now was the ending, and by the looks of things, that was surely under control. The trick to keeping it that way was to appear calm, unfazed by whatever happened next.

Ugly Eyes felt her knees go weak and she felt the urge to fall on the ground. The sight she beheld was a nightmare, yet she remained awake and could feel her heart pound and her mouth go dry. Everything she'd been told about the *Bula Matadi* was true—and even more so. They were hideous beyond belief—particularly the one she supposed was the female. Her skin was white like the underbelly of a frog, and her hair was not the color that hair should be, and it grew like long algae that clung to the downstream side of rocks in the stream. Both the whites wore strange clothes of many descriptions, which surely explained the sweat that gleamed on their brows and the strong goat odor that accompanied them.

No! Was that elephant meat? For a minute Ugly Eyes forgot her panic in the anticipation of a feast. And yes, there was meat, and two African men from a strange tribe and a crippled woman, also African, who talked too much, but then there remained the matter of the *Bula Matadi*, for now they sought to speak to Father—although it was soon clear that Father did not speak their difficult language.

"Is there no one here who can speak this gibberish?" Father demanded in an angry voice. It was fear that made him peevish; this much Ugly Eyes understood.

No one answered.

"Bring me the blind man," Father ordered. And when he was brought, quivering, Father ordered him, saying, "You, Blinded by Spitting Cobra, you claim to know seven tongues. Ask these Belgians what it is they want."

"Call me Charles," Blinded by Spitting Cobra said.

"Heddo, Charles," the woman said, or something that sounded like that.

"What did she say?" Father demanded.

"That first we must feast on all this meat, only then she will tell us what she wants."

Father was furious, for he was not a fool. "Will you drink from the poison cup to swear that your words are true?"

"*Aiyee*, you are not to trust a blind man," cried Blinded by Spitting Cobra, and he slunk away. "Ugly Eyes," Father said gently, "go in the hut and gather your things, for we are going on a trip."

"A trip, Father?"

"Remember to get your favorite hair pick, your spare loincloth, and your toe loom. You may put them in your mother's egg bag; I will make for her another."

"Where are we going, Father?"

"We are going to visit the *Bula Matadi*'s land, to see if there is good hunting in that distant place."

"Can Mother accompany us?"

"Ugly Eyes, surely you jest. Who would there be to inform the chief of our whereabouts? I am, after all, his right-hand man."

"Yes, Father," the girl said with mounting dread, "I was only joking."

Cripple knew exactly why she'd been summoned to the front of the line. But since she'd flat-out lied, there was nothing she could say in her own defense. She may as well just confess—

"*Aiyee! Mamu*, this is most horrible!"

"This is a girl, Cripple."

"But *Mamu*, she is naked above the waist. And she has breasts!"

"So does every other woman in this village, Cripple," the white woman said, with unnecessary irritability.

"Yes, but *Mamu*, these breasts are white, so it is like they are *really* naked—*mene, mene.*"

Her employer sighed. "You have a point. What do you suggest we do?"

"We must insist that she covers them up, *Mamu.*"

The young woman from America sighed again. "But in order to do that, first we must make her feel shame."

"You are correct, *Mamu*. Fortunately, you are a missionary, and causing one to feel shame is precisely your job, is it not?"

Cripple was pleased that the young Belgian police captain, Pierre Jardin, seemed amused by her observation. She knew that the Catholic tribe of Christians was at war with the Protestant tribe, each proclaiming the other to be false and on the road bound for a destination they called *ngena*—which wasn't originally even a Tshiluba word. This place was supposedly a lake, yet at the same time nothing but flames of fire into which the enemies of their god were burned alive, screaming in agony for all eternity.

The young American, however, was not amused. "Cripple, are you trying to make a point again? I already know that you reject God; all I want you to do now is to translate for me."

"Yes, *Mamu*, but I am afraid that is impossible."

"No, it is quite possible. Now do it—*please*. Tell this girl that I am happy to meet her, and ask her what her name is."

"Yes, *Mamu*." Cripple turned to the girl. "The white woman with the large feet and wide hips is happy to meet you, and would like to know what your name is."

"*Unh?*" the girl said, turning to her father.

"Cripple!" the *mamu* practically screamed. "You were supposed to ask that in *her* language, not in *Tshiluba*. *I* could have asked it in *Tshiluba*."

"Then perhaps you should have, *Mamu*, because I do not speak this primitive bush tongue."

"*Mon Dieu*," the captain roared, "then you lied to us! You claimed that you could speak Bushilele. You said that you learned it while playing with a girl who lived next to you in the workers' village when you were growing up."

"But *Monsieur le Capitain*, I am just a heathen, the wife of a witch doctor. Surely you do not believe the words I speak."

"I most certainly will not in the future," the captain said. "*Mene, mene*."

"Stop that," the American girl said. "The question is, *Now* what do we do?"

Cripple looked for the sun, which she knew would be already low in the sky. When it dropped quickly to its bed behind the horizon, the spirits of the Bashilele ancestors would rise from their graves (surely there was a cemetery somewhere near a village this size) and then her life might be at stake. This was especially the case since she had mocked these people.

"*Bakalenge*," she said, "my lords, perhaps we should drop our most gracious gift of elephant meat at the feet of these most hideous excuses for children of women I have ever seen, for truly they offend my eyes. Then while they scramble about like dogs, we should run for our lives, each giving no thought for the other."

The soldiers laughed, causing Cripple to grin.

"Very well, Cripple," the captain said, "but then you will be left behind."

Cripple raised her head high and threw back her shoulders just so, which emphasized her twisted body to perfection. "*Eyo*, but then at least the *mamu* will have her justice. As for me, I do not mind dying; have I not proved that once before?"

The captain nodded gravely. "Indeed you have. And yes, we are very grateful for that. Are we not, Mademoiselle Brown?"

"*Eyo*, we are, but—"

"So we will do exactly as you have suggested. *Men*," he said, addressing his awful laughing soldiers, "have you been listening to our words?"

"Yes, lord," they said, and nearly dropped the sling which held the precious hunks of delicious protein.

Standing at two meters the Headhunter was of average height. He was also of average strength and intelligence and possessed no special gifts of which he was aware—except for one: the Headhunter was a sentient, a *mumanyi*. Although the Headhunter had long ago found that being so tuned in to the moods of the universe that one could know the future was both advantageous and a curse. True, it was his special ability that had enabled him to rise to a position of power in the village, but the Headhunter was also keenly aware that a slip of the tongue could result in his slit throat. No one liked bad news for themselves, no matter how true it was.

So it was that the longer the Headhunter beheld the strange quartet, the clearer his understanding of the situation became. Indeed, his son had sent from the spirit world a solution to the problem of Ugly Eyes' evolving womanhood. In addition, and perhaps to make up for having caused his mother so much unhappiness, Born-With-Cord-Around-His-Neck had sent along a female slave. But as always his son tended to be rash in his actions and had not carefully examined his choice of female slaves. This one was not only crippled, but she had the temper of a setting hen. She certainly would be more trouble than she was worth. It was much better to give her to the *Bula Matadi* and let her drive them crazy. No doubt such a gift would help hasten the day of independence.

The Headhunter waved his arms at Cripple. "You! We do not want you. Go back with the white man, little one."

Next he motioned for the soldiers to come and deposit the meat at his hearth. As he did so he kicked back a dog with the side of his foot. "You, white man's lackeys, bring the elephant meat here. I hope it has been butchered properly, for my wives will be in charge of its distribution, and cutting through any elephant skin will be impossible for them."

Only then did the Headhunter turn to address Ugly Eyes' mother. "Morning Light, you must abide by the knowledge that has come to reside within me. If you do not accept it, you will meet only unhappiness on your journey."

Morning Light immediately sat in the dirt in the doorway of her hut and began to scoop loose sand into fistfuls which she dribbled into her hair as a sign of mourning, for she knew what was to follow. Morning Light was not *mumanyi*, but she did know her husband very well, for she had been his wife for twenty-four years.

"*E*, Husband," she moaned, "I will meet acceptance of my journey."

"Good. Then it is with a heavy heart that I tell you that our daughter, Ugly Eyes, must go on her own journey, back to the world of the *Bula Matadi*. I have decided to accompany her. Once she is safely there, and settled in, I will return."

"Is this a punishment, Husband?"

"No, Wife; this is a gift from your son. This is a solution to a very large problem that we were about to face, but which we did not want to acknowledge."

Meanwhile, Ugly Eyes, who had obediently retrieved her scant belongings from the hut, stood outside at a respectable distance from everyone personally involved and said nothing. Curiously, for the first time her sky-blue eyes seemed more striking than ugly.

Suddenly, much to the Headhunter's great surprise, Morning Light was on her feet, shaking her head. "Give me your machete, Husband, so that I might divide the meat properly. In exchange you may take my manioc knife to keep you safe from these most unattractive foreigners and the traitorous gorillas who serve as their henchmen. Also, remember to take your bow and arrows. Do you wish me to get some poison from the witch doctor's hut?"

Iron Sliver and a few of the other women standing close enough to hear these words gasped before dissolving into giggles. Even the Headhunter smiled.

"You are a good wife," he said. "I could not ask for better."

Theirs was a culture that lacked a word for love in the romantic sense, but Husband had surely spoken words of affection—had he not? Similarly, Husband felt deep affection for the girl he had come to think of as his daughter—as if she were his very own flesh and blood.

Had Husband's ensuing thoughts been turned into words that all could read and understand, they would have been written as follows: *I knew that this day would come, and thus I have prepared for it for a long time. I will accompany my daughter into the strange world of the* Bula Matadi, *and I will protect her with my life.*

Only once have I been farther than the village of Musoko, *and that was when I was on my sacred journey to collect my drinking skull. I ventured then as far as a stream in the direction of the setting sun—a stream that sparkles with diamonds. I collected my skull from a* Mupende *hunter, so that having encountered no* Bula Matadi *on that trip, my knowledge of them, until today, has only been hearsay.*

Most, but not everything I have heard has been bad, and since you are everything good, daughter, there must also be good Bula Matadi *somewhere as well. Together we will seek and find these good people. I will not rest until I have safely delivered you into their hands, for this is the promise I made to my son that day when he brought you to us as a swaddling child.*

So I will go with you, Ugly Eyes, even as far as the earth begins to bend, and if I find suitable material for a torch, I will follow you to the place where the sun disappears each night. Know this above all else: there is no need to be afraid.

SEVEN

◈

The girl was torn between fear and excitement, exhilaration and pain. The white man's *didiba* was woven of cotton and softer than the one Mother wove from palm fibers, but still it chafed against her nipples. Before they'd walked ten paces from the village, there had been an argument between the two *Bula Matadi* about her wearing it. Of course she couldn't understand the words they spoke, but when the anger reached its peak, the female removed part of her own *didiba*—she wore two, one on top of the other— and tied it around Ugly Eyes' chest.

It was an utterly humiliating experience. Never before had Ugly Eyes felt so violated. And now wearing the disgusting garment that drew attention to her breasts made her feel dirty—like she imagined the two village harlots must feel. But they had once been *Batshioke* slaves from down around Kajijji way, not the free-born daughter of a *Mushelele*.

There had been so many feelings to process at once that Ugly Eyes could scarcely remember saying good-bye to Mother, who now lay prostrate in the dirt outside their hut, keening. Iron Sliver, always a good friend, had joined in the keening, as had a number of other women. Still, there were many women who did not know Mother well, and now these women and their children had become emboldened and had formed a rear flank that even harsh words from the soldiers could not dispel—although there were harsh words from the villagers as well.

"*Mutoka!*" *White*. It was on the lips of many, and Ugly Eyes knew that the hurtful word was not aimed at the visitors, but that it was being hurled at her like a fist-size stone.

"Pay no attention," Father muttered. He walked in front of Ugly Eyes, for that was the custom.

"She was a demon who brought bad luck to our village!" Dances Badly was a bitter woman who never had a kind word to say about anyone, and who seemed to be satisfied only by stirring up trouble.

"I should like to kill that woman," Father said, "and give her silly head to the baboon troop that lives in the ravine where the two streams come together. They could use her head for sport. What do you think, Ugly Eyes?"

She attempted a laugh, which came out as a snort that only succeeded in producing unwanted mucus. Oh well, at least the evil cover-up was good for something.

"Father," she said when she was through cleaning herself, "what is to become of me?"

"I do not know, daughter. But no one will harm you; I promise you that."

"Father?"

"Yes, daughter."

"Do you suppose that we will have to enter the belly of the metal elephant? The one with no trunk?"

"It is possible," he said, without a second's pause. "But never, Ugly Eyes, have I heard of a person not surviving such an experience. Although it is said that members of our tribe are particularly afraid of the metal elephant, lacking experience with it as they do. Therefore, some of the old women have given in to fits of screaming. If it is possible, my daughter, do not give in to the temptation, for then you will appear weak in the eyes of the *Bula Matadi*."

"Yes, my father."

Although they walked in silence for a moment, the taunts around them increased. Even the dogs, which knew better than to display any sort of aggression to a villager lest they end up in a cooking pot, were suddenly emboldened and darted in and out of the burgeoning crowd, nipping at the girl's ankles.

"Have you been inside this beast?" she asked her father by and by.

"No, Ugly Eyes."

"Then you must remain strong as well."

"Amanda," Pierre said, "from now on, we must speak only in French."

"*Porquoi?*" Amanda was startled by the dictate.

"Because the poor girl must learn to speak a European language, and as fast as possible if she is to assimilate well."

"You are sure she is Belgian?"

"What are the odds she is anything else? We Belgians by far outnumber any other white community in the Congo. But tell me, Amanda, you were perhaps hoping that she was American?"

"Pierre! I was hoping no such thing! Okay, so maybe just a little."

"But don't worry, Amanda; you speak French very well, and your accent is not so, so terrible. In addition, you always seem to have an extra room or two available at your rest house. Therefore, on behalf of His Majesty's Government—given that we have no hotel in Belle Vue, and my house would be inappropriate—I am requesting the use of one of your rooms. I would be renting it, of course."

Amanda's heart raced. How exciting! Who back home was going to believe this? An actual headhunter's daughter staying under her roof—well, sort of. The fact that the girl was white, and not really the headhunter's daughter, made the story all the more exciting. No doubt the *Rock Hill Herald* would love to do a feature story on *this*.

"There's plenty of room," she said breathlessly. "Isn't this supposed to be the suicide month?"

He laughed. "*Oui*. So hot and sticky that the only people who move are the ones who jump over the falls."

"Maybe it's because of the weather, but when the current guests leave, I don't have any other guests booked until November, when the rains are said to be here to stay. I would be glad to help you in any way I can—you know, show her how to be a modern young lady."

"Good. Now observe, Amanda; watch how this girl walks. What do you see?"

"A beautiful young woman—Pierre! She walks like an African!"

"*Exactement!* It is not just that filthy *didiba* that she wears, or those braids in her hair that set her apart. This girl is more African than you think. Did you notice the scarification patterns on her back?"

"Excuse me," Amanda said. "What kind of patterns?"

"The scars—the marks. From wounds that have healed. They are all over her back. And her cheeks. And she is missing her two front teeth."

Amanda gasped softly. "I noticed the teeth—not the marks."

"Scars," Pierre said, so that she would learn the new word.

"Yes, scars. And look, Pierre, her heels are just as cracked as those of anyone else here not wearing shoes."

"Which is everyone else, since even my soldiers prefer to go barefoot when it is this hot."

Suddenly the enormity of the task hit her. "It might not work, Pierre. What if she doesn't want to be white? It would be wrong to force her. In my country the Indians took a number of white children captive and then later had to release them. Some of the children refused to return to the families of their origin because they had new families now."

"*Mon Dieu!* They chose to remain with the savages?"

"But that's the point I'm trying to make; after a while the Indians ceased to be savages in the eyes of the captives."

Pierre whistled softly. "I assure you, mademoiselle, that I am not your typical colonial racist. I was born right here in the Congo and was raised by a *baba*—an African nanny. But she was a Muluba, *not* a Mushilele. You have been to the workers' village at Belle Vue many times, where most—admittedly, not all—of the people are Baluba. And now you have been here. Can you not see the difference?"

"*Oui*, monsieur. Forgive me, but what exactly is *your* point?"

"Simply that there is no option for failure here, Amanda. The OP will have my head if I return a white teenage girl to live among the Bashilele warriors. Belgium is a very small country—not like the United States. It is possible that eventually even the king will have to be involved."

Amanda stopped walking, precipitating yelps of distress from some otherwise aggressive boys who had been showing off by slowly creeping closer to the *Bula Matadi*. They fell back now, and virtually everyone, including Amanda and Pierre, had a good laugh at their dismay. But the youths were soon at it again, acting out with even more bravado than before.

Good little headhunters-in-training, Amanda thought. *Mama always said I had a big head, every time she dragged a comb through my hair or tried to pull my woolen stocking cap down over my ears. These little guys probably know a good thing when they see it. I wonder how much palm beer my skull would hold. They probably wouldn't have to do much cleaning of it either; Miss Kuhnberger always said I had an empty head, which is why I couldn't remember how to do long division.*

"Were you serious about the king having to get involved?" Amanda asked when they'd fallen back into the rhythm of walking.

"*Oui*, of course. If it came to that. This is a very delicate time in the colony now, Amanda. When word of this girl gets out—and believe me, it will grow wings—she will become a symbol."

"A symbol of *what*?"

"Oh Amanda, I do not mean to insult your intelligence when I say that I find your simplicity most endearing."

Amanda first bit her tongue, then counted to three. That was as far as she could go.

"Well, I very much mean to insult you when I say that I find your Gallic arrogance insufferable, and were you not the only English speaker at Belle Vue, I might seriously reconsider our friendship. As for your request that we continue to speak only French—well, I find the act of doing so very taxing. True, this language can be pronounced with great flourish, but it lacks nuance. Did you know that it has only one third the vocabulary words that English has?"

"*Mais c'est impossible!* This is the language of Voltaire."

"And English is the language of Shakespeare, who, by the way, was a far greater genius."

"*Alors*, Amanda, perhaps we should keep our opinions to ourselves."

"Perhaps so—at least when it comes to patriotic things. After all, it wouldn't be ladylike of me to win all our arguments."

But there really wasn't much Amanda wanted to say to Pierre until they got to the truck.

They were about an hour's walk from the village when Ugly Eyes noticed that the crippled woman was having an especially hard time keeping up. They were walking single file: first the Africans in *Bula Matadi* clothes, then the cripple, then Father, then self, then the white woman, and lastly, the white man, who incidentally, appeared to be the headman in this situation.

At any rate, every time the crippled woman faltered, or paused, Father's rib cage rose and fell with irritation, although he made not a sound. This woman had one leg shorter than the other, and her foot was twisted. This was the first grown woman with a deformity that Ugly Eyes had ever seen. What barbarians her tribe must be, to have allowed her to live past infancy. How cruel of them to subject her to the childhood taunts she must have endured, and the inevitable physical pain that a deformed body such as this was bound to have experienced. Ugly Eyes seethed with rage.

"Father," Ugly Eyes said, "I will carry the dwarf."

Father spat into the grass at the *hand of the men* (that is to say, to his right side). "Daughter, she is the white man's slave; we cannot get involved."

"But Father, see how she suffers?"

"Tell me, Ugly Eyes, is this something that you feel strongly about?"

"Yes, Father."

"You have the gift of knowing, daughter—as do I. But truly, your gift exceeds mine; therefore, you have my permission to do as you wish in this case."

Ugly Eyes said nothing in return because she could not think of the right words to express her jumbled thinking. How proud it made her feel that her father, who was such an esteemed headman, should find her to be so wise. But oh how confusing that was as well; after all, she was but a female, and a young unmarried one at that, with no husbands to her credit.

To her relief the little Muluba woman appeared to recover her strength for a few steps. Then alas, the poor creature fell forward on her face, like a child just learning to walk. There she floundered in the dirt path like a fledgling while the African *Bula Matadi*, who had now stopped and turned, just stared. Even the whites did nothing except to call out to the poor creature.

"*Tch, tch, tch,*" Ugly Eyes said, and brushing past Father, swooped down and scooped up the broken little bird in her strong, young arms. Much to her astonishment the full-grown woman felt practically weightless.

"*Aiyee*," Cripple protested, her arms beating in vain about the head and shoulders of the strangest Mushilele girl she had ever seen. "Put me down," she yelled in *Tshiluba*. "Put me down, you giant turd of a colobus monkey!"

"Cripple!" Captain Pierre grabbed one of her hands and held it still. "This girl is trying to help you—I think. She's offering to carry you."

"*Eyo, muambi*. She wants to carry me to her cooking pot. Is it not time for the evening meal?"

The captain laughed. "You have a delightful imagination, Cripple. "But you are like an old hen that no longer lays but has been kept around to sit on the eggs of the young hens that refuse to brood. Your meat will be far too tough to eat; even if it is tenderized with all the papaya leaves in the Kasai."

"*Aiyee! Mona buphote buebe!*"

"What did she say?" the white *mamu* demanded. "I did not learn these words in my *Tshiluba* language school."

"I cannot translate this for your ears," the captain said, and laughed.

Cripple was not appeased by his good humor. "Will you make this strange child put me down?"

"No. It will be dark soon and then the hyenas will be out."

"See what you have done?" Cripple said, directing her words to the white face just inches from her own. The Headhunter's Daughter didn't even bat an eyelash, which made Cripple all the angrier. "*Muambi*," she cried, "this Mushilele does not bathe; never have I smelled such stink. Even you whites do not offend me as bad as this one."

"Good," the captain said. "Then you will stay awake, which will make it easier to transfer you into the truck when we reach it."

"*Baba wetu, baba wetu*," Cripple moaned. "Surely now this is the end of me."

When they got back to the truck, they found a pack of jackals prancing around it. One brave individual had actually jumped in back and was trying in vain to loosen the securely bundled elephant meat. Other than that, everything was just as the rescue party had left it. This astounded Amanda. Such a state of affairs might not have been the case had one been able to transpose the scene to Cherry Road, back in Rock Hill, South Carolina. Of course back home the precious commodity would have been something quite different than elephant meat—like maybe a hi-fi stereo.

"Where are we all going to sit?" Amanda asked.

"You, and I, and Miss Bossy Pants will sit up front. The others can stand in back, behind the elephant meat."

"Yes, but what about the girl?" Amanda said. "And please, Pierre, try to think charitable thoughts about Cripple. You, more than anyone, should know that she really is a diamond in the rough."

"*Mais oui*, but diamonds stick to grease; that is how they are mined in Kasai Province. Every time I'm through dealing with Cripple I feel greasy."

"Oh, stop the dramatics, Pierre. Anyway, this Mushilele girl cannot ride in the back."

"Why not?"

"Because she's white, silly." Although they were thousands of miles apart, there were some things about South Carolina culture and Belgian Colonial culture that were identical; segregation of the races being one of them. Personally, Amanda saw nothing wrong with the races mixing upon occasion, but at Belle Vue where the whites were the minority, it did make sense to maintain one's distance. One couldn't, for instance, invite a black into one's home socially, because then all the Africans would want to see what the inside of a white person's house looked like.

"I see," said Pierre. "So Cripple gets to sit up front in my truck, as does this white Mushilele girl. I suppose you get to do so as well—am I right?"

Amanda's heart pounded. She had never assumed anything *but* that she would get to ride in the cab.

"Yes, of course."

"Then where does that put *me*? I am, after all, the silly owner of this truck. And if I am to ride in back, which of you three ladies will drive?"

Ladies? Was Pierre mocking the other two women, or did his Gallic sense of gallantry really extend to women of color? Amanda had heard that the Portuguese were more tolerant in that regard, but not the Belgians, half of whom were Flemish and were said to have brought with them to the Congo the more Germanic views on race.

"I am a perfectly good driver," she said crisply. "I possess an International Driver's Certificate—although it is back at the rest house."

"*Alors*," Pierre said, "then our problem is solved. I will ride in back with my soldiers and guard the elephant meat with my life."

If looks could kill, Amanda shot him a look that could have killed a pair of pachyderms, had any live ones been handy. Unfortunately, it was too dark for the handsome young captain to read the passion in her expression.

"Are you being sarcastic?" she demanded.

"Quite possibly," he said.

"Have the ladies get in," she said, and without speaking to him again climbed up to the driver's seat and retrieved the keys from their "hiding place" behind the sun visor.

"The girl will sit next to you," Pierre said.

Amanda bristled at the directive. "If she wants to, then she may," she said.

"No, Mademoiselle Brown. The white Mushilele *cannot* sit next to the door; there is too much danger that she might jump out. I have seen it before with natives who have never ridden in automobiles. They are terrified of the noise and the motion. It was the same way with our grandparents, no? And back then the autos did not even go so fast as we drive now on these terrible Congo roads."

The trouble was that the girl did stink. The combination of wood smoke and body odor was bad enough, but with every bump, every sudden jostle, her unwashed, scarified, scab-covered flesh seemed to seek out Amanda and press up against her, and for far longer than was necessary. But remarkably, the girl did not let out a peep when the truck roared to life. And even when Amanda misjudged the location of a deep rut that the truck had to straddle, and the axle nearly broke, the strange white girl remained eerily silent.

Then, just a few kilometers outside Belle Vue, all hell broke loose—literally, to hear Cripple tell it. One minute they were driving along a fairly smooth stretch of hard packed clay, anxious to get home with their elephant meat and tales of the strange white *mamu*, and the next minute a demon was flapping about the cab.

Yes, Amanda had screamed. Who wouldn't have? But the boldly patterned demon that thrashed about their faces was merely a bewildered nighthawk that had been blinded by the headlights. Cripple had been just as frightened; she'd practically wet herself and had shrieked like a banshee. However, the bizarre young woman sitting between them had remained as still and silent as a stone carving. That's when Amanda knew for sure that repatriating the girl was simply not going to be possible.

EIGHT

She's beautiful!" The American teenager strained to get a better look at the creature squatting next to the wood box in the kitchen; only her father's arm prevented her from getting any closer.

"We need to leave her alone for the night," Dorcas said. As the oldest white present, she represented the voice of wisdom.

There really was no point in waking up the OP at this hour of the night, was there? This was, after all, first and foremost, police business. Besides, Pierre knew from past experience that the OP could be as congenial as a cape buffalo if aroused from a deep sleep. No, there was nothing so important that it couldn't wait until morning except for a heart attack and acute appendicitis, and the white Mushilele suffered from neither.

The question remained, however, of where to leave the girl for the night. All the jail cells were currently unoccupied, and although they were undoubtedly better than anything the girl had ever slept in, somehow it did not seem right. And since he couldn't very well invite an unmarried white girl to stay with him, well, that left only one other solution as far as the young captain could see.

"Amanda?"

"Yes?"

"Do you have room for the girl here?"

"Yes—but do you think she will stay?"

"This is outrageous," said Mr. Gorman. "This is a savage we're talking about. She can't stay inside—not with my daughter and wife here."

"Then perhaps your wife and daughter should sleep outside," Amanda said.

"Why you impudent little thing! I will be sending a telegram to the Mission Board in the States first thing in the morning in which I will be reporting your abominable behavior. I am sure that the Board will demand that you return on the very next plane."

Amanda blanched. "I'm very sorry," she said. "I often speak before I think. It's my worst habit; one that I pray that I outgrow. Please forgive me, Mr. Gorman. Mrs. Gorman. Peaches." Mother and daughter nodded, but the father didn't seem to have heard her.

"Peaches can move in with Father and me," Mrs. Gorman volunteered. "And we can shove the bureau in front of the door. I'm sure we'll be just fine. But it's you and Dorcas that I'm worried about."

"May the Lord guard my tongue," Dorcas said. "We're talking about a Mushilele girl—at most a Mushilele woman. She's unarmed. She's not an army of Amelekites, for Pete's sake. She's as afraid of us as we are of her—perhaps ten times more so. She isn't going to come anywhere near us. No, the real question is, Where is her father going to spend the night?"

"Her *father*?" Mrs. Gorman said. "Where on earth did he come from? I didn't hear any planes land today."

"Don't be daft," Mr. Gorman said. "She's referring to the native who came with her. That great big fellow just outside with the six-foot bow and the monkey-skin quiver full of arrows."

"He's not really her father, is he?" Peaches said. "I mean, not *really*."

"Of course not, dear," Mrs. Gorman said to her daughter.

"Now run along, honey. I spotted a collection of Grace Livingston Hill novels in the living room this morning. Why don't you pick one out and take it to my room?"

"But Mother, you said those were trash—"

"Now be a good girl and just do as I say." The spoiled teenager stomped away in a huff, in total contrast to the poor but apparently calm Mushilele girl Pierre had found himself forced to bring in.

Orders from the top aside, looking at her now in Amanda's kitchen, it was clear to Pierre that this strange hybrid girl could not be anywhere else except for somewhere in the civilized world. It would have been morally wrong to leave a girl of her complexion, of her genetic heritage, to be raised by the Africans out in the bush. It just wasn't done. Case closed. Besides, her very existence under these circumstances bespoke of a crime, and that, of course, had compelled him to act in the first place.

Ugly Eyes could bear it no longer. She had done everything as Father had commanded her to do up until now. She had followed him in silence. She had climbed into the metal elephant, and when it bucked and roared into life, she closed her eyes and shivered, but she did not cry out. When the nighthawk flew in through the metal elephant's eye and the silly foreign women screamed, even then Ugly Eyes had remained as silent as the striped antelope that haunts the forest shadows.

But now it seemed that the *Bula Matadi* wished to separate her from her father. The young one, who had been gabbling at Ugly Eyes in her incomprehensible tongue, had grabbed one of the younger girl's wrists and was attempting to pull her deeper into the strange house built of stone. This meant that Ugly Eyes could no longer see her father.

Ugly Eyes felt her knees go weak. At the same time her heart began to pound between her ears, and she felt as if her body would burst out of her skin if she had to endure this feeling for one more second. Something had to happen; anything! So that's why Ugly Eyes lunged forward and bit the younger *Bula Matadi* on the arm. She had no intention of eating her—or even just killing her—but something had to happen.

The young *Bula Matadi* screamed and dropped Ugly Eyes' wrist. Perhaps that might have been the end of the violence had not the old man—not the one with the gun—jumped into action and struck Ugly Eyes with the back of his hand. Hard. Hard enough to knock her across the large stone room. Then all the women screamed, and this time the young man—the one with the gun—hit the old man. Then there was silence, except for the deep breathing that comes with intense emotion and sudden exertion.

At that point Ugly Eyes was grateful that Father heeded his own council and did not come inside and become part of the fray. Father could have—would have—killed everyone, even the young *Bula Matadi* with the gun. Only one person in Ugly Eyes' village owned a gun; that was Born With One Fist Extended. He had built his own gun; having made it from memory preserved from his service in the *Bula Matadi*'s army. Born With One Fist Extended had actually managed to take down a she-buffalo with it by hitting her at the base of the skull where it meets the back of the ear. That was the occasion of a great feast, and was also the only time that Ugly Eyes could remember when her father's position in the tribe had been threatened.

Ugly Eyes struggled to stand before Father could see her lying on the floor. "You are very fortunate," she told her onlookers. "Had this happened in our village, you would not live to tell your children about it."

She turned to the old man who had struck her, and took some small pleasure in the fact that now, under the younger man's intense stare, he seemed to have drawn back into himself, like a chicken in a rainstorm.

"You, old man," she said, "have an especially large head. Your skull—after it has been cleaned thoroughly by 'the ants that travel' will make some lucky man a very nice drinking cup. It is so large that it will not have to be refilled. As for the rest of you—bah, you are a mixed bag at best. There is not one man in our village with an appetite so strong that he would take to the bed the most desirable of you. You are as white and ugly as the grubs that feed on logs that litter the forest floor. Truly you disgust me."

The Headhunter marveled at all that he saw that day. The *Bula Matadi* were a clever race to have produced such astonishing things—even if they did so on the backs of other peoples. A metal elephant! One could slice off as much meat as needed, yet the beast did not die. To the contrary.

There was a secret location on the stomach where one could grab a strip of skin and pull. The stomach then opened wide and as many as three people could climb inside and be seated. Perhaps the most difficult thing to believe was the fact that somehow this man-made beast could be made to obey, to move along the *Bula Matadi*'s wide trail at the speed of a plunging eagle.

With such a means of locomotion at their disposal, the Bashilele could relocate an entire village under the cover of one night! Never again would the Headhunter's people have to live in fear of marauding tribes or vengeful *Bula Matadi*. Of course first one had to learn the ways of the white men and that would require a great deal of courage, for they were a strange, dangerous, and unpredictable people. But a people, nonetheless—of that he was sure, unlike some of the more ignorant members of his tribe. Ugly Eyes had taught him that. And as Ugly Eyes learned the ways of the *Bula Matadi*, she would teach them to him.

Someday she might even take a *Bula Matadi* man as one of her husbands, and in the course of time bear that man children— *yala*! Would those children also be white? Perhaps so—although most likely not. Ugly Eyes had been living a long time with the Bashilele people, and she was one of them. Her whiteness was but a thin layer that did not extend down to her soul or to her woman parts; of that the Headhunter could be sure. In the meantime, why was he not showing a father's concern? Was he not afraid for Ugly Eyes? Was she not as much his daughter as if she had been born of his wife? These were silly questions to ease the mind; Ugly Eyes was not only his daughter, she was much more than that! Let it be known that Ugly Eyes was as brave as any son—and as clever as any two sons. Yes, let that be known.

In the meantime—and this he had made very clear to his daughter—they were not to give the white man the satisfaction of knowing that anything he did, or said, had any effect on them, the representatives of the Bashilele people.

In the end it was decided that father and daughter should be kept together *temporarily* in what used to be the woodshed (in the days before the Missionary Rest House was hooked into the boundless electricity supplied by the falls)—no matter how improper it might appear to Mr. and Mrs. Gorman to have a black man spend the night alone with a young, nubile white girl. Normally, this strange girl's whereabouts would have been of no further concern to Cripple (given that she'd lied about speaking the Bushilele language)—but since the woodshed was where she kept the uniform that the white *mamu* now required her to wear, it was ordained that the two strong souls should meet again.

"*Aiyee!*" Cripple cried upon opening the door to the woodshed the following morning. The white Mushilele girl was supine upon a very comfortable-looking sleeping pad on the cement floor, covered by a real blanket. She appeared to be alone; still, Cripple half expected the girl's father to leap down from the rafters and lop off her head. She glanced up and was vastly reassured by the same cobwebs that had not seemed so friendly the day before.

Meanwhile the girl jumped to her feet and was hastily attempting to dress in some of the real *mamu's* clothes. Frankly, it was more than Cripple could bear. First the luxuriously soft sleeping pad, and now these rich clothes! Even Cripple had yet to be favored by any of the white woman's castoffs.

"What has this wretched creature done to deserve such favoritism?" she cried. "Anyone can be born with a sickly white skin. I too would have been born with such a hideous condition, had but I known the treasures that lay in store for one such as this."

"Then truly it is a shame that you did not listen to your mother's womb," one of the spiders in the rafters said. "I listened, and as you can see, I have been richly rewarded."

Cripple raised a clenched fist. "So now even you spiders mock me?"

"Oh you silly Muluba woman," said a voice closer at hand. "How much palm beer did you consume last night?"

Cripple dropped her fist and stared at the white African. "If it were possible that you could understand me, I would not speak thus; I drank no beer last night, nor did a drop of honey wine pass my lips. I am not a betting woman, but if I were, I would bet the lives of my sister wife's children that you spoke just now. For either that is the case, or I have crossed over to the land of departed souls and we are both dead."

The white girl clapped her hands and laughed. What impertinence that child showed!

"We are neither of us dead, *Mamu*," she said. "It is me, the wretched white creature that you tore from the bosom of her mother yesterday in the Bashilele village."

"Nonsense," Cripple said. "You are speaking to me in *Tshiluba*, which is my own tongue, not yours. You would have no way of knowing my language."

"*Mamu*, how is it that you supposedly came to know *my* tongue?"

"Well, I had a friend—but I lied." Cripple's ears burned with humiliation. "You overheard that conversation? Why did you not say something?"

"*Mamu*, it was not my conversation."

"*Tch*, you are most annoying. So tell me then, from whom did you learn to speak like a civilized person?"

"I learned to speak thus from my mother and father, *Mamu*. But I learned *your* tongue—this primitive tongue—known as *Tshiluba*, from my mother's dear friend, Iron Sliver, who learned it from her mother."

Cripple's legs felt exceptionally weak, even more tired than they had the day before after the long trek to and from the village. Without further ado—and really, as befit her rights as the elder of the two—she plopped down on the soft mat. My, but it really was soft. No wonder the whites were unable to perform their own work; they'd been pampered so much by their own inventions that they had lost the ability to do anything labor intensive. Indeed, it was a wonder that their arms could even lift a spoon.

"Is your mother's friend—this woman, Iron Sliver—is she a slave?"

"*Nasha, Mamu*. But she was a slave until she married. She is the chief's sister; they were both captured as children."

"*Aiyee!* If she is a free woman, why does not she leave?"

The white creature smiled licentiously. "We have a saying, *Mamu*. Those who take a Mushilele husband will never leave the tribe of their own accord."

Cripple felt the urge to jump up and strike the child—along with the urge to laugh. Lacking the energy to do the former, she engaged in the latter. After all, the girl was sporting breasts; true, they were not the round, full breasts of a woman, but *mabele* nonetheless. She would understand soon enough what this loose talk was all about, if she did not already.

"Do your parents also speak my language, strange white one?" she asked.

"Of course they do!"

"*Kah!*"

"Your surprise baffles me, *Mamu*. Your unpleasant language— which frankly grates on my ears like the noise of so many crickets—is the dominant language of this region of the Congo. Therefore a great many in our village have gone to the trouble of learning it because someday it might become useful for our survival."

"But yesterday neither you nor your father seemed to understand a word of it! And it does *not* grate on your ears."

"Yesterday I obeyed my father; today he is not here, as you can see. By the way, I have a name, and it is not 'Strange White One.'"

Cripple lay back upon the mat. How soft and welcoming it was. How gently it cradled her twisted frame. With this for a bed, she could sleep like a kitten and wake each morning with a smile on her face.

"I suppose you wish to tell me what your name is," Cripple said.

"My name is Ugly Eyes."

"*Kah!*" Cripple sat. "That cannot be!"

"*Eyo*, it is exactly so, just as your name is Cripple."

"How did you know thus?" Cripple demanded.

"So you were called yesterday," Ugly Eyes said.

"*Mesu Mabi* is the name of the white woman who brought you here. It is for her that I work—"

"You are her slave?"

"*Aiyee!*" Cripple struggled to her feet. "You are an ignorant child; you have so much to learn. Who will teach you the *Bula Matadi*'s ways?"

"My father says that perhaps it is the spirits of my white ancestors who have come to claim me. They will see to it that I learn the *Bula Matadi*'s ways. To that end, is it not possible that this woman who shares my name wishes also to be my teacher?"

Cripple shook her head in wonder. "You are indeed a strange person, Ugly Eyes, for you have the look of one who is young, but the tongue of one who has survived for many years. Tell me the truth, child; where did you come from? Are you the product of a powerful witch doctor's curse?"

"There are those who believe this is so, and there are those who believe that I am nothing more than the abandoned off-spring of the *Bula Matadi*. At any rate, I was found in the forest, as an infant, by the older son—now dead—of my beloved mother and father."

"Ah. How old are you now, child? Do you know?"

"*Nasha.*"

"Have you begun to bleed?"

"*Nasha.* But my mother says the time is very near."

"She is right," Cripple said. "A mother knows these things. Now back to your name—what do you think of Ugly Skin as your new name? For you must admit, your skin is hideous to the extreme."

"*Kah!* I think Ugly Skin is a horrible name," the girl said, "and it does not fit my skin at all. The answer is no; I will not change it. You cannot force me. The *Bula Matadi* cannot force me."

Now this was a girl who could go far. She was brave, she was headstrong, and she had a powerful self-image; something Cripple had never been privileged to possess. Surely she would make a powerful ally. Possibly even a friend—if one could truly get to the bottom of who she was.

"Why is it that your father—this head-hunting savage—wished to keep secret the fact that you speak my civilized tongue?"

The girl had the effrontery to clench her fists as she spoke. "I will remain calm before the *Bula Matadi*, so that I might learn their ways, but you, you Muluba forest monkey, I do not have to act thusly with you."

"*Aiyee!* Let it be known that this creature has feelings," Cripple said. She was doing her best to act cavalier, while instead she felt guilty for making the girl feel bad. What's more, she felt inexplicably maternal.

"I am a person," the girl said simply.

"And so you are," Cripple said. She smiled at the girl for the first time.

The girl returned the slightest of smiles. "My father believes that I will learn many additional things if it is believed that I do not understand *Tshiluba* which, as you know, is the main trade language of this region."

"Your father is right," Cripple said, without a hint of sarcasm. "Come, let us go greet the *mamu*, whose name is also Ugly Eyes. But do not be afraid, strange one, for I will remain at your side, and I will not give away your secret."

NINE

◈

Amanda saw Cripple enter the woodshed to get her uniform. She would have called out to stop her if it would have done any good. But the woodshed—which was really a rather tidy little brick building with a galvanized iron roof—was set well back from the main house, and therefore well back from Amanda's bedroom. And then there was the noise of the falls. It would have been a waste of breath.

When Amanda first arrived in Belle Vue as the hostess of the Missionary Rest House, she was actually put off by all the racket. What folly it seemed to build a rest house where one could barely carry on a decent conversation, let alone think. But of course it was all about the view; the lawn swept right to the edge of the precipice. It was as if the landscape architect was daring the guests to dash themselves against the rocks far below.

Fortunately, this was not really the case, but merely the state of Amanda's mind. She had arrived in the Belgian Congo weighed down with a guilty conscience, having been riding in a car full of drunken teenagers when a fatal accident occurred. Although the accident wasn't Amanda's fault, the fact that she had escaped with relatively minor injuries, when so many others had died, made her feel like a murderer. But a lot had happened since her arrival, just a few months ago, and by now the roar of the falls was merely a constant in her life, something even to be missed when the time came for her to leave.

It did, however, make calling out to Cripple an exercise in futility. Then again, perhaps it was just as well that she not alert Cripple to the fact that the Mushilele girl and her father were in the shed. It would be amusing to see just how quickly Cripple emerged, and what her expression would be. At home it had become fashionable lately for Northerners to come to the South (even to Rock Hill) and comment on the racism they observed. Jim Crow, they called it. But Amanda had never witnessed ethnic prejudices quite as explicit as that displayed between the various tribes here in the middle of Africa.

"Oh my stars!" she cried aloud. "This just can't be!"

But it was. Cripple, with a smug smile on her face, and the white Mushilele, as impassive as ever, had emerged from the woodshed holding hands. Like schoolgirls! Amanda was at once relieved, overjoyed, and envious. How could she not be? Cripple had been *her* discovery, and introducing this feral child (well, she amounted to one, didn't she?) to civilization was supposed to be *her* job as well. Now it appeared as if Amanda's first project had stolen her second project right out from underneath her, and probably all because Amanda had been all too successful.

Amanda dashed through the Missionary Rest House, paying scant attention to her surroundings. Unfortunately for Protruding Navel, she did not see him coming through the kitchen door and into the dining room.

"*Aiyee, Mamu,*" he said, for what else can one say, when it is a white woman who has knocked you to the floor? You cannot give a white woman the back of your hand, and tell her that it is your wish that a male goat will find her attractive and follow her into the bush when she goes off to do her business.

"*Eee*, I am so sorry," Mamu Ugly Eyes said. "Protruding Navel, please forgive me."

The apology came immediately, a fact that pleased Protruding Navel immensely. In his position as head houseboy he had served many missionaries—such as the ones who waited for him now on the front patio—and had observed that some of them were more respectful of the African than others. Protruding Navel was not in the mood this particular morning to be poked like a toad with a sharp stick.

"Mamu Ugly Eyes," he said expansively, "I am on my way to take the breakfast orders from the guests. They have already been served their juice—although the *mukelenge* did not like his; he poured it on the ground."

"*Nasha!*"

"*Mamu*, do you call me a liar?"

"I do not! I am merely saying that such behavior is hard to believe. What was wrong with the juice? I made it myself."

There it was, was it not? Had the juice been squeezed by Cripple or by Protruding Navel, then perhaps it could be easier to understand why it was that the fat missionary from the distant mission should pour it wastefully on the ground. In retrospect, Mamu Ugly Eyes was not so different from the others; she was just better at disguising her true feelings—for a while.

Protruding Navel hung his head provocatively. "*Mamu*, it is not my place to repeat such things."

"*Feedlesteeks!*" It was an English word that Mamu Ugly Eyes said when she was frustrated—which, it seemed, was very often. "Protruding Navel, you will repeat this; I demand it."

Is it only a white woman who could dare demand that a man do such a thing—or anything? Among the *Bakuba* people there is said to be a great queen; perhaps she too could demand obedience from her male subjects. However, such was not the case with Protruding Navel's more sensible tribe, the Bena Lulua.

"*Mamu*," Protruding Navel said, "does not the *Book of God* forbid gossip?"

"It is not gossip if it is true," the *mamu* snapped.

Protruding Navel resisted the urge to laugh. He had the *mamu* right where he wanted her. She was so easy to manipulate sometimes; she was so much like a child.

"He said your juice was weak, *Mamu*. Bitter water, he called it. But this was after he spat it on the grass; the very grass that I myself must cut since the yard boy is not permitted that close to the patio. And as I said, he poured out what was in his glass, and as he did thus he had a terrible expression on his face, perhaps like that of a dying monkey—although I must hasten to assure you, *Mamu*, that as I am not a heathen forest dweller, but instead a citizen of the workers' village of the great city of Belle Vue, I have not seen many dying monkeys." Protruding Navel paused to catch his breath. "Of course I would not tell you any of this, except that you forced me to, *Mamu*."

"*Eyo*. Indeed, I did. Now please get back to work—"

"*Mamu*, there is much talk in the village about this strange European."

Protruding Navel observed his employer straighten and cross her arms. "So fast?"

"*E*, like a *tshisuku* fire in the dry season. They think it is a bad omen. Some go so far to say that you have brought a curse to Belle Vue."

"A curse? What kind of curse?"

"Perhaps an illness, like the sleeping sickness, or boils, maybe even smallpox."

"And what do you think, Protruding Navel?"

It is the fool who answers quickly. "Mamu Ugly Eyes, you know that I am a Protestant—like you—and therefore a true Christian, and as such I do not believe in these primitive superstitions. But *if* I were to believe in such nonsense, I suppose I might believe that you have brought a *mukishi*—a ghost—into this house. It will make this house its base, *Mamu*, but it will also sneak into the village at night and steal the lives of babies, as well as the elderly, and even some of the people's livestock."

"Protruding Navel, this is absolutely preposterous! Surely you cannot believe this. *Babies?* The *elderly?* Here they die on a regular basis. Their deaths cannot be blamed on this girl. I will not allow you to blame her. I forbid it! As for the livestock—why, if I did not know you to be a good Christian, this would sound to me like a clever way for you to steal goats and pigs while putting the blame on an innocent child."

Protruding Navel felt the veins along his temple throb. Never had a woman spoken to him thusly. How fortunate for Mamu Ugly Eyes that she wore the skin of the oppressors. But the world had begun to tip; Protruding Navel could feel the destinies of nations sliding beneath his feet to opposing poles. Someday soon everything would be upside down. Black would be the new white, and white the new black. That is what the Communists taught.

Perhaps even this very place would be his, and Mamu Ugly Eyes would be his housekeeper. In that case, because she was a young woman, there would be no need to use the title *mamu*. Just her name would suffice.

"Ugly Eyes," he could say, "I do not care for this jam; bring me a different flavor at once!" Then he would clap his hands like the whites always did when they were impatient. "Chop, chop," they always added in their own language.

"Protruding Navel," Mamu Ugly Eyes said, breaking through his daydream, "are you even listening to me?"

"Yes, *Mamu*, I have heard every word, and you have deeply offended me. Did I not say that I was a Christian, a follower of *Yesu Clisto*?"

"Yes, of course. I am so sorry, Protruding Navel. It is just that I feel so strongly about the heathen superstitions that some of the villagers believe in."

"Do you refer to Cripple, *Mamu*?"

"*Eh?*"

"Is she not a heathen? Please remember, *Mamu*, that these are her own words; not mine."

"*Eyo, eyo!* Cripple is a heathen! Now I really must go, Protruding Navel, because I hear Cripple and the ghost girl in the kitchen now."

"Very well," Protruding Navel said. "Perhaps we will talk again soon." He waited until she turned her back on him before smiling. Indeed, there were many things that he had yet to say to her.

The OP's binoculars had gotten quite a workout, both the night before and this morning. That was certainly one of the advantages of living in the official quarters of the Director of Mines; the view across the river to the Missionary Rest House was unparalleled. If the OP felt the slightest twinge of guilt for spying on the white girl who'd been rescued from the ferocious Bashilele, it was far outweighed by his sense of duty fulfilled.

Yes, of course Captain Pierre Jardin had been a part of this; there was no getting around that. It simply wouldn't do to have someone as important as the OP wandering around in the jungle—or wherever those savages lived. Who knows what could have happened? The very fact that the rescue party had been charged by a mad bull elephant was proof enough just how dangerous that excursion had been. And let's not forget the driver ants—*sacre coeur*! There was that young upstart now!

The binoculars! The OP jumped to his feet, whipped his helmet off, put the glasses down on his chair and did his best to cover them with his helmet. Thank God he had a large head.

"*Bon jour*, Monsieur OP," Captain Jardin said with a smart bow. After all, the army, the police—all were here to back up the Consortium. As to whom the Consortium ultimately answered to—well, one might consider taking up philately for the answer.

"*Bon jour*, Pierre. Would you like some coffee before we go?"

"*Oui, merci.*"

Merde! That son of a bitch had the intuition of a woman and was probably already onto him. He could feel it. Better to confess now than to make it seem really strange later.

"Ha, ha, these binoculars are a joke," he said as he reclaimed them and at the same time donned his helmet. "But not these helmets, eh? Of course you don't wear one, what with your regulation police captain's hat, but I find that this thing is a lifesaver. Did you know that I get a new one every year?"

Captain Jardin glanced at the white cork helmet with what appeared to be admiration. "They are very attractive, sir. The coffee? *S'il vous plait.*"

"*Ah, oui! Garcon,*" he called. Boy! He had a new table boy since the move—some fellow by the name of Laurent, or Lucifer, or something pompous and European. The OP couldn't be bothered to learn the man's name just yet; not until he was sure the fellow would work out.

With the fresh coffee now just a memory—as well as some warm croissants and butter produced by Consortium-owned cows—the OP insisted that he and Captain Jardin get right down to business. The morning had wings, after all. Then again, didn't all the mornings in Belle Vue? Money, money, money, that's what the ticking minutes represented. In less than two years the day of independence would dawn and then the land would stop hemorrhaging diamonds—well, at least into European coffers.

He let the captain drive—the better to appreciate the experience. Everything seemed more intense: colors brighter, sounds clearer—for a moment he felt an odd, intense sort of love for the Congo, even though his deceased wife Heilewid was eternally trapped somewhere beneath the falls, and all that remained of her sister was the burned stump that was buried in the white cemetery up on the hill straight ahead.

The OP forced himself to savor the long dirt drive that skirted the gorge on the African side of the falls on its way to the Missionary Rest House. How lucky the missionaries were to have originally received this lease from the crown, and then to have just recently had it renewed for the next one hundred years. As everyone knew, this was the Protestant missionaries' reward for doing such a good job of establishing elementary schools in the villages surrounding Belle Vue.

The OP was not a religious man, although like most Belgians of Walloon extraction he was at least nominally Catholic, but as a mining official, much like a government official, he held himself above the missionary wars for the souls of the people. Still, he couldn't help but feel a twinge of envy every time he drove up to the rest house.

The view up here was unsurpassed in all of Kasai Province. Should King Baudouin and Queen Fabiola decide to visit their colony one last time before turning it over to the natives, the OP would do his best to strike a deal with the young missionary who ran the rest house. If he was successful, Their Majesties would never forget their visit to Belle Vue, or the man who had arranged it.

"Pierre," the OP said, as they pulled to a stop in the circular drive just outside the front verandah. "Do you think she has my coloring?"

TEN

◈

Monsieur OP, the girl has been living in the sun for the past thirteen years; forgive me, but she has the coloring of a peasant. However, I have been reflecting on her features and there is, I think, a great deal of similarity in the profile. Also, you both have blue eyes, do you not?"

"Don't ask me, you idiot," snapped the OP. "I have yet to see the child!"

"Well, sir," Pierre said, struggling mightily not to call the OP an idiot in return—or worse, "the truth is, I'm not sure what color *your* eyes are."

"Ah," the OP said, "now we're getting somewhere. The problem lies in the fact that you've been unable to look me in the eyes ever since that day when my wife's killer climbed down from the gallows as a free woman. Isn't that the case?"

"Screw yourself," Pierre said. "Look, I haven't told *anyone* your secret—not even the woman with whom I wish to be involved, the woman who has willingly agreed to play a huge role in this girl's rehabilitation. So don't be giving me any crap about the Muluba woman, Cripple, being responsible for your wife's untimely demise. We both know it was probably suicide. Leave it at that."

The OP grunted, but mercifully did leave it at that.

"Voila!" Pierre said with a good deal of relief, now that they had finally arrived. "Here we are. And there they all are; gathered around that massive round table that is said to once have hosted Prince Albert."

"Do you see her?" the OP said. His voice came out as a squeak, despite the fact that he was supposedly still a virile man, not yet fifty years old.

August 24, 1945

The war in Europe was finally over—although just barely. But the riches of the Congo had been left intact, were still there for the taking. Heilewid had given birth to a beautiful baby girl just three months earlier, in Luluaburg. She was home now with him in their villa overlooking the river and they were managing just fine—thanks to the help of a very experienced *baba.*

Last Born Child had come highly recommended by a Belgian family in Luluaburg that Heilewid had met during the last few weeks of her pregnancy. Because Heilewid had suffered three miscarriages by going into premature labor prior to this pregnancy, her doctor had strongly advised her to stay near a hospital during the last trimester. What surprised the OP was how fond his wife became of this other Belgian family, given that they were Walloons. After all, she was a card-carrying Fleming who despised Walloons, regarded them all as racist snobs—her husband excluded.

To have Heilewid so fired up about this family and their fantastic *baba*—this ancient crone of a woman called Last Born Child—well, that was like Christmas, his birthday, Easter, and Armistice Day all rolled into one. That's how hard it was to please Heilewid now that he'd gotten her to join him in Africa—never mind that by doing so he might have been responsible for saving her life during the war. Although her culture was Flemish and her ancestors had lived in Antwerp for generations, Heilewid's maternal grandmother was Jewish.

On August 24, 1945, when the OP rose early from his bed because he couldn't wait to hold his infant daughter in his arms on that cool late-dry-season morning, the war in Europe may have been over, but the two young parents in the middle-of-nowhere Africa were about to experience unbearable grief. "Carnage of the heart," he told his priest, in the last confession he would ever make.

As for Heilewid, it was the day she began her long, solitary descent into hell.

Ugly Eyes gazed at the faces of whites seated around the table as if seeing them for the first time. Last night she had been so tired, so stressed, that now she could not remember if any of them were the same people—except for the young white woman who also went by the name of Ugly Eyes. As for the others, it was true, what Mother and Iron Sliver often said, before dissolving into fits of laughter: *"Which is uglier, the white man or the belly of a toad? Ha, must you ask?"*

The old white man was particularly ugly—and toad-like. He was corpulent, his puffy body giving him the impression of having no neck. And although he wore the obligatory white cork helmet, even under cover of the verandah roof, he was deeply tanned everywhere except for under his shirt. Ugly Eyes knew this, because she watched him lean forward to shovel the food from his plate, watched the shirt gap just enough to expose the pasty white skin covered with moles.

Were the other two women his wives? She didn't think so. One appeared much older, but how was she to know for sure? For one thing, the woman hid her breasts, as if she were ashamed of them! And even though this woman's face bore more wrinkles than Ugly Eyes had ever seen on a live human being, she appeared to be in possession of all of her teeth. Father would very much appreciate a skull like hers from which to drink his palm wine; the teeth in the top jaw would add such a festive decoration.

The other woman was fat, like the man who was possibly her husband, except that she had a neck and there was both fear and curiosity in her eyes. Sometimes one, then the other, of the emotions would take over, so that her movements were abrupt and unpredictable, much like those of a cat.

Ugly Eyes had had a cat once; Father had traded three of his own arrows for it from a traveling Mushilele from the much larger village of Badi-Banga. The cat was supposed to hunt the rats in the thatch roofs of the village huts, but it preferred the much easier prey of domestic chicks and ducklings. Later everyone agreed that getting another cat just to eat rats would not be the best use of Father's much sought-after arrows.

But there was also a girl at the table—maybe not a whole lot older than Ugly Eyes. Of course Ugly Eyes couldn't even speak one word of this girl's language, but she understood her perfectly. The girl's eyes were half closed and her arms were crossed in front of her chest. Her pale thin lips were extended and every now and then she parted them just enough to emit little puffs of air. "Go away," she was saying, just as clear as if she were speaking Bushilele. "I do not want you here. You do not belong here! This is my village; not yours!"

Fortunately, Ugly Eyes was able to say quite a bit in this girl's language as well. She let her eyes settle on this girl's pale face, and then closed them halfway for a millisecond. After that she smiled slowly before looking away and never looking back.

Judging by the anger she heard in the girl's voice a moment later, Ugly Eyes knew that she'd guessed right; Ugly Eyes was indeed fluent in at least one language spoken by the whites.

Mastermind smiled. Yes, thirteen years had passed since the plan had been put in place, and something had gone terribly wrong, but *perhaps* it was not too late to salvage something. There are no guarantees when committing a crime of this magnitude; no guarantees at all—except, perhaps, for an eternity spent in hell. Well, that was a risk that came with the trade. The *trade*—ha! This was the only crime that Mastermind had ever committed. Would ever commit for that matter. Frankly, a life of crime was more work than Mastermind had bargained for.

What a fool the OP was for expecting another reaction. Of course the girl wouldn't show a hint of recognition. Why should she? There was no reason for him to assume that she was his daughter, except that she was *approximately* the same age. But she wasn't even found in the same territory, amongst the same dominant tribe.

It really was ridiculous to think that somehow a three-month-old infant could disappear from her cradle in Belle Vue and then pop up in a remote Bashilele village thirteen years later. This was either something for the anthropology books, or it was a fairy tale, but it couldn't be happening to him. It could not be his child.

And she had just proved it. Had it been his, there would have been at least a spark in her eyes—a glimmer that reminded him of Heilewid. But these eyes regarded him with the same impersonal cautiousness with which a lizard would look upon him. He wasn't sure, but was that the tip of her tongue flicking through the space where her two front teeth ought to be? *Mon Dieu!* Was she trying to seduce him?

"She doesn't speak anything intelligible," Mr. Gorman said in perfect, unaccented Flemish.

The OP nearly fell backward in his chair. He was a Walloon, and French was his mother tongue, not Flemish. Still, he was a Belgian, and had been forced to learn Flemish in school. That, and the fact that he had been married to a Jewish woman from Antwerp, who had grown up speaking Flemish—all these things combined made the OP a fair judge of Flemish accents. If it were not for the fact that he knew—or thought he knew—that Mr. Gorman was an American, he would have assumed by just this one sentence that the man was a native-born Fleming.

"Where did you learn to speak like that?" the OP demanded.

"As you know, sir," Mr. Gorman said, continuing on in Flemish, "we missionaries are required to spend six months in Belgium studying French before coming out to the colony. As the colony is ruled by two ethnic groups, I elected to learn Flemish as well."

"And your French, monsieur? How is that?"

"Passable, I hope," Mr. Gorman said, switching to that language. "I wish I'd had more time in your lovely country, but alas, there was a war brewing, and I did not wish to get caught up in it."

"Incredible!" the OP exclaimed. "And yet you do not speak Bushilele?" he asked, switching to English, so that everyone at the breakfast table could understand.

"No, monsieur. Our mission considers it a minority language. I speak only Tshiluba, Kipende, Tshokwe, Lingala, Kituba, and Swahili."

"You have tried all these languages on her, I presume?"

Meanwhile, the girl in question was sitting an arm's reach away, just as still as a golden honey-covered statue.

"Yes, a few words of each. She showed no reaction, monsieur."

"Of course not," Dorcas said. "The poor thing is scared to death."

"Nonsense," Mr. Gorman said. "She looks fine to me. Mother," he said to his wife, "how does she look to you?"

"She looks almost normal," Mrs. Gorman said, "except for those awful tribal markings on her face. It's a good thing they just got started and did just one on each cheek."

"I think that a plastic surgeon could take care of that," Mademoiselle Amanda Brown said quickly.

"A *what*, dear?"

"She means a movie-star doctor," the Gormans' daughter said. "Geez, Mama, don't you know anything?"

As much as the OP disliked all three of the Gormans, he felt a twinge of pity for the mother. Children showed their parents no respect these days. It was as if in facing up to the atrocities of the war, today's youth had not only lost their innocence, but their manners as well.

"Don't worry about her hair, sir," the mademoiselle said. "After breakfast I plan to undo the cornrows and wash it—with *real* shampoo. That is, if she'll let me. So far she hasn't allowed me to touch her."

"I like them corn things," the teenager said. "Makes her look like a native, and ain't that what she is? Ooh boy, can't you just smell her? I can hardly eat my breakfast."

"Peaches!" Mrs. Gorman said with surprising sharpness.

"If she were my child," Dorcas Middleton said, "I'd send her to her room."

"But Peaches isn't your child," Mrs. Gorman said softly. "You chose not to have children, remember? And oh, how you've made me suffer for my decision to have one—just one. 'You're not devoting enough time to the Lord's work,' you said. You must have said that a million times."

"To be fair," Mr. Gorman said, "she's backed off in recent years."

Apparently, Mrs. Gorman had managed to work herself into a state of tears over this issue. "That's only because the mission board finally separated us; now that we're serving on different mission stations I don't feel quite as picked on."

"May God guard my tongue from speaking evil," Dorcas Middleton said. Now she too had tears in her eyes.

"Well," the OP said, "you Americans certainly know how to— what is the word—*upset*, maybe, a welcome party."

"I think the word is *upstage*," the mademoiselle said. She smiled at Pierre, and the little shit smiled back, which annoyed the OP immensely. So much for hoping that his friend was no longer infatuated by the nubile young woman from the American South.

It wasn't that the OP disliked the mademoiselle—it was nothing personal, at least—but she still employed that woman, Cripple, who'd been implicated in the death of Senor Nunez, manager of the Consortium company store. Yes, Cripple had been vindicated, but—in a very strange, *deus ex machina* sort of way. From here on out the OP would just as soon have no further dealings with Cripple—or her American employer.

It was a very strange breakfast, with insubstantial foods by and large, although a ball of *bidia*—manioc mush—was provided, seemingly for Ugly Eyes' benefit. Only the young male *Bula Matadi* ate from it; he cut a large slab and put it on his very own plate first. Imagine that, each person having their own plate! What riches the white man possessed, and to think that someday they would all belong to the Bashilele.

Ah yes, Father, she related to him silently, *we do indeed each have our own plates. And cups! Even the female persons. And we have miniature spears, and small paddles with which to scoop up another mush—this one not cooked until it is stiff, as it should be. It is called* ohta-meela.

Over this ohta-meela *one is to sprinkle something very sweet— something sweeter than the juice of the cane. Also, over this thinner mush, one pours milk—but it is not goat's milk, nor is it the milk from any known animal. Father, this concoction tastes as awful as you can imagine, but when they set a bowl in front of me they smack their lips like apes and go "mmm, mmm." I must try hard not to laugh, because it reminds me so much of little Kahinga when she strains to have a bowel movement and it will not come.*

What was *that*? Ugly Eyes clapped twice with happiness when Father stepped suddenly from behind the trunk of a thick mango tree that shaded the outdoor eating table. Where were his bow and his monkey-hide quiver of arrows? Where was his machete? Never mind those things for now. For now he was holding a cone that was shaped from banana leaves. The smells that escaped from the cone made Ugly Eyes' nose want to dance.

Father cautiously approached the group, then as befitting her status, he offered the delicacies first to the ancient crone. She peered into the leaves, but shook her head.

"*Nasha kakese*," she said, which was a Tshiluba phrase meaning, "not even a little bit." From this Ugly Eyes concluded that the crone was rude, and not wise.

Everyone else reacted similarly except for the young *Bula Matadi*, who carefully removed something from the leaves and put it on his plate. He even remembered to say *tuasakidila*.

Then, with much apparent pleasure, he ate it, and another one like it. He even persuaded the other Ugly Eyes, the young white woman from the day before, to take a bite. Everyone laughed at that, even the rude crone.

Father, then you spoiled it all by speaking.

ELEVEN

◈

*W*owee," the Headhunter said. That's all. It was just a greeting. Like *bon jour* in French, or *muoyo webe* in Tshiluba.

Then that horrible Gorman girl had to spoil the morning by mocking the poor man. It was bad enough that he was about to have his daughter torn from his bosom, but to then have that creature taunting him, why that was simply beyond the pale. If Dorcas had her way, even the Protestant missionaries would take a vow of celibacy, because really, when you thought about it, the Belgian Congo was no place for children. Especially white children.

"*Wowee kazowee*," the girl said. "It's the funniest sounding language there is, isn't it, Mama?"

"I suppose so, dear," Mrs. Gorman said. "But remember what I said about being kind."

"But Daddy, *you* think it sounds funny, don't you? You said so just the other day!"

Mr. Gorman held a fat finger aloft as if recalling something of grave importance. "Funny," he pronounced, "is a nun, a priest and a rabbi showing up at heaven's gates and expecting admittance. Imagine the looks on their faces when Saint Peter tells them you have to be saved first, and that it is too late for them."

Dorcas Middleton frowned at the gluttonous man. "Do tread

carefully, Mr. Gorman. There are, after all, two RCs present at the table."

"What is an RC?" asked the OP.

"Why, Monsieur OP," Dorcas said, "all these years in the Congo, and you've never heard anyone mention RC?"

"It stands for Roman Catholic," their young hostess, Amanda, said. "Actually, I think it's rather a pejorative."

"Forgive me, mademoiselle," the OP said, "but what does *that* mean?"

Amanda tossed her lovely blond hair to the other side of her neck. "In a word: disrespectful. Dorcas," she said, "would you mind terribly scooching your chair over so that we can fit another one in? I think that the girl's father would like to join us."

"Yes, I do mind terribly," Dorcas said. "I suppose that 'scooching' is one of the new slang words you brought with you from America—oh never mind that—but you can't seriously expect us to acquiesce to the presence of an unwashed native. Besides, he isn't her real father."

"But he *is*. My friend Beth back in Rock Hill, South Carolina, is adopted, and her dad is as much her real father as that man who got her mother"—she paused and looked at Peaches—"well, you know."

"He's not even wearing a shirt," Mrs. Gorman said. "I think I'm about to get sick. As if these horrible birds this Belgian has been eating haven't been enough."

"*Excusez moi, madame,*" Pierre said, not without sarcasm. "These horrible little birds are what you missionaries refer to as quail, although they are really francolin. In Tshiluba they are called *nkuadi*. They are to be seen all the time on the roads, especially in the early morning and late afternoon."

"Yes, yes, *nkuadi,*" said Mr. Gorman. "Dear, I've shot hundreds of those; you cook them all the time."

Mrs. Gorman pursed her lips. "Oh. Well, they don't look the same. What did he do? Roast them?"

"Yes," Pierre said. "They were quite delicious."

"It's against the law for him to fraternize with us anyway," the OP said.

"Is that true?" the pretty American asked of Pierre.

He nodded. "*Oui*, Amanda. We do, in fact, insist on separation of the races—so that they don't get the wrong ideas, you understand. But I suppose we could make an exception just this once. Although frankly, I don't think that he would be comfortable sitting with us."

Even though she was from South Carolina, Amanda Brown was just too young and naïve to accept the fact that in the Congo, customs were different. That didn't make them right; it was merely a fact, rather like rendering unto Caesar what was Caesar's. To force the Mushilele to join them at the table would, in fact, be an act of genteel cruelty.

"We should at least give him the opportunity to refuse us," Amanda Brown said. She then displayed her naiveté by giving up her own chair. "Sit," she said and began to gesticulate like a traffic cop. "*Asseyez vous.*"

It was as plain as the buttons on her dress that the poor man was terrified. His dark eyes darted from the rescued child to Pierce and back to the girl again.

"*Somba*," she said in Tshiluba.

"Perhaps you speak yet another language," Mrs. Gorman said.

"Do you know Spanish?" Mr. Gorman said.

"I would like to marry a Spaniard," Peaches said.

"Over my dead body," Mr. Gorman said. "Papists, every one of them, just like the Portuguese, and the Bel—well, you know."

The OP cleared his throat loudly and looked Mr. Gorman straight in the eyes. "My deceased wife, Heilewid—may she rest in peace—was of the Jewish faith."

"Are you sure?" Mr. Gorman said.

"Monsieur, she was my wife; I am quite sure."

"What I meant to say was: a Jewish Belgian sounds like such

an oddity. That's like saying there's such a thing as a Jewish Irish-man, or a Protestant Frenchman."

"Monsieur, I believe there are."

"Hmm. Well, if you insist."

"Which I do," said the OP.

"Monsieur OP," Dorcas Middleton said, "as fascinating as this conversation is, it is doing nothing to address this dilemma. Look, the poor man is becoming more agitated by the second."

"It's his daughter I'd worry about," said Mrs. Gorman.

If Father had not spoken, then the silly girl could not have mocked him. As for the others, who knew if they were mocking him as well? That was less clear. One did not have to be able to under-stand the white man's tongue, however, to understand that with one exception, the whites did not appreciate Father's gift, and did not want him there.

The whites! Yes, Ugly Eyes would continue to think that she was not one of them. Even the crippled Muluba agreed.

"Your skin is the color of a manioc pancake," she had said. "And your eyes are indeed ugly, but you are truly one of us." *Kadi wewe udi muan'etu mene mene.*

It was too much to bear. Surely these people (who comported themselves no better than baboons) could see that Father was a dignified man, one who commanded respect in his village. It was said that if one were to assign a long dry season to each finger and one to each toe, and then count these long dry seasons, one would still not reach Father's age.

Did these monkey people know how to dig their own iron ore and smelt it into metal? Did they know how to grind that metal on a stone wheel until they had achieved arrowheads for every purpose: fish, small birds, large birds, rodents, small antelopes, monkeys, large antelopes that were to be chased until they bled out, and even insects? Did they know that there was even a special arrowhead for fools such as themselves?

Jabber, jabber in their strange tongue that seemed to have no clear beginning or end to the words that comprised the discordant phrases. Such a language would be impossible to learn unless one was born into it. Whatever the circumstances were that surrounded her birth, Ugly Eyes knew that she was not, and could never be, ever be a part of those people gathered around the table there that morning in the shade of the mango tree.

Although Amanda Brown was the official manager of the Missionary Rest House, and she was, for all intents and purposes, the hostess at this rather historic breakfast, she certainly did not feel in charge. If she had to blame any one person it would be the annoying teenage girl who had tried to imitate the Headhunter's speech. Really, everything had gone pretty smoothly up until then.

But that girl! She was going to give her parents trouble bigtime when she got back to the States! Just you wait and see. That loose talk about pregnancy, and then wanting to marry a Spaniard—Peaches was going to do anything she could to push the envelope, and Amanda doubted that the naïve Mrs. Gorman was going to be up to it. Things were undoubtedly a whole lot different in the States these days than the last time the teenager was there; that had to be one of the difficulties of raising a kid in the Congo bush. How do you get them to adjust once you get them back into civilization?

Amanda tapped her water glass with her bread knife. The clear sound elicited a muffled yelp from the "rescued girl," the one who had yet to be given a proper name.

"You may be excused," she said with a smile. "Dinner will be served at noon. I hope to see most of you then."

"Good heavens, dear," Dorcas said, laying a hand protectively on Amanda's arm, "you may be seeing quite a few people before then."

"What do you mean?"

Dorcas stood and pointed in the direction of the bridge that spanned the great falls. A caravan of cars was patiently wending its way through the walking traffic, which at any time of the day consisted of dozens of natives. Wow! There was no end to that line of cars. Literally. It went all the way up to Boulevard des Allies, and then branched out in both directions. Everyone in Belle Vue must be on their way to someplace important. But *where*? Were they fleeing from some danger?

"Pierre," Amanda said, her voice quavering. "What is going on?"

"Damn it," Pierre said. "*Pardonnez moi, mesdames*," he said, bowing quickly to each woman in turn. "They're coming here, I'm afraid. Quick, we must get the girl inside."

"Here? But why?"

"I know," Peaches said triumphantly. "They wanta get a good look at her, that's why."

"That is exactly the case, mademoiselle," the OP said. "You are very perceptive for one who is such a—how do you say—?"

"Hey watch it, buddy," Mr. Gorman said.

"Thank you, Daddy," Peaches said.

The OP flushed. "I agree with the captain; we must get that girl inside."

"How?" Amanda asked. She cupped her hands to her mouth. "Cripple! Cripple. *Eleh kahia!*" Put a fire under it!

Was it possible that the white Mushilele giggled? Amanda shook her head. Just four months ago, back in Rock Hill, she never would have believed such a scene was possible. Ah, and there was Cripple now, brandishing a stick, for heaven's sake. A stick! As if she'd been summoned to herd chickens.

"Ya," Cripple sang out, as she whipped the Mushilele girl lightly about the ankles, "go into the house quickly before you embarrass the new *mamu* with your unsightly presence."

Much to Amanda's relief the girl did seem to get the picture, but she walked slowly—practically dragging her feet—all the while muttering something in rapid-fire Bushilele.

"Cripple," Amanda asked, "do you have any idea what she is saying?"

"*Mamu*, as I told you before, I do not speak the speech of monkeys."

"Cripple! That was not a nice—"

"*Eyo, Mamu*, I should not have spoken with such frankness in front of the *bakalenge*—the lords."

"Ooh!" Amanda said in frustration. "Hurry up. Just get her inside!"

"Come along then, monkey girl," Cripple said to the Headhunter's daughter. With a flick of her switch she actually managed to *eleh kaphia* under the feet of her young white charge.

Amanda watched in growing relief. It was plumb amazing. Either serendipity had stepped in, or Cripple had found her calling; that of playing the part of keeper to a kidnapper's victim.

Or was that even the case? Pierre had been unwilling to commit to that theory. There wasn't enough to go on, he said. In fact, there really wasn't anything. A white child—a young woman really—of definite European heritage—is found tucked away in a remote village deep in the African bush. Virtually no one speaks the language. Officially what can be made of it? Which conclusions can be drawn? Nothing! None! The girl might just as well have come from the moon.

Amanda felt a hand at her elbow and turned. It was the OP.

"Mademoiselle," he said gently, almost fatherly, "perhaps you should go inside now as well. Allow me please to deal with these inquisitive people."

Amanda smiled and nodded. *Een-queez-ee-teev*. The OP could be charming—gallant even—when he wasn't being stubborn, bordering on ruthless, in his quest to overturn the mission's lease on their sixty hectares of prime real estate along the Kasai River. But that was another issue entirely, wasn't it? Yes, that would have to wait.

* * *

Bulelela. It was indeed true that Husband was only a mediocre witch doctor. How could he deny such accusations when there were other medicine men in the village that were far more powerful than he? Why should anyone pay for a curse that had only a small chance of affecting its intended victim? Of what use was a potion that brought no relief to a body wracked with pain?

There can be no denial that Husband's father, and his father before him, were both witch doctors of great stature amongst the Baluba people. It was common knowledge that the special powers a witch doctor possessed were passed down through the generations. Of course, the witch doctor was also required to apprentice, during which time he would learn the many incantations required by his office, and also familiarize himself with a vast quantity of herbs and roots.

Kadi—but—when he was a boy just ten long dry seasons in age, Husband's quick mind discovered the power of the witch doctor. By observing his father interact with his clients, Husband saw that it was only the people who *truly believed* in his father's words, or the potions he sold, who were affected by them.

How did most people come to believe in such things? They believed because it was always thus *and* because the witch doctors projected such frightening images when they danced in their straw-and-palm-fiber costumes, their faces hidden behind wooden masks surrounded by enormous headdresses.

There was power in these dances; one could feel it. There was power in the strange gravelly utterances that were emitted from behind those masks. But the power, Husband observed, was something his father created. When his father was not dancing, the costume and mask hung lifeless from pegs in the potion hut next to the dovecote. *Bulelela*, the same words, the same potions—these things were virtually useless in the hands of skeptics.

This partnership of salesmanship/belief, Husband soon learned, was the ingredient necessary in any witch doctor–patient (or client, as the case may be) relationship. Unfortunately, Husband had been born happy, with no wish to deceive anyone. In fact, his mother had wished to call him *Mumuemue*, because he'd been born with a smile on his face, but that was not an appropriate name for a future witch doctor. (Instead he was called *Tshibungu*, which is a type of dried gourd used in divining.)

One might rightfully ask what an unemployed, mediocre witch doctor does during the day in a workers' village. The answer is nothing out of the ordinary. When he is through with his breakfast and has seen his two wives off to work—Cripple down the hill to the Rest House, and Second Wife off to work in the fields, her children in tow—Husband takes Amanda, the youngest child, and meanders over to the palaver hut. There Husband selects whichever chair seems most likely to remain in the shade the greatest part of the day, and settles in to spend the day snoozing and occasionally participating in the art of male story-telling. This is all that is expected of him; in fact, to do otherwise would be considered strange, and Husband already has been accused of enough strange behavior.

On this morning Husband carried baby Amanda aloft on his shoulders. The child, a boy, is named after Amanda Brown, the young American missionary who runs the Rest House, where Cripple is employed. From the high path that leads to the palaver hut Husband could see the bridge that connected the two Belle Vues, the mist created by the falls, and a line of automobiles waiting to cross over to the African side. Immediately his heart began to pound.

After all, there were only two options that Husband could think of that could be behind such a dramatic European migration: either the whites were fleeing from something, or they were running to something. In the latter case the Missionary Rest House could conceivably be their destination. If it wasn't, whatever was causing them to flee would undoubtedly be cause for Amanda Brown to flee as well.

In either case, at that moment he felt a strong need to be at Cripple's side.

Ugly Eyes—she who could really lay claim to the name, for she had worn it all her life, worn it like a second skin—this Ugly Eyes took in all there was to see in the sitting area of the Missionary Rest House. And sticking close beside her, as close as the stench of a dog's breath is to its face in order that they might whisper unnoticed, was the funny little Muluba woman, Cripple.

"They are incapable of squatting on their haunches," Cripple whispered.

"Truly? Is that so?"

"*Eyo*. They are a very strange people, these whites."

"Eh?" Ugly Eyes began to shiver. After all, what really was her connection to these people who were incapable of squatting, and who had to bring food up to their lips with metal implements every bit as sharp as arrowheads? Perhaps there was a similarity in the color of her eyes and skin, but likewise, were not the mouse and the elephant both *mufika*?

"But not only that," Cripple said, "look at the ornaments on the walls. Can you see that each contains the likeness of a place?"

"I do not understand," Ugly Eyes whispered.

"Look. There is a river, and there a house. Behind it are hills." Ugly Eyes stared at the rectangles which hung suspended from metal pegs. They were, for the most part, brightly colored, but she could detect no images.

"They are the color of the water poured off manioc leaves," she whispered. *Mayi wa matamba*. "That is all I see."

Her new friend groaned. "*Aiyee!* Then you have eaten too many manioc leaves. There are images to be seen; not just color. *Tch!* Let us move to this other ornament. Do you not see the face of a person?"

Ugly Eyes was astounded. She saw nothing but a dark square

with strange light markings on it. But in any case, who would want the face of a person gazing at them all the time? Perhaps it was a curse and could not be avoided. In that case, where was the altar with the countermeasures: the antelope horn, the baboon skull, or the little pouch containing the powders prepared by the white man's witch doctor?

"Cripple, I do not see a face of a person. But I wish to return to the sleeping room, for this is truly an evil place."

At that Cripple snorted into her hands. "Ugly Eyes, you are indeed uncivilized—a *musenji*! How fortunate you are to have me, Cripple, as your teacher. Behold, this is not an evil totem, but a likeness of Mamu Ugly Eyes and her family. Follow my finger. This is the nose of Mamu Ugly Eyes. These are the eyes. And here the mouth. Now do you see?"

Ugly Eyes tried her best to imagine a face—*the* face of the white *mamu* superimposed on the square of confusing patterns and shades of black and white, but she could not. To begin with, the square was altogether much smaller than the *mamu*'s face, and it was flat.

"Concentrate," Cripple commanded.

"Surely this is a trick," Ugly Eyes exclaimed, because for a second she saw the likeness of a woman seated on a chair and next to her a man. Now the images were gone—wait, there they were! Somehow the exact likenesses of five people had been captured and put on this little totem. Or were they perhaps trapped inside, and if so, how could Ugly Eyes be two places at once, and at once be both so small and yet of normal size?

"*Aiyee*," the Headhunter's Daughter moaned. "*Echi chidi bualu bukole!*"

It was with dread that Ugly Eyes realized that she and Cripple had allowed themselves to get carried away. They had been far too loud and the young white girl, the one who was about her own age, was coming straight toward her with a triumphant look on her face.

TWELVE

The OP counted fourteen cars. That was one heck of a welcome committee. Just how the news had spread overnight—Belle Vue did not have an operating telephone system—absolutely mystified him, but he knew he'd never find out. Chances were though, it was the night watchman who'd initially let the cat out of the bag. No doubt from then on it spread from servant to servant.

Well, at this point what did it matter? He'd admit that the girl was here, but he wouldn't let anyone close enough to bother her. Already she'd had enough stress for one day. Like she needed to be poked and prodded by some fat Flemish hausfrau, ha!

"Attention!" he shouted, waving his arms. "This is not a circus sideshow. The girl is a human being. She is inside, and she will not come out. Does everyone understand? *Bon!* Now go back across the river, and if you are scheduled to work today, then please go to your jobs."

The OP watched with satisfaction as everyone—except for Hans Bruebeggar—obeyed without protest. As for Hans, well, he was Flemish, and had been in the Congo longer than anyone working for the Consortium, including the OP. He just wasn't OP material.

"With all due respect, Monsieur OP," Hans said, "you are the

dictator of Belle Vue and the Consortium, but you have no au-
thority over the Protestant missionaries. *N'est-ce pas?*"

The OP looked Bruebeggar straight in his bloodshot eyes.
The man was a drinker, favoring Johnnie Walker Red—perhaps
because the name described his face. No, that was a cheap shot.
The OP had to get over his anti-Flemish feelings if he was ever
going to be a truly effective manager, because, face it, the union
of Flanders and of the Walloons was here to stay.

"You are correct, Monsieur Bruebeggar. I have no control of
your actions on this side of the river, and as it is Saturday, and you
have the day off, neither can I dictate your activities. However,
in order to return to your house, you must either cross *my* bridge,
or take a detour of some one hundred kilometers. It is a hot day,
monsieur, but at least it is not raining. Now, the choice is yours;
bon chance."

"You bastard," Hans Bruebeggar said, and made a meaty fist,
which he waved in the OP's face, before turning around and
heading back across the mighty Kasai River.

As the OP watched his employee drive angrily off he felt a
curious mix of power and tenderness. The feeling of power he
welcomed—he'd come to rely on that; it was like oxygen. The
feeling of tenderness was frightening; it was like being awakened
in the dead of the night and being told that there was a spider
under the cover with you, but you didn't have a flashlight, and
there was no electricity. Just you, darkness, and a poisonous spider
that could be anywhere and bite at any time.

Love and tenderness were terrible things.

"Cripple," Mamu Ugly Eyes said, "the master's daughter says that
she saw you and the white Mushilele whispering together. Is that
true?"

"Which master?" Cripple said. Her eyes were wide and innocent, although in her voice could be heard the insouciance of Protruding Navel. "Is it the handsome young police captain, the rich

king of diamonds, or the missionary whose belly exceeds mine but which does not carry within it a child?"

"Cripple, you are wasting my time! You know that it is the fat man—*aiyee*! You see what you have done to my tongue?" It appeared as if Mamu Ugly Eyes was fighting back a smile.

Cripple clapped her hands and laughed happily; truly, Mamu Ugly Eyes was the source of much amusement. But why stop there? Because Mamu Ugly Eyes had taken Cripple into her sleeping room for the conversation, they were quite alone.

"*Aiyee*," Cripple said, pointing to the bed. "*Mamu*, are you not afraid?"

"Afraid of what?"

"*Mamu*, there is space beneath your bed. Like so!" Cripple gestured with her hands to indicate the amount of airspace between the box springs and the cement floor. "At night it is the gathering place of many demons."

"*Tch!*" Mamu Ugly Eyes was learning how to reply like a good African. "Where did you get such a silly idea, Cripple?"

"From your sacred book, *Mamu*."

"From the *Book of God*?"

"*Eyo*, from the *Mukanda wa Nzambi*. Are there not demons mentioned in this book, *Mamu*?"

"*Eyo, kadi—*"

"It is true, *Mamu*, that I am but a lowly heathen. Quite possibly I am the biggest sinner that you will ever have the privilege to meet, for I have no intention of repenting. Nevertheless, despite my heathenish ways, I am not an ignorant woman. As my brother, whose head was as hard as a mahogany stump, sat inside the school of the Catholic Fathers and struggled to learn, I sat outside on the grass and soaked up their words like a head cloth soaks up the dew if one forgets to bring it in for the night."

"I am sure that you did, Cripple," Ugly Eyes said.

"*Mamu*, one of the many things which I learned was this: in your world of beliefs, your chief demon—the one who you call

Satana—gets very much annoyed by direct confrontation. Even though you do not belong to a real religion, such as Catholicism, I am sure that he is very much disturbed by your presence here, and will do everything in his power to wage a spiritual war against you. For you have come to give rest and renewal to the hard-working Protestants who—although not quite real Christians—are still close enough to make the Prince of Darkness very, very angry with you, the caregiver. Do you not agree with my analysis, *Mamu?*"

Mamu Ugly Eyes sighed. "*Eyo,* I quite agree. You are very perceptive, Cripple. I think that, despite statements to the contrary, you are indeed a wise woman."

"*What* statements, Mamu?"

"*Yala!* Perhaps I spoke without thinking. In that case, you must please disregard what I said. Because we almost—but not quite—Christians are not allowed to engage in gossip. Now, where was our conversation before I made such a terrible error in judgment?"

"You were telling me what a wise woman I am, *Mamu.*"

"*Eyo,* so very wise."

"Now, speaking as a wise woman of many more years than you possess, I must ask you: do you not desire to feel a man's body pressed next to yours in such a big bed as this?"

"*Kah!*"

"It was only a question, *Mamu.* But if not a man, then perhaps a goat. Just for the company, you understand."

"Cripple, are we through here?"

"I believe so, *Mamu.* But it is a terrible waste of space, just the same. You would do well to get some hens. They would lay many eggs on such a soft surface while you slept beside them. Everyone would benefit, I assure you. Even the young white *mamu,* for she did not like the gruel you set before her and called breakfast."

"What? My oatmeal? How do you know this?"

"Because it was my job to wash the dishes, *Mamu.* And because you have no chickens, first I must scrape off all the food you white people waste so that we can then throw it over the cliff and feed the big crocodile.

"Anyway, Mamu Ugly Eyes, the young white *mamu* did not eat but a few spoons of the gruel. One could not blame her, given that its taste was of bird poop mixed with sand. However, the child within me was hungry and as of yet does not distinguish taste, so together we prevented this shameful waste of oatmeal, cow's milk, and sugar."

The white *mamu* closed her eyes tightly and stood silently for a moment, but her lips moved as if she were inwardly saying an incantation. Cripple hoped she wasn't being cursed; life was hard enough without having an almost-Christian white person siccing one of her demons on you.

"That is *not* why we throw it over the cliff," Mamu Ugly Eyes said. "What *else* am I to do with the scraps from their plates?"

"*Mamu,* is it not better to serve these people only as much as they will eat?"

"Yes, but—but—our village does not work that way."

Captain Pierre Jardin badly needed something stronger to drink than a glass of grenadine sans alcohol, which was all the Missionary Rest House had to offer. This was exactly the kind of situation he had hoped to avoid by selecting a sleepy little town like Belle Vue as his first post eight years ago. Since then, he could still count on both hands—okay, throw in the toes as well—the number of times he'd had to deal with "situations" involving whites. Most of the occasions had featured the Consortium's *Le Club* and, of course, liquor was involved. Only twice were the cases entirely of a personal nature: a wife beating, and "the love which dare not speak its name"—but which did, and *loudly.*

Of course this was not counting the diamond incident, which happened *after* the young American's arrival. No doubt that one week alone shaved years off the young police captain's life. What was it about Americans that drew trouble to them like they were magnets in a junkyard of scrap iron? Well, for one thing, they didn't mind their own business. The Belgians—and the other Europeans, for that matter—stayed on the "white" side of the river, whereas the Americans insisted on getting their lease on the African side.

That was just one example, but a good one. Over the years the Missionary Rest House had been the drop-off site for orphans, the dying, the diseased, the starving, the homeless—and it wasn't even a mission, but a vacation spot for missionaries hoping to escape just this sort of thing for a few days. Nobody dared drop off diseased and dying people on the steps of the Belgian-owned houses.

Mais oui, this white Mushilele girl was not the doings of Mademoiselle Amanda Brown, but she *had* offered to help with her rehabilitation. And now look, it was sheer madness. Like a Shakespeare comedy, yes? That huge American, Mr. Gorman, had him cornered in the kitchen, and was interrogating him right in front of the help. Interrogating *him*.

"Aren't you going to do anything about it, Captain?" the American bellowed. That was another thing: Why did Americans always have to speak as loud as drunks?

"Mademoiselle Brown is speaking with the woman, Cripple, now," Pierre said.

"But shouldn't *you* be doing something," Mr. Gorman said. "Aren't *you* the one in charge?"

He heard Protruding Navel snicker, even though he was quite sure the man didn't understand a word of English.

"Yes, Monsieur Gorman," Pierre said, "I am in charge. It is precisely because this is the case that I must request that you— what is the English? Ah! Butt out, yes?"

"Captain!" Mr. Gorman growled. "I am shocked. You may be assured that I will speak to the OP immediately."

"As you wish, monsieur, but it may interest you to know that the OP is not my boss."

Pierre could swear that Protruding Navel snickered again.

"Then who is your boss?"

"Ah, monsieur, I shall leave that up to you to investigate in your spare time—now that you are on vacation. *N'est-ce pas?*"

Protruding Navel started laughing so hard that he doubled over at the waist. In fact, he was so far gone that he soon had to lean on the counter for support.

"What is that boy up to?" Mr. Gorman demanded, and rightly so.

It really was unacceptable for a houseboy to behave like that. Pierre had been asked to overlook cases in which adult houseboys had been whipped for being too cheeky to their employers. Upon occasion the whippings got out of hand, or the whip came in contact with an eye, and compensation had to be made—sometimes to the houseboy's extended family, sometimes to his entire clan. One was free to read between the lines there.

In a nutshell, if one put a stop to insubordination in its early stages, quite possibly it could amount to the same thing as having to put down tribal unrest later down on the path.

"Protruding Navel, come with me," Pierre snapped, using his most official voice. "*Maintenant!*"

Still laughing, the Lulua houseboy followed him outside. Pierre led him away from the house and the woodshed, to what some might say was perilously close to the edge of the river gorge. Here the roar of the falls was loud, but not so loud as to preclude a shouted conversation. A third party trying to listen in, however, would not have been able to hear.

But it was only when Pierre got the man to stand right alongside the gorge that the fool quit laughing.

"*Muambi*," the houseboy said, suddenly quite solemn, "do you not agree that our waterfalls here at Belle Vue are the most splendid in all of the Kasai?"

Pierre was astounded at the man's cheek. "*Pardon?*"

"Of course I have not had the opportunity to see as many waterfalls as you, given that I lack your means of transportation. Nonetheless, based on all the comments I've heard throughout the years of my employment, I stand by my conclusion."

Captain Pierre Jardin was a young man of twenty-eight, but unfortunately, he was no longer naïve. It may have taken him a moment, but now he had caught up with the sly houseboy, Protruding Navel, son of a minor Lulua chief. Somewhere, somehow, Protruding Navel had learned to speak English, and had been so amused by the preceding conversation that he had been unable to contain himself.

"Where did you learn to speak English?" Pierre asked. It was no surprise that the second he opened his mouth to speak English, the houseboy turned his head away from him.

No matter, Pierre thought; there were ways. "I will pay you a week's salary if you tell me," he said.

The arrogant man snorted, but wouldn't take the bait.

"Very well. I'm sure that I will find another Lulua monkey in the village who knows how to speak English. How about your wife? Is she a monkey too?"

"*Nkima?* You call us *monkeys?*" It was the worst insult in the book; it was the worst thing Pierre could have called an African, because the word had a history. *Macaque!* Monkeys. That's what Belgian housewives said—sometimes to their faces—of the Africans they encountered on the streets of Leopoldville, Luluaburg, and even Belle Vue. It was the Belgian equivalent of "nigger." It was worse than "shit." It was a fighting word—except that you weren't allowed to fight if you were a black.

But Protruding Navel was on fire now. The veins along his temples twitched. His dark eyes flashed, and yes, he was looking at Pierre now, looking at him as if he wished to throw him over the cliff, throw him to his death on the rocks below, so that ultimately Pierre would become crocodile food along with the table scraps.

"Ah," said Pierre, "a thousand apologies. But I did not call you, or your wife, a monkey. I asked if she was one. Clearly the answer is no, because in order to be a monkey, she would have to be Flemish, *n'est-ce pas?*"

The two men stared at each other, as if they were engaged in a contest, and then suddenly it was over and they were laughing and shaking hands. But no more, of course. No backslapping—after all, Protruding Navel was still a black.

"Yes, Captain, I do speak a little English," he said in a very heavy African accent.

"So then, one more time please, where did you learn?"

"Monsieur, I learn this from just my ear, *comprenez-vous?*"

"No teacher?"

"Just listen to missionaries. They very funny sometimes. Like now."

"Yes. But *excusez-mois*, Protruding Navel. How was *Muambi* Gorman very funny just now?"

"Because, monsieur, he thinks progress is to be made by investigating the little Muluba woman, Cripple. Yes, progress—if one is a stick of dynamite." He paused, and both men laughed. "Can you not see it now, monsieur? Cripple and Muambi Gorman matching watts?"

"Uh? Do you mean 'wits'?"

"Perhaps. But this English is not the speech of your peoples. Am I correct?"

"Touché."

"So maybe for now, we are both right."

Pierre nodded and extended his hand again, but Protruding Navel was no longer in the mood for pleasantries. He took off like a virgin from a French monastery, or, perhaps because he was sure now that he was no longer wanted on official police business. Oh well, Pierre could understand that as well; if he were in the houseboy's shredded cloth shoes, he would do the same thing. He wouldn't fraternize with the enemy one more second than he had to, that was for sure.

Alone at last, Pierre stole a few precious moments of solitude. The arrogant man was right; there was no finer setting for a city in all of the Congo, except perhaps up in the mountainous Kivu Province. A horseshoe-shaped falls could not compare with the Mountains of the Moon, with their fabled gorilla bands. But then again, those mountains probably couldn't compare with Everest. It was all relative, wasn't it?

And wasn't *relative* just another word for perspective? So what if Cripple and the headhunter's daughter were really communicating somehow. Ultimately, that was a good thing. In the meantime it was merely a puzzle that needed to be worked out. More worrisome was discovering Protruding Navel's propensity for acquiring languages. This was just the kind of thing that had probably never occurred to the stuffed shirts in Brussels; quite possibly there could be other secret geniuses like Protruding Navel. Who knew what that might mean as the days dwindled, and independence for the Congo loomed closer?

Taking hold of a jacaranda sapling that clung to the very edge of the precipice, whether by design or by nature, yet not quite trusting it, Pierre edged as close to the drop-off as his stomach would allow. From his vantage point, the cliff plunged straight down—even undercutting him somewhat—for at least sixty meters. What was that in feet? About two hundred, maybe slightly less? Then below that the land continued to fall steeply in a jumble of rocks and debris for another fifty meters. At the very bottom was a wide, seasonal sand bar, one that would be under water in another month if the rains continued on schedule.

C'est incroyable! Ce crocodile est deux fois grand comme il etait la derniere fois. Captain Pierre Jardin gazed respectfully down at the largest reptile he had ever seen. All right, so it couldn't be the *same* crocodile, since it was twice as large as the last one he'd seen there, but *mon Dieu*, where were these monsters coming from? Usually only man-eaters got this large. The Missionary Rest House was going to have to stop throwing its rubbish over the side of the cliff; Pierre had been trying to get them to compost it for years. Maybe now that Amanda was in charge, things would change.

He made a mental note to check with some of the villages along the river to see if there had been an unusual number of fatalities amongst women laundering clothes in recent years. In the meantime, he would remember to be thankful that Amanda lived high above the canyon walls.

THIRTEEN

When Amanda returned to the sitting room, she was greeted by a gang of demanding eyes. Yes, that's what they were: a gang. They were all trained on her, and they all wanted to know the same thing: Were Cripple and the white Mushilele girl communicating together in Tshiluba? What was going on? Were they somehow being duped?

"I'm afraid I didn't learn very much," Amanda said.

"But she's your—what *is* this crippled woman to you?" Mr. Gorman asked.

Amanda felt her cheeks redden. "She's my maid, I guess."

"You *guess*?"

"He's only asking this because most houseboys are men," Mrs. Gorman said. "And if they're young, you can spank them."

"Why, I never!" Amanda said. "It wouldn't occur to me to spank an African. Aren't we called here to shine a light in this, the heart of darkness?"

"The child is right," Dorcas said, "although I haven't heard it put so quaintly for quite some years."

"Humph," said Mr. Gorman, as he gave the old woman a look of moderated sourness.

For some reason his expression reminded Amanda of putting sugar on grapefruit. She'd never much cared for this fruit before coming to the Congo, but now she adored it. Maybe if she dumped enough Christian love on crusty old Mr. Gorman she could at least learn to tolerate him.

"What are they doing now?" Mrs. Gorman asked.

"Cripple is giving the girl a bath," Amanda said.

Mrs. Gorman recoiled in shock. "A *bath*? That's impossible; it's utterly unchristian."

"I don't understand."

Young Peaches rolled her eyes dramatically. "You can't have an African looking at a white girl's baby-maker."

Her *baby-maker*? What century were these people living in? This was almost the nineteen-sixties, for crying out loud. Had they even heard of Elvis Presley or Jerry Lee Lewis? If Amanda were to use the scientific word for that part of a girl's anatomy, every other female in the room would faint dead away, and as for Mr. Gorman, he'd probably have a heart attack.

Nonetheless, Pierre had put her in charge of the girl's rehabilitation and she would do the sensible thing. "Black or white, a woman is a woman. Y'all have *babas* here in the Congo, just like we have mammies in the South, and my mammy saw me without my clothes on plenty of times."

"Yes," Mrs. Gorman said, her face as white as froth on the falls, "but you were a little girl. Am I right?"

"She is trying to be delicate," Dorcas said. "She is afraid to reference pubic hair."

"Dorcas!" Mr. Gorman exploded.

"Oh Mama," Peaches whined, "and I'm just an innocent child."

"Bother you are," Amanda said, using a Briticism she had learned in the movies and of which she was rather fond. She was suddenly fed up to the gills with her guests. She would have thrown them all out, except that of course that she couldn't, because strictly speaking they weren't her guests; they were the guests of the Missionary Rest House. They were hardworking servants of the Lord, and her job was to give them a place to rest and refresh themselves; not to judge the narrowness of their minds.

"Why, I never!" Mrs. Gorman said crossly, or was that a sly smile playing around the corners of her lips?

"Oh come on, everyone," Dorcas said. "The girl is right again; this foundling—for that's really what she is, is not our business. By the way, I have decided to go across the river this morning, instead of after dinner. Would anyone like to ride along? I'll be going to the general store and then to the garage to have some work done on the car. One can walk from there to the company club grounds and have a soda by the pool while one waits."

"Will there be any boys my age there?" said Peaches.

"Yes, I'm sure there will be," Amanda said, and then she caught herself. "Well, there usually are. The Gaston twins are fourteen and their parents are keeping them home this semester."

"Isn't that highly unusual?" Mrs. Gorman said. She sounded genuinely alarmed. "Shouldn't they be off at a boarding school?"

"What did they do?" Mr. Gorman boomed. "Get thrown out?"

"No—I mean, yes," Amanda said. "It really isn't my place to talk about it."

How ironic was that? Back home, in Rock Hill, South Carolina, Amanda had loved nothing better than to gossip with her friends. It was a skill she had learned at her mother's knee. As one grew older, one perfected one's craft until, as a fully integrated adult woman in the community, it was possible to gossip with impunity just as long as one spiced it with wit, and then sugarcoated it with charm. But Amanda had come to Africa to atone for her sins, not to revel in the sins of others.

"Hmm," said Mr. Gorman, sounding not at all convinced.

"Mama, can I please go with Auntie Dorcas? Daddy, please?

Pretty, please, with sugar on top?" Peaches was a ball of energy. No doubt she could have run all the way across the bridge if given permission.

"Well, I—" Mrs. Gorman started to say, speaking slowly.

"You ladies go ahead and enjoy yourselves," Mr. Gorman said, giving Amanda quite the shock. "I never did see much sense in dabbling about in a shared bath and then cooking in the sun like a wiener on a stick."

The three ladies looked at Amanda, but of course she had to refuse the offer to accompany them. Not that she would have seriously entertained the offer for a second, anyway. How often did one get the chance to study a real-life Tarzan—make that Jane? In this movie, however, there would be no need to hire men in chimpanzee suits to play the part of the apes; those parts went to the white community of Belle Vue.

Harry Gorman thrived on being a contradiction. After all, he hailed from a town named North, South Carolina. Having been the victim of an armed robbery when he was just six years old—his parents were shot in a home invasion, right in front of his eyes—Harry grew up as an ardent pacifist. However, his was a hunting culture, and Harry was able to delineate quite clearly between the killing of animals for sport and the taking of human life.

Similarly, he was brusque in his manner—a bit of a loudmouth, when it came down to it—but at the same time, he was a humble follower of the man from Galilee. And just because Harry yelled at Mrs. Gorman and Peaches, that didn't mean that he didn't love them; *au contraire*, a more passionate family man you'd be hard-pressed to find out on the mission field.

So when Harry went hunting for the Headhunter, it wasn't so hard to convince himself that he did so in his capacity as a father. There was at least a part of him that wished to communicate with the man heart to heart. But since the other so-called father was a Mushilele, one of the tribe known to be headhunters, Harry did not have much hope. Only Satan could convince a man that it was all right to kill another man as a right of passage. Only Satan could convince a man that it was okay to drink one's palm wine from a human skull. Satan and his helpers on earth: the village witch doctors.

Oftentimes the natives were spiritual slaves to these witch doctors. They lived their lives in abject fear of the witch doctor and the power of his curses. Harry also knew that these curses weren't just a bunch of mumbo jumbo, either. They were very real. In his twenty-one years in the Belgian Congo, Harry had witnessed perfectly healthy people fall deathly ill overnight because of a witch doctor's curse. He had seen a man's arm shrivel practically before his eyes. He was there when a woman, cursed to her back, fell on the ground, foaming at the mouth, and died twenty minutes later.

If the Headhunter was under a protective spell, it might even be dangerous to talk to him. Yet what worried Harry more was the possibility that the girl was similarly protected. What else could explain the fact that she, with her skin the color of yellowed ivory, could live undetected for thirteen years in a Bashilele village?

Harry slipped out the back kitchen door, the one facing the woodshed, and took stock of his surroundings. To his left was the lawn; that narrow, level bit of land that led to the precipice and the falls. To his right the land rose steeply, save for a half acre or so, tightly planted with mango and citrus trees. The Missionary Rest House had been built at the base of a great *tshisuku*-covered hill, atop of which perched the workers' village.

The Headhunter had found quail in the *tshisuku*—the elephant grass—and Harry thought of the antelope it must contain. There would be time to hunt on the morrow, and in a safer place, because the hillside was too close to the village, and undoubtedly the *tshisuku* here was crisscrossed with native trails. So focus, Harry told himself, *focus*. He was always talking to himself. Wasn't everybody his age? And look, it paid off. There, sticking out behind the green-and-white blotched trunk of that mango tree. That is the tip of a bow.

Harry could creep up on a grasshopper and grab it. That was a skill he'd perfected as a child, just in case he had to run away and live in the woods. You never really knew when the home you lived in would be invaded again, or if the people Foster Care stuck you with would treat you mean. After all, adoption was out. Nobody wanted to adopt a harelip, even after the surgery.

Cripple could work wonders, not miracles. She had engaged Protruding Navel in many conversations regarding the *mamu's* clothes, but neither of them had been able to figure out the workings of the garment-of-shameful-breasts. This was to be expected, as neither of them had actually seen it worn. However, Protruding Navel, having been employed by several white women of varying breast sizes and shapes, proclaimed himself to be the more informed of the two on the subject.

In Protruding Navel's considerable opinion, the band was worn up, along the top side, to help flatten the breasts. The cups then hung down like the mud flaps of a truck, but essentially to protect them from being bumped. Any suggestion that the breasts might be hoisted and enhanced by an article of clothing struck the man as lewd—unchristian to the extreme; certainly something no Protestant would ever do.

"Come," Cripple said to Ugly Eyes, when she had dried her off with the softest of cloths, "come and I will show you the most amazing sight." She led the girl, who by then was truly almost white, to the *mamu's* closet and flung open the door.

"Behold! A forest of dresses hanging from sticks! Have you ever seen such a thing in your life? Of course you have not; you are a savage from the *tshisuku*-dwelling Bashilele. Nonetheless, are they not beautiful?"

"*Aiyee*," said Ugly Eyes, and then she did the oddest thing; she backed away, as if she were afraid of all that brightly colored cloth.

"They will not bite you," Cripple said, repeating a joke she'd heard the *mamu* say. "Except for one!"

"*Baba wani!*" Ugly Eyes cried and flung her arm over her eyes.

Cripple thought she would burst a gut laughing. Perhaps she would have, had not the *mamu* pounded on the door and demanded that she account for the racket.

"Cripple! *Nudi nenza tshinyi?*" What are you doing?

"Nothing, *Mamu*. We will be out shortly. In the meantime, please attend to your guests, for they are *bakalenge*, lords, and as such are far more important than I am."

"Stop that," Mamu Ugly Eyes said, and then Cripple could hear her walk away from the door.

"Cripple," whispered the new Ugly Eyes in astonishment, "you dare to speak to a white woman like that?"

"*Tch*," Cripple said. "I said nothing that was untrue. And when I am through with you today, you too will be a *mukelenge*—a lady. I shall have to call you *mamu* and show you the respect one normally reserves for one's parents. I will have to say yes, when I mean no, and no when I mean yes. I will have to stand when I can no longer feel my feet, and then I will have to walk home, only to sleep on a thin mat woven from the fronds of the *malala* palm. I will have to serve you and the other lords sumptuous feasts—with meat—three times a day, but I will eat but twice, and perhaps twice a week there will be meat—if we have been fortunate."

Ugly Eyes had big feet and she stamped one now, just like a white woman. "Then I will *not* be a white woman. Believe me, Cripple, I will never treat you as you have just described. Give me back my *didiba*—my loincloth—and I will return to my village."

"*Aiyee!* Such a sensitive one you are. Perhaps it is because of the pasty color of your skin. Do you not recognize a joke when you hear one? Of course not! Well, never mind; that will all come in due time. For now let us return to the matter of the dresses on sticks. You must choose one to wear."

"*Kah!* They are not mine!"

"And the sky is not yours, yet you breathe the air. Now choose. Hurry, we do not have much time if we are to surprise the *mamu* with a good impression."

The poor girl was truly a *musenji*, a barbarian. She was completely without the knowledge needed to choose a dress. Cripple had never worn a dress, so she was not exactly an expert herself, but she had seen Mamu Ugly Eyes in the blue dress. She knew that it buttoned in the back. She also remembered that after Mamu Ugly Eyes was all buttoned up in her pretty blue dress, she then stepped into a strange white skirt, and then pulled that strange white skirt up under the skirt of the dress.

Now that white skirt was a puzzle—truly, truly it was. It superficially resembled the costumes that the fertility dancers wore. Like the costumes, the white skirt was stiff and stuck out in all directions; it swayed with every movement Mamu Ugly Eyes made. However, unlike the costumes, the white skirt was not made from straw, but some strange web-like material made by the white man.

"Cripple," the new Ugly Eyes said, "do you not think that there are too many things to ponder in a place such as this?"

"*E*," said Cripple, for that was exactly what she was thinking. Of what use were the underskirt and the breast protector? Surely a dress was enough.

But even then the dress was almost more than Cripple could handle. Although she was barely more than a child, this Ugly Eyes had larger breasts than Mamu Ugly Eyes. Stuffing the breasts into the dress so that they were placed properly, and getting the girl to put her arms through the sleeves, was like trying to catch a fish without a hook. Finally Cripple was able to stand back and survey her work.

"Now we must do something about your hair," she said.

"My *hair*? What about it? Iron Sliver, my mother's friend, toiled a long time to weave these braids. Do you not admire her handiwork?"

"*Eyo*, my little barbarian, but you are not a basket; you are a white lady. I shall remove the braids and give you the hair that you were born with. In the meantime you must think of a new name."

"A new name?"

"Yes, of course. Have you ever heard of a white lady called Ugly Eyes?"

"Cripple, until this *mukelenge* came to my village, I had never seen a white woman. Truly, I tell you; I know nothing of their names."

"Then I must help you select something more dignified."

"Like what?"

"*Mamu Mabele Manene.*" Mistress Big Breasts.

"*Bulelela?* Really? Is that more dignified to the white man's ear?"

"*E.*"

Amanda must have thanked God a dozen times that the other missionaries had decided to spend the morning in town—except for Mr. Gorman. That still left the OP and Pierre to entertain, and of course, entertaining Pierre wasn't any work at all—not anymore. Amanda flushed just to think of it.

But it was true. It seemed like just being near Pierre was all she needed to have in order to pass the time. Conversation was just a bonus. Then there were those rare moments when his skin brushed up against hers, sending sparks of electricity throughout her body, even to those places she dare not think about—in fact, was told she *shouldn't* think about until after marriage. Such was the power of Pierre.

So really, that left only the OP that she had to entertain. Why was the Operations Manager even here? After all, the girl was found in a Bashilele village far away from his private little kingdom of Belle Vue. The girl was not his subject, and for that matter, neither was Amanda.

And indeed, Belle Vue was ruled exactly like a feudal state. In the two months that she had been in the Congo, Amanda had become well aware that the OP was in charge of *everything* that had anything to do with what went on in town, both European and native sectors—everything, that is, except for those few hectares that comprised the Missionary Rest House and its environs. Those had been leased directly from His Majesty's government for a period of ninety-nine years. That was forty-six years ago.

If, and when, the Belgian Congo gained its independence in two years, as some predicted, then the fate of the Missionary Rest House was anybody's guess. Until then, the Home Mission Board made the rules, and the current Hostess—in this case, Amanda Brown—implemented them. In fact, she even had the power to make rules of her own, although, of course, later they might be overturned by the board. The point being that if she wanted to, Amanda could require the OP to don a paper hat and recite a nursery rhyme before he could enter the Missionary Rest House.

The frustrating thing about this business was the fact, of which the OP was probably blithely unaware, that Amanda was quite possibly risking her very soul by disliking him so much. And it wasn't even anything personal that he had done to Amanda, but to Cripple.

That racist man had sat calmly in the grandstand, watching Cripple climb the gallows to her certain execution. True, he had lacked the power to commute her sentence, but he could have stood up and protested. He could have done something; but he didn't. There is always *something* that one can do to make a difference. Amanda knew that from experience.

If only she could tell him off face-to-face. Pierre, however, absolutely forbade that tactic. Even though the OP had no power over Amanda, and there was virtually nothing he could do to her that either Pierre or Amanda could think of, the captain would not back her up. Yes, this felt like a form of betrayal, although Amanda was doing her best to compartmentalize those feelings.

Now the time had come for the great unveiling. So to speak.

Cripple—bless her heart, the woman was as slow as molasses on a cold day in January—had finally signaled that the girl was ready to come out. It had taken Cripple an hour and a half to bathe and dress the girl, plus many whispered conversations through a cracked door.

Amanda had approved the use of her royal blue cotton dress with the scoop neck and the dropped waist. She'd given Cripple permission to use her hairbrush even though she couldn't imagine why, given that the girl had rows of tightly woven braids.

What about shoes? Cripple hadn't asked about shoes. My goodness, what a mistake Amanda had made to turn the girl over to Cripple; there had been no conversations at all about leg shaving, or anti-perspirants, or all the other necessary things a white girl needs to know.

"Cripple, come on out," Amanda said. She sounded far gayer than she felt.

Much to Amanda's surprise a white woman stepped out of the room first. Amanda's first thought was, Where did she come from? Her second thought was, What is this woman doing in my dress?

It wasn't until after she heard the OP say: "*Mon Dieu, c'est ma fille! Ma fille est belle!*" that she realized the young woman standing before her was none other than the Headhunter's Daughter.

Her hair now sprung loose in golden curls, some of them reaching as far as her shoulders. Her developing figure, stuffed into a dress a size too small for her, was almost shockingly buxom. Funny, Amanda thought, but she looks sexier now than when she was topless. If I was her mother, I wouldn't let her out of the house in that dress.

"*Voila*," Cripple said proudly, "*elle est magnifique!*"

"Yes, she is magnificent," Amanda said.

She turned to the OP, who stood staring with his mouth open and his eyes glazed. Unfortunately, Amanda was acquainted with the "dirty old man" syndrome, thanks to "Uncle" Casey at church back home, who sat next to her in the choir and performed lewd acts under his choir robe that were meant to get her attention.

"What do you mean by saying, 'She's my daughter'?" Amanda snapped.

"Yes, what did you mean?" Pierre said.

The OP glanced at them and then turned back to the girl.

FOURTEEN

The Headhunter could have grabbed the clumsy white man, flung him to the ground, and then slit his throat with the homemade blade he kept in its monkey-skin scabbard. The man had a big head; his skull would have made a fine wine mug. One of his hairy ears, even when dried and shriveled, would have made an impressive addition to the thirteen already on his belt.

This is not to say that this Mushilele was an immoral man. *Au contraire*; never had the Headhunter taken the life of a fellow Mushilele, whether man, woman, or child. All thirteen of these ears represented men who had dared encroach upon Bashilele territory. Since he was not now on Bashilele territory, and his daughter was not in any immediate danger, the Headhunter allowed the missionary to creep up behind him. But only so far.

"*Muoyo webe*," he said to Harry. Life to you.

The big white man recoiled. "You speak Tshiluba?"

"*Eyo*," the Headhunter said. "I am a Mushilele; not ignorant."

"But they said you couldn't," Harry said, still speaking in Tshiluba.

"Perhaps they are right," the Headhunter said. "Perhaps this is all a dream."

"*Really?*" Harry said.

The headhunter couldn't help but laugh and then immediately realized he had taken the joke too far. The big white man was furious for having been made the fool.

"You heathen," Harry exploded. "What are you even doing here?"

"My daughter is here," the Headhunter said, his face ridged. "I am here to see that she is safe."

"*Safe?* Of course she's safe," Harry said. "She's with her own people."

"They are *not* her people," the Headhunter said.

"And you heathens are? You live like dogs, like naked monkeys. What do you know about raising a white girl?"

The Headhunter tried to lean his bow against the trunk of the mango tree, but it wouldn't stay. Recalling that he still had his knife strapped to his waist, he let the bow slide to the ground. Then he stepped away from the tree and held his hands out in front of him. He hoped that Harry recognized that this was a peaceful gesture.

"*Muambi*, you are a father, are you not?"

"*E.*"

"I have seen your daughter. She will bring a good dowry, but you must act quickly. She will soon no longer be desirable."

"*Mona buhote buebe*," Harry said. Behold your stupidity.

"*Aa!*" The Headhunter started to laugh. It startled him to learn that a white man knew such an insult. "You speak Tshiluba very well, *Muambi*. But now I wish to return to the matter of my daughter. Even a blind mudfish can see that her skin and my skin do not match, but I held her in my arms when her mind was not yet formed, and she did not see the difference between her skin and mine."

"*Tatu*," Harry said. Father. "I am sure that the Belgians will give you a *matabisha*. A reward. But listen closely to me, for I speak the truth. The *Bula Matadi* are not to be trusted. They will say that their reward is very generous, when for a fact it will be like one ear of corn for an elephant. Instead of accepting such an insult, you should allow me to conduct proper negotiations on your behalf. Of course you and I will consult privately so that these sons of Flemish monkeys will never know that I am the real mastermind behind this scheme."

"I do not want a reward! I do not wish to negotiate away my only child! I only want her safety and—"

"Nonsense. You would be happy to sell her for a handful of goats and some fat ducks, would you not? As for her happiness? I'm sure that she will be well taken care of."

The Headhunter felt his toes curl in the thick grass, so great was his frustration. "Forgive me, master," he said, "but to guarantee her happiness is foolishness. I can wish only that she is safe, and well fed, and healthy. To wish for more is to tempt the spirits."

"*Tch,*" said Harry, sounding deceptively like an African. "There are no spirits; only *Nzambi, tatu wetu mu diulu.*"

The Headhunter had no wish to discuss theology at the moment, even though he was mildly curious about this father god in the skies. Perhaps such a god could be persuaded to hold off a severe thunderstorm while a hunt was underway. Last season two hunters in their prime had been struck by lightning, and both of them had been wearing protective leopards' teeth around their necks.

To indicate that he had heard but did not necessarily agree, the Headhunter grunted.

"Eh? said Harry. "What must I do to get you to leave? Call the *Bula Matadi*?"

It crossed the Headhunter's mind again how easy it would be to kill the white man. If he slit his throat, there would be too much blood. Far better for the Headhunter to bring the knife up behind the ear and enter the skull at the soft spot there. Then, even though the white man was fat, the Headhunter could carry him to the edge of the precipice and throw him to the croco-dile. Of course, before doing that, the Headhunter would take a moment to separate the grinning head from its corpulent owner. He would then take the head into the *tshisuku* and bury it somewhere deep enough that hyenas and jackals would be discouraged from digging it up.

"No, master, I do not wish to speak to the *Bula Matadi*," he said.

Mastermind couldn't help but rejoice. The plan, like a puzzle, had been composed of distinct pieces. Unfortunately, the pieces had been scattered for thirteen years, but now all of them were accounted for. Now it was simply a matter of fitting the pieces back into their proper places. In fact, with the child's *baba* out of the picture—one could only presume the Bashilele were responsible—there was one less loose end to worry about. But oh, the payoff! In the intervening years new mines had been discovered, and the ransom, when delivered, would be ten times the amount it would have been all those years ago.

The OP's eyes must have radiated pride, shame, joy, wonder, love—surely too many things to explain. And of course he had no proof—except a feeling, like an invisible web that connected him to the girl, a web that had always been there, just never had been spoken about.

"Thirteen years ago," he said, "almost fourteen years ago, I was assigned to Belle Vue as Operations Manager. Shortly afterwards my wife, Heilewid, became pregnant. It was a very difficult pregnancy and we had to make many trips into Luluaburg to see the doctor—as we had none here. But then when the baby was born—I mean soon after—she went missing. This girl"—he pointed directly at her—"this is she. I know it. I feel it. Besides, there have been no other reports of European girls gone missing in all these years."

"What was your daughter's name?" Amanda asked.

"*What?* She was a baby, just three weeks old. She wouldn't remember it!"

It was Captain Jardin who put a hand on the OP's shoulder in an attempt to calm him down. "Monsieur OP," he said, "I think that the Mademoiselle Brown is merely curious—in addition to being perhaps a touch rude."

"*Oui, oui,* she is very rude," the OP said. Fat hot tears filled his eyes as he recalled the morning of the abduction. "Her name is Danielle Louise." She was named after her grandmother— Heilewid's mother."

The OP heard the black housekeeper whisper something to his daughter, something that he couldn't understand. After an adult lifetime in the Congo the OP still couldn't understand the local language, which was fine with him, because the natives all spoke French. That is, either they did speak French, or found someone who did. But what was the point of the maid whispering to his daughter, if the girl couldn't speak the language either?

"Excuse me," he said in French, "what were you saying to my daughter just now?"

The African woman was certainly not one to be intimidated. She even stepped forward—hobbled, to be more exact—and did her best to straighten her bent frame.

"Monsieur OP," she said, "do you not recognize me? I am the Muluba woman who gazed down upon you from high up on your gallows. You may feel free to address me as madame, or you may use my name, which is Cripple."

The OP felt a pang of loathing. "You were arrested for my wife's murder."

"The governor set her free," Amanda said.

"Mademoiselle," the OP said, "I recall that this was really your doing."

"*Mon ami,*" Pierre said, "the past is past, *non?* Now you have an exciting future to look forward to."

"Perhaps," said the OP. After all, his daughter looked every bit as happy to be there as the crippled one had looked on the day of her scheduled execution. "*Alors*," he said, "*j'ai une idée merveilleuse!*"

Husband knew his place. That did not mean that he liked it. He certainly did not approve of it, but there was only so much that one man alone could do. After all, by himself, Husband was not a movement; he was not Cripple.

He was not even master of his own feet. Now, as he waited at the back door of the Missionary Rest House for someone to answer his knock, Husband shifted nervously from foot to foot. Like a small boy he rubbed the soles of his shoes against his shins in turn. Husband could feel the calloused pads of his feet against his hairy legs, but not vice versa.

At last the screen door was flung open by Protruding Navel, the head houseboy. This man of the Bena Lulua tribe was in Husband's eyes of less worth than a caterpillar; at least the caterpillar could be eaten.

"*Tch*," the houseboy said, rolling his eyes in disgust. "What does this disgraced Muluba witch doctor want?"

"I have come to see my wife," Husband said.

"Your *wife*? This is the house of an American missionary. Does she know that she is married to the likes of you?"

"My wife is Cripple, a fact which you know very well. As for your joke, *Monsieur Tablier*—Mr. Apron—it was not funny. Intermarriage is against the law."

The man named Protruding Navel clutched the once white apron with both hands. "It is a job, the pay is good, and there are many nights when I am sent home with extra food for my family."

"Eh, that is so. Cripple too returns with food—but what we are to make of it, that is often a great puzzle. This *sow-wah-clout!*" Husband spat on the grass to the side of the back steps. "*Aiyee*, I once tasted monkey brains that had been left too long in the sun. Believe me; the brains tasted better."

The houseboy roared with laugher. "Yes, yes, they have some very strange flavors. The *mamu* must eat small quantities of a thing called *cho-co-laht* or she will become very unhappy; she will even whip us."

"*Aiyee!* Even Cripple?"

"Especially Cripple."

"Then I must speak to her at once."

"I'm afraid that is impossible," Protruding Navel said. "She is working. Did you not see all the whites in their cars on the front road? They have all come to see this strange creature plucked from the midst of the heathen Bashilele."

"You will fetch my wife, Muena Lulua," Husband said to Protruding Navel. He chose to address him as an individual of the Bena Lulua tribe, rather than by his given name. It was meant as an insult.

However, the man in the apron—he who did woman's work—this man had the gall to gaze with insolence into Husband's eyes. During that length of time a good wife could have fried caterpillars in palm oil until they crunched between the teeth, launching waves of pleasure that seemed to sweep beyond the mouth even, causing the entire body to shiver with ecstasy.

Protruding Navel was a man without prejudices. The Belgians, the Americans, the Baluba, the Bashilele—all of them were equal in his sight. That is to say, they were equal to each other, but not, of course, to the Bena Lulua. It mattered not to Protruding Navel if these aforementioned tribes fought amongst each other, just as long as he still had a job that paid him every Saturday evening, and that his hut was still standing at the end of each and every day.

Therefore, was not Protruding Navel a progressive man? Some might even consider him an evolved man, worthy of receiving special status by the colonial government, given only to those blacks who had managed to lift themselves up above the level of savagery. One must also never forget that Protruding Navel was the legitimate son of a Bena Lulua chief—a minor chief, and of a small village—but a real chief nonetheless.

Tch! Still, as important as he was, Protruding Navel could not ignore the fact that he was fond of the American with the meaningless name, Amanda Brown—but now called Mamu Ugly Eyes—and that stubborn Muluba woman named Cripple. That annoying little woman was supposed to be Protruding Navel's assistant, but she seemed to do whatever she pleased, whenever she pleased.

At any rate, for the past six years Protruding Navel had been saving up to purchase a house—a real house with a tin roof—in the Jacaranda Grove section of the workers' village. This house was only steps away from one of the village's four public water faucets. If they lived in this house then Protruding Navel's wife, who was expecting her third child, would not have to carry her laundry or her water for more than a kilometer, as she did now. This house did not have electricity, but it had wooden shutters that could be closed at night against the mosquitoes, and best of all, it had two rooms! Imagine that; *two* rooms.

But in order to get this house Protruding Navel had to make sure that everything continued on as it was. The status quo had to be maintained. Thus it was that when he saw two men rolling about on the grass at the edge of the Missionary Rest House property; one of them white, one of them black, Protruding Navel was horrified. Not knowing what to do in this case he picked up a large fallen branch—one bereft of leaves—and began thrashing both men soundly.

"You fools," he cried.

"*Aiyee!*" the Headhunter groaned as he tried to shield his face.

"Stop it," roared the enraged missionary.

Protruding Navel was, of course, horrified at what he had done, and would have stopped immediately—perhaps even run away from the scene—but then it occurred to him that this would be the perfect opportunity to beat a white man. Down came the stick—*thwack, thwack, thwack*—across the missionary's blubbery back.

"You heathen Mushilele," Protruding Navel shouted. "How dare you try and harm this white man, this emissary of God? I should beat you even harder for this." *Thwack, thwack, thwack.*

"Ow! Damn you to hell, you son of a bitch!" Despite his great size, and the steady onslaught from the houseboy's makeshift cudgel, the white man had managed to get to his feet. "How dare you strike me?" he roared. "I am a white man! A *white* man."

Protruding Navel gave each man another whack. The missionary received his blow across the bottom, and as a result he lurched forward but remained standing. The Headhunter was smitten across his broad shoulders and knocked temporarily back to the ground.

Having regained his balance the missionary advanced on the houseboy like a man intending to do severe bodily harm. Alas, the time for games was over. No longer could Protruding Navel hide behind the excuse that he had suffered momentary confusion. This white man was not so easily fooled. With flight as his only other option, Protruding Navel closed his eyes and held his clenched fists by his sides. The offending stick now lay on the ground at his feet.

However, the *muambi* did not strike the lowly servant, as was his right in this case. "Extended Belly," he sputtered, "or whatever your name is, you are going to be very sorry for this! Believe me."

"*Eyo, muambi.*"

The white man was silent for a long time. Finally, Protruding Navel couldn't stand the silence, so he opened his eyes. Much to his distress he saw tears in the *muambi*'s strange green eyes. How was a mere houseboy—even if he were a chief's son—to deal with such an embarrassing turn of events? He need not have worried too much, for things only got worse.

FIFTEEN

The Headhunter's Daughter wanted nothing more than to go home, to return to her village. Perhaps the only thing she wanted more was to see her father again, for she was not sure at that point that he had kept his word—that he had been *able* to keep his word—and remain within hearing distance of her cries. Oh how glorious it would be to see her mother, her *baba*, again, and her *baba*'s best friend, Iron Sliver. Even the annoying village children, even the cruelest among them, would be a welcome sight.

"Be patient," the little crippled one was saying. "It will be all right."

Yes, but for whom? Ugly Eyes felt naked in the blue dress selected for her because it didn't even come down to the knees. Only the village harlot dared wear her *madiba* above her knees, and she was mocked and spat upon by the other women. That was certainly not a life to which one should aspire.

Then there was the matter of the breast garment. It was meant to draw attention to the breasts, and surely it did, for it generated strange lumps beneath the cloth of the dress that should rightly scare away any man who was not possessed by malevolent spirits. It made the hair on her arms and neck stand on end.

As to her hair; it was frightening. Her hair closely resembled the dried grass sewn around the perimeter of the witch doctor's mask. That was meant to give the impression of a lion's mane. Who was the girl who wished to look like that? It was not Ugly Eyes.

Simply said, it was all too much. Too much had happened since yesterday; too much was happening that very moment, too much which was strange and frightening. Ugly Eyes could no longer contain herself.

"I want to go home," she said, in a loud, clear voice. She spoke the words in Tshiluba, the trade language, so that the white *mamu* named Ugly Eyes, and the *Bula Matadi*, would understand.

There fell a silence such as there is immediately following a flash of lightning. Then the white *mamu* gasped and clapped her hands to her cheeks.

"You *do* know Tshiluba! Why did you and your father—wait, does he speak it as well?"

"Lady *mamu*," Ugly Eyes said, "we are the Bashilele; we are not savages like the Bapende people. Of course we speak the regional language in addition to your own. It is a pity, however, that you do not speak our language since it does not assault the ears as does Tshiluba."

"*Aiyee*," the little one cried. "See how this white woman lies!"

"I am *not* a white woman," Ugly Eyes said. She wanted to look each person in their face, but instead could look only at her own feet.

"Yes, you are a white woman," Mamu Ugly Eyes said. "If not that, then at least a white girl."

"I am an albino," said the real Ugly Eyes. This was a notion that she longed to believe, but could not. Mother and Father had shown her the difference. They had taken her to visit a real albino, and held her healthy arm up next to his blistered skin. The difference was indeed clear, but the truth so unwelcome. Where *had* she come from? Surely not from people such as these.

"No, you are not an albino," the white *mamu* said. Sadly, even she could not be fooled.

"What is your name?" demanded the *Bula Matadi*.

"Ugly Eyes."

"Who told you to say that?" the white *mamu* said, suddenly very agitated. "Did Cripple tell you?"

"*Aiyee*," Cripple wailed again. "Not me. Why, until just a few minutes ago I was unaware that this bush rat was capable of speech."

Ugly Eyes smiled. "Cripple, you and Iron Sliver would make fast friends, for you both enjoy the advantage of quick wits. But you are a witness to the fact that it was me who spoke first of this name."

"Is this true?" the *Bula Matadi* said.

"*E*," Cripple said.

It was then that the old white man—the one who had the gall to claim that he was her father—said something. Since he spoke in one of the foreign languages, Ugly Eyes didn't understand a word. However, she hoped it had to do with him withdrawing his claim to her, so that she could return to her village. At once! She would gladly walk that distance, by the way.

"Permit me to translate—please," said the *Bula Matadi*. "This man is the chief of this village. His name is Chief Raging Baboon." The *Bula Matadi* paused to glare at Cripple for giggling. "Chief Raging Baboon has offered to give a big feast in your honor at his house tonight. The entire village is to be invited. Of course, as his daughter, you are to be the guest of honor."

Ugly Eyes squelched an impulse to spit on the *Bula Matadi*, because she realized that he was merely the translator, and not responsible for these words. Besides, he was a very attractive man—despite the color of his skin.

"This man is *not* my father. If he wants my father to attend this feast, then someone must invite him."

Cripple laughed openly despite cautionary looks from both the *Bula Matadi* and the young white woman.

"I will give him the message," the young *Bula Matadi* said.

SIXTEEN

When Protruding Navel, coward that he was, opened his eyes, the white man was gone. But so was the Headhunter. Protruding Navel had heard the sound of scuffling, and grunting, like the sound of pigs mating in the banana grove, and then a thin reedy screech, like that of a hawk as it calls for a mate. Then silence—well, but for the roar of the falls. There was always the falls.

For some the constant noise of water striking against rocks was soothing, whereas for others, it brought on the pains that threatened to split open one's head. Generally, it was the women who suffered more from this disease, but Protruding Navel also suffered from such pains.

Sometimes it was a thunderstorm that brought on the suffering. Other times it could be a simple act, such as beating *Mamu*'s braided rugs, of which there were many, and from which great clouds of dust flew up, as if each rug contained a miniature drought's worth. Yet another source of these intense pains was stress, and as far as Protruding Navel could reckon, absolutely nothing in his life until then had been quite as stress producing as beating a white man with a mango branch as thick as his thumb.

On another day Protruding Navel might have investigated the

sudden, almost mystical absence of the other two men, or even considered the thin reedy cry of the hawk, but today he had all he could do just to keep from gathering his knees to his chest and calling aloud for his *baba*. In order to appear as a semblance of a man, if only a lazy, sleeping Lulua man, Protruding Navel stretched out in the shade of a mango tree, put one of the *mamu*'s "borrowed" handkerchiefs over his face, and pretended to sleep. With any luck, in due course, real sleep would follow.

Madame Cabochon checked her reflection in a car window one last time. It was important that she present a flawless appearance; after all, she was *the* most beautiful woman in Belle Vue—bar none. It was a fact even, not just an opinion. Everyone thought so; you could see it in their eyes. In the men's eyes you could see lust, whereas in the women's eyes it was envy or hate. Yes, there were a couple of men who were unaffected by her great beauty in a sexual sort of way, and perhaps one woman who was, but even these individuals still made it clear that they too worshipped at the altar of Madame Cabochon's perfection. Surely Madame Cabochon was worthy of being encased in glass and exhibited in a museum somewhere.

She was like an alabaster vase clothed in purple silks and satins. Her flaming hair spilled down her back like a miniature replica of the Belle Vue falls, drawing attention to the shockingly low V cut of her dress. It was virtually impossible to tear one's eyes away from Madame Cabochon. That's what they would say when they recalled the party that the OP threw for that savage daughter of his.

So what was an exquisite beauty like the madame doing in the Congo in the first place? She had the good fortune of being born in Coquilhatville, in the north of the country, on a palm oil plantation. Like Captain Pierre Jardin, she had the Belgian Congo in her blood. So rather than "return" to Belgium when she reached the age of majority, she married a member of the Consortium and moved to Belle Vue, where she was perfectly miserable. *Except* for events like tonight.

"Francois," she said, having approved of her reflection long enough, "do you hear the music? I don't recognize it. American, no?"

"Screw American," her husband growled—in French, of course. Francois was not in the mood for anything American. When he'd heard that missionaries had been invited, he'd almost refused to come. *Almost*, because he really had no choice, without arousing suspicion. After all, it wasn't common knowledge that Francois's mother was German, and as far as he knew, nobody was aware of the fact that just before the Germans marched into Brussels, the Cabochon household had hung a large flag of the Third Reich from their second-story windows.

It was indeed toe-tapping rock 'n' roll from America that the gorgeous Madame Cabochon heard. She couldn't wait to get down into the thick of things, shed her husband, and start shaking it up a bit—perhaps with that cute Captain Pierre Jardin. *Mais oui*, so he had eyes for the young American hostess of the Missionary Rest House, but so what? The word *missionary* said it all, did it not? No missionary could compete with Madame Cabochon. That was like having a nun compete with Cleopatra.

"Ah Francois," she said, succumbing to the beat. "Promise me, you won't be a *drag*." She said the last word in English. She'd learned it on the shortwave, along with "rock 'n' roll." Congo born and bred, but still up on things, eh?

But Francois was not altogether pleasant. Instead of answering, he forged ahead. What a pity that he didn't care for her; what fun they could have had as a couple just getting to where the real action took place. Because to reach the terrace where the phonograph and buffet tables were set up, one must wend one's way down the hillside through a series of gardens and terraces lit by torches. It was so dramatic! Really a lot of fun! And with servants in full livery to point the way at every turn.

"Excuse me." At a dark turn in the path, where the torch was unlit, and there was no servant to point the way, a figure stepped forward and thrust an envelope in her hands.

"Who are you?" she asked.

"Give this to the OP," the figure said. Then it was gone.

It had happened so fast, that recreating it in her mind was really pointless. The messenger was African, male, but so what? That could have been any of the servants, or none of them. As for the envelope—damn! It was sealed.

Madame Cabochon, her heart pounding from the encounter, slowed her descent as she pondered the ramifications of her two choices. If she withheld the envelope, so that she could read its contents, she might find herself with a powerful possession. On the other hand, the contents could spell trouble, something that only the OP could avert. At the very least, by delivering the document to its rightful owner she would cement her husband's position in the company, if only by the smallest fraction, and every little bit helped these days.

Alors, she would do the right thing!

Cripple reached the workers' village just as the first of the jackals came bounding out of the *tshisuku* and onto the road behind her. What wondrous news there was to share with Husband. Who but Husband would believe what strange things Cripple had seen and heard in the white woman's house that day? *Yala,* it would be an evening of recounting like no other.

But when Cripple finally hobbled into the family compound, she found no fire, no bubbling pot of bidia calling to be stirred, no laughing children—no crying ones for that matter—only Husband sitting in the dark on his slant-back wooden chair, his head in his hands.

"Husband!" Cripple cried. "What is it? What has happened?"

"It is Second Wife," he said. "Her brother came to take her home."

"What? I do not understand."

But Cripple did understand. Ever since Husband had allowed himself to be caught up in a white man's plot to smuggle an enormous diamond out of Belle Vue, the family had had less luck than a stewing hen. First Husband lost his job at the post office, and then a windstorm blew their hut's roof halfway to Angola. In a culture where a brother had more rights to his sister's children than did their biological father, it was time to step in.

"It is only temporary," Husband said. "There were no discussions about returning the dowry."

"Of course not," Cripple said. She bit the inside of her cheek. How much *had* Husband paid for Second Wife? Five goats? More than that? *Aiyee*, she must not think of such things. The girl Morning Joy was truly a joy to be around. And the baby, the one Second Wife had recently named Amanda, who could not help but love that cheerful little boy?

"Cripple," Husband said without looking up.

"Yes, Husband."

"Do you think that your missionary might have a job for me?"

Cripple sighed softly and then carefully considered the question. Meanwhile, the village noises of happy families, laughing women, crying babies, bleating livestock and soft beating of drums filled the void that seemed to suddenly exist between Cripple and Husband.

"I will ask," she finally said. "But remember, Husband, that you are a witchdoctor, and she is a Christian. The same might be asked, what need does a snake have of an eagle?"

"Which am I?" Husband asked.

"It was a white man's question, of the sort not meant to be answered." She paused long enough to let him know that she was on to something new. "Husband?"

"Yes, Cripple?"

"Is it only money that we lack?"

"*Tch.* No. It is face. Second Wife's brother cannot allow her children to live in the house of a failed witch doctor, one who can not even keep his job with the *Bula Matadi*."

"You are not a failed witch doctor! How many potions did you prescribe this week? How many curses did you put in place, or lift?"

"Two people came to see me, an old man and a woman with a baby. I sold the woman a small antelope horn for the baby to wear as an amulet against the night spirits, and I prepared a potion for the old man to drink so that his tree might once again become firm and hard, such as it once was, and no longer the soft useless sapling that it is now—"

"Husband," Cripple said, not caring that she interrupted, because Husband almost never beat her, "does this tree of which you speak press its foliage against his groin, so that it grows upside down?"

"*Kah!*" Husband slapped his thighs, he laughed so hard. "Cripple, the priest at my Catholic school would not approve of you."

"Husband, nor would I approve of him."

"Nevertheless, Cripple, we cannot stay in this house, for when the rains come to stay we shall drown like the toads that fall in the privy. And as we do not own this land, we have nothing to sell or trade that is of any value except for a few useless potions and bits of animals tied on to raffia strings."

Cripple sank to her haunches. "But Husband, what are you saying? These things—these potions and animal parts—they are full of magic. Surely they have value."

Husband sighed, and suddenly the village sounds were far less soothing. Cripple thought that she already knew the answer—at least part of it. For many years already it had troubled her mind that such ordinary things, items gathered by Husband's own hands, should somehow become magic simply because he declared them to be so. An antelope horn was a horn—simply that. Yet there were indeed herbs and potions—such as the aphrodisiac— that did appear to work.

"Wife," Husband said, "I have powders that soothe, and some to ease pain, and the one of which we spoke that makes the male member hard, but as for the spirit world, it is you, the heathen, who seems to be better connected than I."

"*Aiyee*," Cripple said, "now that it is dark, let us not speak of that world." She struggled to her feet. "Come, rise if you wish and light the kerosene lantern. Meanwhile I will look for food in what remains of the hut. Surely Second Wife will have left us something."

"*E*, Cripple," Husband said, rising quickly from his chair. "You are a good wife. I need not worry."

"*Kah!* Husband, indeed you must worry, for I have become as forgetful as an old man of fifty years!" Cripple hastily unwrapped her head cloth. "Look what the white *mamu* has generously supplied for our supper!"

She proudly displayed a feast of two chicken legs, four boiled eggs, a third of a loaf of homemade bread, a slab of Blue Band margarine, and two very ripe, somewhat spotted bananas. Husband squatted to better examine the goods.

"Wife," said Husband, "truly I am astounded. What is the meaning of this? What is it that the white *mamu* desires of you?"

"Husband, it is not what she desires; it is something else that she offers."

Husband looked longingly at the chicken legs and then back into his wife's eyes. "Cripple, you are a very wise woman. But a wise woman seldom marries a fool. I know that you find her offer most attractive, am I right?"

"Very much so."

"At the same time, you dare not refuse her demand—for indeed there is a demand as well. Am I right again?"

"Yes, Husband. You are so often right," Cripple said, in just the right tone to make Husband smile with satisfaction.

"Then please explain."

"There is to be a *fete* given in honor of the new white *mamu* tonight. I am to be there as—ah—"

"Servant?"

"*Nasha!* I am there to give her comfort should she need it; she is just a child, after all, and the ways of the white man are still very strange to her."

"Where is this fete? At the Missionary Rest House?"

"*Nasha.* It is at the house of the OP."

"*Kah!* Cripple, that man would have seen you dead!"

"Then think, Husband. Is this not the perfect revenge? The Muluba woman, Cripple, alive in his very own house and with his white Mushilele daughter?"

Husband jumped to his feet. "What dangerous words leave your mouth, my wife? Behold, the night has ears!"

"No, husband, it is true! You will see; you will hear. All Belle Vue will hear of this, for tonight all the servants will bring back this news. Believe me; Protruding Navel's tongue is now more tired than a bitch in heat."

"How will you get there, my wife? Will you walk all the way down the hill, and across the bridge in the dark with the jackals and hyenas nipping at your heels? And you a cripple?"

"*E.*"

"You will not."

Cripple's heart pounded. This was her one opportunity to see a Belgian fete. In fact, she hadn't ever been in a Belgian house, and the only *group* of Belgians she had ever been around were the ones who had come to watch her hang. Husband was not going to stop her from attending, and neither were the hyenas. If she had to, she would feed Husband to the hyenas, or vice versa.

"Husband," she said, careful to not raise her voice, "if I do not show up tonight, I will lose my job. Then we will have even less to eat, which, as you know, will not be good for that which now grows inside me."

"*Eyo*. But you will not walk there, because I will carry you. Now, shut up—please—and eat a chicken leg and at least one egg before we start out on your adventure."

The OP was as proud as one of the long-tailed birds that flitted about on the lawn in front of his office. It was only the males that had these ridiculously, dangerously long tales, and they used them to impress their mates. What the OP had was a gorgeous daughter, if you overlooked the fact that she was missing her two front teeth and had a raised scar that slashed across each cheekbone.

The Bashilele had a natural grace, and she was a quick study, this one, so if you made it past her hair—which the American girl had further managed to tame—and the girl's mouth was closed, you were in for a bit of a shock when she did smile. The feedback was universal: she was breathtakingly beautiful except for her teeth. Well now, that wasn't so bad, was it? That could be fixed. Assuming, of course that fatherhood was something he really wanted. *Perhaps* that had been the case at one time, but even if so, he'd outgrown those feelings years ago.

This creature before him—well, she was just that: a bizarre creature. A chimera. Half savage, half the ideal of European perfection. But as for her being his daughter for longer than it took for his plan to work—

"Monsieur OP," Madame Cabochon said, lightly touching his elbow.

The OP turned, his troubled thoughts suddenly soothed. Now here was a real beauty, through and through. As stupid as a draft horse, of course, and about as graceful on the dance floor, but what did that matter? When Madame Cabochon missed a dance step she had a habit of falling into her partner's arms like an invalid stolen from her sick bed. With Madame Cabochon's charms draped across one's body, adherence to form was no longer the burning issue.

"Ah, you are a vision in purple," the OP murmured, his words rendered indecipherable by proximity to the gramophone.

"I believe this is yours," she said, and made a great show of placing the envelope in his hand. One or two people actually applauded at her fine performance.

"What is it?" he asked.

"How should I know? One of the blacks passed it off."

"Which one?"

"*Which* one? You can't be serious."

The OP ripped the thick, creamy white envelope open with a calloused forefinger. Well, whoever wrote it certainly had good taste.

"Undoubtedly an invitation," the OP said grimly. "Dinner with someone I see every day. Someone with the wit of a stone, and a wife like a cabbage, and a cook who studied in an English boarding school. Just because I'm a recent widower, every hausfrau in town—pardon me, madame—thinks I'm fair game."

Madame Cabochon reached up and gently brushed a strand of hair back off the OP's forehead. "I'm more than just a pretty face, Monsieur OP; I'm also rather well educated. My advanced degrees were in Ancient Greek and Latin—although I minored in Aramaic."

For just a second or two the OP fanaticized pushing Monsieur Cabochon over one of the low stone walls that traced his many breathtaking terraces. A couple of spots were remote enough that no one would hear the man's screams over the sound of the falls and the phonograph.

"Ah, if only you were single, Madame Cabochon," he said, and gave her a kiss on the cheek that held promise. At the same time he gave her a gentle push that sent her in the direction of one of the many liveried waiters bearing trays of fancy hors d'oeuvres. Since the OP was the Consortium's top dog in Belle Vue, and the town's only grocery store was company owned, one could bet that the food being served was of the finest quality available.

When it was clear that her attention was diverted, the OP opened the paper. The writing had been executed in India ink. The lettering was perfect—almost too perfect. It was, not surprisingly, in French.

Dear Monsieur OP,

This note will undoubtedly come as a surprise to you, so take a moment to digest what I am about to say. And that is this: I have proof that you were involved in the kidnapping of your daughter back in 1945. I kept careful records of all our conversations and every scrap of correspondence. In fact, I was able to record two of those conversations—the most crucial, I believe— and I am keeping them in a safe place.

Should something untoward happen to me, every bit of this information will be released to the police—both here, and at the provincial level. After all, at that point, what will I have to lose?

So what are my demands, you might ask? Well, they are much like our original demands—but adjusted for the price of inflation. In other words, I am asking for the equivalent of $1,000,000 in uncut diamonds to be delivered, via special courier, to my agent across the border in Angola. You have three days to get this parcel together.

Sincerely yours,
Mastermind.

The OP felt sick. He staggered to the nearest terrace wall, and then, bracing himself by placing his hands on his knees, he retched into the hibiscus shrubs immediately below. At least such was his intention. Specks of his stomach contents, however, became airborne by an updraft and wafted across the terrace, creating an unpleasant moment for the revelers.

"My apologies," the OP shouted down at his disgruntled inferiors.

What an unfortunate turn of events; one must never debase

oneself in front of one's employees, for if the curtain of mystique is rent, the peasants might revolt. The OP shoved the offending piece of paper deep into the pocket of his dinner jacket, where he found a silk handkerchief just right for dabbing at his mouth. The trick now was to dab casually. There, like that. Because he was top dog and he willed it to be so, his dignity was now restored.

"I'm sure that had to be awkward," a voice at his elbow said.

SEVENTEEN

Even in her best Sunday dress Mrs. Gorman was not appropriately attired. To put it simply, she was a missionary. Her job was to spread the Good News, and that was easier to do if she did not draw attention to her body. The Belgians, on the other hand, were free to show their smooth shoulders and flaunt their suntanned backs. A few of the women even felt free enough to expose shocking amounts of décolletage.

Shocking was exactly the right word to describe it. That's the word Mrs. Gorman would use in her letter to her sisters who lived in Charlotte, and to whom she wrote every week in her elegant handwriting. Of course they would be seeing Mrs. Gorman soon—hopefully within a month—oh, my fathers, there went another one, with her cleavage exposed practically down to her navel! So shocking! So thrilling, even. Mrs. Gorman was entranced.

If only Mr. Gorman's whereabouts could be confirmed. Protruding Navel had insisted that he'd seen Mr. Gorman in the side yard conversing with the girl's father—but that was *before* lunch. Since then no one had seen either man. However, the Gormans' car was still parked in front of Missionary Rest House, which was both a good sign and a bad sign.

On the plus side, it could mean that Mr. Gorman had set off on foot with the Headhunter, on one of his evangelizing forays into the bush. This would certainly not be unlike him. Once when Mr. Gorman had seen an unexpected opportunity to witness a band of Bapende hunters passing through the mission, he'd dropped everything to join up with them, and was gone for two weeks. When he returned he claimed to have baptized eight of the men. "Collecting scalps for Jesus," he called this kind of work.

On the negative side—well, gosh darn it, there was that very wicked chasm behind the Missionary Rest House. Everyone in the mission with any lick of sense had urged the Mission Board back in Raleigh not to approve the appropriation of this site, or the building of the Missionary Rest House there, but the view gawkers had the loudest voices, and had won the day.

Now, quite possibly, Mr. Gorman lay smashed somewhere at the bottom of the gorge or, worse yet, he might already be in the belly of the behemoth reptile that waited greedily at the bottom. Thankfully, Mrs. Gorman had been in training all her life for just such an evening as this. Only unfaithful Christians worried; the faithful ones put their trust in the Lord and lived their lives with joy and the knowledge that everything works out for the best for those who truly love the Lord.

So there was no point in worrying, no point at all. Enjoy the evening, be a light unto others, and yes, by all means, experience a little shock. Just don't let anyone see you looking, or they might get the wrong impression.

From the safety offered by the leafy shadows to the left of the portico, Cripple stared in amazement at the gathering of whites. Not since the scheduled day of her execution had she witnessed such a vast number. Then, as luck would have it, her mind had been on other things and she had not had the luxury of taking it all in.

So many Whites, yet they all looked the same. How did they

manage to find their own mates in a throng such as this? Or perhaps they were encouraged to do just the opposite; indeed she had
heard tales of a Christian sect across the Big Sea in which the
men were allowed to take many wives and Jesus did not mind.
If this sect were to come to Belle Vue and recruit, maybe then
Cripple might consider becoming a Christian. Until then, however, she would remain a happy heathen.

Yala! What was she doing thinking about such trivial matters
now! She was there as a *mulami*—a shepherd—for the new Ugly
Eyes. The real Ugly Eyes. What did the OP call her? Danielle.
Not too difficult to say, but still a silly name, as it had no meaning.

Cripple tried making up a few names. "*To-ma-lah. Ma-don-
ah. Lin-si.*" What foolishness. *Aiyee!* It was so hard not to be judgmental. But she who judges will be twice judged; so said the wise
old women who passed on the secrets of living the happy life to
which Cripple aspired.

Happiness was not the birthright of any creature—except
for those who could fly, such as birds and butterflies. (For those
who were ashamed of flying, and therefore flew at night—such as
bats—theirs was a curse). Everyone else had to work to be happy
within his or her own rules and the traditions handed down by
their elders and their stories; for even monkeys and leopards had
rules for being monkeys and leopards, did they not?

Tonight all attention should be solely on the girl. Was she
happy, or unhappy? Neither. The girl was terrified. Cripple could
not only see the fear written on the young woman's face, but she
was sure that she could smell it as well.

Although the new Ugly Eyes was standing next to Mamu Ugly
Eyes, she was obviously on display. By turns the whites stepped
up to greet her and, of course, to get a good look at one of their
own who had somehow managed to survive in a Bashilele village. Cripple could not understand the words that the colonists
spoke to Ugly Eyes, but she observed with approval that the *mamu*
translated some of these words and that Ugly Eyes appeared to

respond to these words by nodding or shaking her head. However, it did not escape Cripple's attention that the *bakalenge*—the Belgian masters—maintained a greater distance than is normal when speaking, as if Ugly Eyes were a strange wild beast that might suddenly leap forward and bite.

Once, in the workers' village, Tshilembi, the hunter who lived next door to Cripple, returned from a hunting trip bearing a fawn with five legs. All that afternoon and evening the village boys poked at the fawn with sticks to make it walk, even though it could only drag the fifth leg. The next morning it lay dead in the wicker pen Tshilembi had built for it. The death glaze had stolen the fawn's sight, and its tongue protruded grotesquely from its long slender muzzle.

As Cripple looked at Ugly Eyes, the memory of the fawn returning, it suddenly occurred to her that perhaps the baby antelope had been a warning, a foreshadowing of Ugly Eyes, daughter of the headhunting Mushilele. Instead of the marvel of a fifth leg, this girl had the white skin of a Belgian. Like the fawn, however, the girl did not belong where she'd been captured and taken, and like the fawn, it was possible this girl could die.

Undoubtedly a fawn with a fifth leg would, sooner or later, be taken down by a leopard, or a hyena, for it could never run as fast as a normal antelope. But in the meantime the fawn would be free, a stranger to torment. And what of Ugly Eyes? Was her destiny to live her life as an African with white skin, and not only an African, but one steeped in the traditional ways? How long would it take this "fawn" to perish in captivity?

Bualu bukole! Something must be done. Cripple was never one to second-guess herself. What was the point in doing so? One could always change directions later, and if not, then whatever it was that had been futilely attempted must be regarded as not in one's destiny. It was as simple as that. Really, life was very simple if you didn't think about it too much. Act first from the stomach, and then see what the head has to say.

"Ugly Eyes," Cripple called from the shadows.

It took three tries, but then two pairs of ugly eyes strained to find her in the shadows.

"Not you, Mamu Ugly Eyes," Cripple hissed loudly. After all, *Mesu Mabi* does not roll off the tongue without some syllibency.

There followed an awkward moment when Cripple considered hobbling away from the OP's house as fast as her deformed leg would carry her. It seemed as if the white *mamu* was angry and was for sure going to call for help. Instead she gave her young charge a gentle push in Cripple's direction, while stepping forward alone to greet the would-be gawkers.

"*Aiyee*, Cripple!" Ugly Eyes sounded both happy and immensely relieved to be away from the spotlight. "What are you doing here? Why are you clothed in darkness? Where is my father?"

"*Kah*, so many questions! Ugly Eyes, you must focus on what I am about to ask you. Is that understood?"

"Cripple, I am not a child."

"Exactly so. Therefore, Ugly Eyes, I must ask you, do you desire your freedom?"

"To return to my village? To Mother, and Iron Sliver, and all of my friends?"

"*Eyo.*"

"And my dog as well?"

"*E*, unless your mother has eaten it, you foolish heathen."

"Cripple, are you not a heathen as well?"

"*E*, but I am a Christian heathen, a civilized dweller of the village of Belle Vue; whereas you are a bush heathen of the Bashilele plains. But enough of this talk. If you wish to return to your people, meet me later tonight in the mango grove when the moon goes to sleep."

"We laugh and we cry," Ugly Eyes said. It was the literal meaning of "thank you." She glanced back at the whites who had come to stare at her.

"And what of my father? What if he cannot be found?"

"*Tch!* Enough thinking like a child. Put yourself in his place; what would you want your daughter to do? Would you prefer that she get away from these people, or would rather that she waits here while she is poked and prodded like a five-legged fawn and her father gets drunk in the village on palm wine?"

"*Truly?* A five-legged fawn?"

"A five-legged fawn."

Cripple took a deep breath in order to calm herself. It was surprising just how effective that tactic was at the moment, for suddenly she felt entirely peaceful. She imagined it was much like a suckling child felt as she drifted to sleep before the second breast could be offered.

It was clear now that she'd been right to offer the Mushilele girl an escape plan. The wearer of this white skin was nothing more than a child. She was surely not a woman. Perhaps Ugly Eyes would be sold into marriage soon after reuniting with her true family, or perhaps the Belgians would return to her village and exact a punishment of one kind or another, unless she was returned to them. Unlike Husband, who was a hereditary witch doctor, Cripple did not possess the ability to see the future, yet she knew inside her bones that the strange creature before her would not meet a happy ending. But such was the fate of the five-legged fawn, was it not?

"When the moon sleeps," she said, giving the girl a gentle push back to the world of the whites one last time, "meet me in the mango grove."

Pierre Jardin couldn't recall ever being so happy. He'd been re-signed to a life of bachelorhood, stationed here in an outpost of the Belgian Congo as he was. He wasn't complaining—he liked Belle Vue: he spoke Tshiluba, he got along with most of the whites, the blacks weren't yet killing each other, it was only half a day's drive from Luluaburg, where he was born, and it was a bush town—that part he actually liked as well. Where else could you kill a rogue elephant while doing your job?

But having been resigned to never getting married made it all that much sweeter to suddenly have the most beautiful, seductive woman in the world practically fall into your lap. True, she was an American *and* a Protestant missionary, but she was also Amanda Brown. *Oo la!* If you thought you knew American missionaries, then you'd never met Amanda Brown.

Amanda was—well, she was gorgeous! Ravishing! There she was, standing against the railing of one of the eastern terraces, the last rays of the sun glinting off her hair. They say that the French girls are the best dressed, but Pierre would have to disagree; it is the American girls who know how to enhance their hourglass figures. Besides, the neckline of Amanda's dress was not only flattering, but it was positively shocking—possibly even scandalous. In fact, she had worn a light silk scarf over her shoulders until she was quite certain they were alone.

"*Ma cheri,*" he said. "Are you trying to seduce me?"

Amanda laughed. "Pierre, we haven't even been on a proper date!"

"This means a malt shop, yes?"

"Yes."

"Hmm. Perhaps with a little Belgian ingenuity the Consortium clubhouse could be turned into a worthy stand-in. What do you think?"

"Oh, but it must have drive-in speakers, and waitresses on roller skates. Try arranging that."

Pierre had never even held Amanda in his arms, much less kissed her. Tonight, what with the teasing, the moonlight, and her provocative dress, he knew it was time to take their relationship to the next level. Just a smooth, gentle embrace and a series of light, teasing kisses. He stepped forward, his arms half extended, his eyes on hers—but then out of the corner of his right eye he saw the most horrible, unimaginable thing happen.

"What is it?" Amanda demanded as she whirled.

"A man," Pierre said. There was no point in trying to deny it, not with the woman with whom he was hoping to start a relationship.

"Where is he now? I don't see him!"

"Look away, Amanda. Look at me."

The stubborn girl would not do as he said. She was looking down, and down was where Pierre knew the monstrous man-eating crocodile made its home. But the crocodile wasn't just man-eating, it ate any mammal, fish, or bird that got swept over the falls and was thereby rendered incapable of escaping. This was not a bad thing; it was, in fact, a good thing. This croco-dile is what kept the catchment basin clean. The giant crocodile was Belle Vue Falls's garbage disposal, and as such had been al-lowed to survive unharmed since the town's establishment. Even the Americans at Missionary Rest House relied on the beast to consume their refuse.

"Pierre!" Amanda screamed. "Pierre, you have to help him."

"No one can reach him, Amanda. He can't be helped."

"You must!" she shrieked.

He grabbed her and yanked her away from the railing. Then he scooped her up and carried her along a fern-and-orchid-embroidered trail until they reached an alcove without a river view. He set her gently down there but continued to hold her in his arms while she sobbed hysterically. In an effort to calm her he kissed her hair and muttered soothing words in French that were every bit as meaningless as "there there."

This was not the way their first embrace was supposed to have unfolded. These were not the kisses he'd been dreaming about. Oh well, that was only a plan, a wish; this was real life.

After many minutes the sobs became raspy as Amanda fought to breathe. Soon it became apparent that she desperately needed to blow her nose. *Mon Dieu*, what was a gallant Gaul to do under these circumstances? Pierre carefully unbuttoned his shirt, which had been imported from Paris, and offered it to Amanda as a handkerchief.

True, it wasn't a malt shop with roller-skating waitresses, but he reckoned it wasn't a bad gesture for a first date either.

Both eyes were swollen shut so the man had to feel for any indentations there might be in the rock above him. Unfortunately every nook and cranny was the potential home of a scorpion or a poisonous centipede the length of his forearm, or one of a dozen varieties of snakes. He had no way of knowing, but he'd already managed to pull himself up about thirty feet from where he'd finally landed—this despite a broken leg and a dislocated shoulder.

Mai Manene they called this falls: the Big Waters. A better name for this place was *Mai a Mutoyo*: the Noisy Waters. The man had shouted to make himself heard until he had no voice left; he could not produce as much as a croak or a whimper. Fairness was not something that the man expected from life, yet it occurred to him that even a dying infant could make *some* sound that another could hear.

Then at last the man's right hand found a spur of rock that had smooth edges, and behind which there might have been a ledge. It was something to hope for. If he could stand to move his broken leg, and if he could find a crack or pit for a toehold, he could perhaps make more progress in the next few minutes than he had in the last two hours.

And there it was! A crack just wide enough to accommodate his foot, and what's more, it seemed to rise at an angle in the right direction. However, fate is no respecter of persons. As the man breathed a sigh of relief, in that same millisecond his concentration was broken and he relaxed his hold on the cliff face just enough so that he slipped and plunged to his death on the rock at the bottom of the abyss.

Such a small thing, that exhalation of a single breath. Yet such an important thing for the monstrous Nile crocodile waiting patiently below. Or, perhaps, it had been waiting impatiently. Who is to know? Surely not the dead man, who was not omniscient, and for whom reptilian fantasies were beyond his ken. Who, then, is to live and tell this tale?

Perhaps it was the man peering over the edge of the abyss.

Iron Sliver's brother had been in the hunting party that was absent from the village the day that Headhunter and his daughter left for Belle Vue. Although he had been born a Muluba slave, Little Bully was the chief of the Headhunter's village.

Although most decisions that involved the welfare of the village as a whole were made by the council of elders, old men all of them, there were occasions when Little Bully acted unilaterally. These happened to be occasions when Little Bully thought that he knew better than everyone else, or when time was too precious to waste on a consensus opinion. At any rate, by the time Iron Sliver and the Headhunter's wife were through telling their stories, the chief of Musoko village had already made a crucial decision.

He clapped his hands, signaling his messenger to his side. "Alert the drummers. They must communicate the following message to the people: tonight we move the village deeper into the bush in order to escape the wrath of the *Bula Matadi*. We will dismantle every hut, including the palaver hut and the women's bleeding hut. Every chicken and duck must be rounded up. Every goat and sheep must be securely tied. We will leave nothing behind."

Unfortunately, it so happened that the Headhunter's wife was standing within hearing distance of this conversation. No sooner did the breath of the last word cool his lips than she pounced on him like a leopard hiding in tall grass.

"*Mukelenge*, please, may I speak with you?"

"No, for surely you have heard there is no time. I must get this village moved before tomorrow's light."

"*Eyo, Great Mukelenge Little Bully Chief of Musoko,* I have heard, and I understand your reasoning, but it is false."

Now without being summoned, it was the chief's bodyguard who stepped to his side. Little Bully pushed the overzealous warrior away in annoyance. But when he turned again to the woman, he could almost feel his face harden into a beaten copper mask, so great was his disdain.

"Woman, it was you and your husband who brought this trouble upon us, was it not?"

The woman did not answer. She could not answer, could she? What can an honorable guilty person say in their own defense, except the truth? And were not the Headhunter and his wife amongst the most honorable citizens of the village? Little Bully enjoyed watching his neighbor squirm.

Finally, enough time had passed so that he was obliged to put an end to the game. "You may leave your house standing," he said. "Or you may wish to send it ahead with my slaves. But then where will you wait for your man? On top of an anthill? The very first night a leopard will come along and take you back to her weaning cubs. There they will bat you about like a child's ball. Is that what you wish, widow woman?"

The last two words had not been intentional, and they made him shudder with cold, despite the heat of the day. It was the shared opinion of many in the village that Little Bully's predictions were far more likely to come true than were predictions from the witch doctor—this despite the fact that Little Bully did not engage in fortune-telling.

The chief was a freed slave, captured as an infant, and it was widely surmised he descended from a line of hereditary witch doctors in the tribe of his birth. These hereditary gifts—or powers—were not something that Little Bully particularly enjoyed, as they enabled him to see his own stony path to destruction along with everyone else's.

"I am not a widow!" the Headhunter's wife cried angrily. "But if it is your intention that the village flee, and does not leave so much as a trace for the *Bula Matadi* to follow, how then can my husband follow me when he returns?"

Little Bully knew then, without a doubt, that she need not worry about staying behind for the sake of her husband. "You will not be seeing your husband again," he said matter-of-factly.

Her eyes widened and just as the drums began to talk she let loose a scream that was so anguished that even he, who had been ripped from his mother's teat while suckling, was moved. For the duration of her cry, the sun paused on its journey across the sky out of respect, and the birds folded their wings, and those still in flight fell to earth. Because of the pain in her cry a lioness jumped off a buffalo's back and trotted away hungry.

But a mere woman cannot scream forever. The next thing the Headhunter's wife did was drop to the ground and roll in the dirt. When she was sufficiently covered with it, so that it was clear to all that she was mourning, she began to keen, rocking backward and forward, as if keeping time to her own invisible drummer. Occasionally, without varying her rhythm, she scooped up handfuls of sand which she dribbled down on her head.

Iron Sliver, who had been harvesting wild mushrooms in the short grass, was hurrying back to the village when she heard the drums announcing their sudden departure, but when she was yet a full sprinting distance away, she heard her best friend's piercing shriek. Iron Sliver was a good friend, but not a foolish woman; she knotted the mushrooms she'd collected securely in a corner of her waistcloth before racing home to her friend's side. There she carefully deposited half of the delicious mushrooms in a clay pot inside the Headhunter's house, and half of the mushrooms in a pot in her own house. Then she joined her friend on the ground, wailing and throwing handfuls of sand in the air.

The Headhunter's wife had expected no less from her friend.

However, should the Headhunter's wife decide to remain behind, then she would expect Iron Sliver to move on with the village. They would say good-bye, but not in a long, exaggerated, drawn-out manner. Such displays of emotion were not the way of the Bashilele people. Nonetheless she very much appreciated her best friend's solidarity and her cries of anguish grew even louder now that she had support.

A crowd of spectators grew, but so did the number of women who actively participated in mourning the great headhunter's passing.

At last it was time for Mastermind to make an appearance—if that's what you want to call it—at the OP's party. Mastermind did not require finery in order to impress. What's more, Mastermind spoke softly, so softly as to be unheard by anyone but the OP. Besides, the OP was standing on the lowest terrace, looking out over the falls and the cliffs beyond, when Mastermind startled him by speaking. At first he hoped it was a joke; one that his conscience was playing on him. The alternative was that he was going mad.

"Perhaps you have already guessed, Monsieur OP, but I am the Mastermind."

He grinned; embarrassed that he might be experiencing a public breakdown—just like his deceased wife. May she rest in peace. When he turned and saw Mastermind just behind him, he yelped like an injured dog.

"*Sacre coeur!* It's only you; I thought for a minute that my mind was playing tricks on me."

"What kind of tricks?"

"I thought you said—" He stopped abruptly. What a fool he could be.

"That I was the Mastermind? But I am. Monsieur OP, don't look so astonished; it is not a becoming look on you. What were you expecting anyway, a cape and a mustache?"

"No, but you—this is impossible! Surely you are not working alone?"

The Mastermind gave him a look as cold as any Belgian winter. "Believe me, Monsieur OP, I have spent a lifetime outwitting men far more intelligent than you; I am not falling for your silly trap. Not that it matters, for I am not so stupid as to come here alone. I am one, and I am twenty. Thirty, if I snap my fingers. Now tell me; did you get the letter?"

The OP fancied himself to be a good judge of human behavior. After all, one cannot climb this high in an organization such as the Consortium without a thorough understanding of the way people worked. Just where had he learned all that? By carefully observing a troop of baboons. And what exactly had he learned? The importance of bluffing in getting one's way; it was as simple as that.

It was all about one's attitude, and it was precisely because the OP was himself such an expert on attitude that he was able to determine that the Mastermind was not bluffing. Clearly the OP was outnumbered—outmaneuvered even, for the time being.

"Yes, I got your letter," he growled. "I will start working on getting the parcel together tonight. How shall I contact you?"

"Wait! Did you see that?" Mastermind asked.

"See what?"

"Across the gorge—there, on the American side. It looked like a man falling."

"It was most likely a rock," the OP said. "Or a dead tree limb. The river is constantly eating away at the landscape. For the Consortium, that's a good thing, because often it's the hungry river that exposes the diamonds that are deposited along its banks."

"Yes, I'm sure you are right," Mastermind said, suddenly all business again. "I understand that you rise very early."

"I'm too old to benefit from any beauty sleep, and too young to practice for the grave."

"I see. In that case, Monsieur OP, meet me at the gravel pit at four in the morning. We'll talk more then. Oh—and bring what product you've managed to lay your hands on by then."

"*What? Product?*"

Poof! Mastermind disappeared into the throng of party guests, just like the rabbit the OP had seen disappear at a carnival side-show in Brussels when he was a boy.

EIGHTEEN

Husband was a man of renown for his patience. Until recently he had worked for the white man by day, cutting grass around the post office, and never once had Husband shown the *Bula Matadi* that he felt himself to be his equal. In the evening he'd been served by two wives; one of whom possessed a tongue sharp enough to cut through a stalk of sugar cane, and the other—well, the other was Cripple.

Aiyee! Cripple was more trouble than any three wives! Still, any man who could put up with a woman such as Cripple and not beat her, now there was a man of infinite patience. Husband had waited faithfully outside the compound of the OP, hiding in the shadows as all good non-essential persons should do on a night like that, and when Cripple's services were no longer needed, he'd given her a ride home.

He had listened to her exciting stories and asked the right questions, but she had a request that stumped him.

"*Why* will you need the machete tonight?" Husband asked in disbelief.

"Husband, it is better that you do not know."

"Cripple," Husband said, his patience finally worn away, "must I sit on your neck and beat you?"

"If you do so, Husband," Cripple said, "then I will turn my head and bite your behind. Like so." Because Cripple's body was already twisted, she had a head start on turning her head.

Husband's laugh began as the sputter of a diesel generator that was first springing to life, and it finished with a roar that was sure to attract the neighbor's attention. Only a man of great self-control—such as Husband—was capable of reigning in his emotions thusly.

"Wherever it is that you are going, Wife, there I am going as well."

Husband could see Cripple's jaw tense in the reflected light of fire. She responded almost immediately, but he was not surprised by the speed of her response. Husband knew that she had probably made up her mind long before she'd broached the subject with him. Such was the way of Cripple.

"I walk to the gravel pits tonight," she said. "The machete is in case we are attacked by hyenas—or a leopard."

Husband stared at his beloved first wife in horror. "*The* gravel pits. The very same gravel pits which are haunted by the ghost of a white woman?"

"Are there any other? Husband, the white girl—the white Mushilele, but yet not of their blood—it is important that this very same girl must return to her village so that she may live a few days more with her tribe."

"*E!* And that is all you will be giving her—a few *days* more! Wife, do you not see the futility in this plan? Do you not see the danger that you are putting these people in? True, they are only savages, these Bashilele, but they are not our enemies, like the Bena Lulua. They do not lock us in our thatch huts and burn us alive simply because we agree to work for the Belgians—because we are smart enough to work for the Belgians, and they are not."

Cripple nodded. "A few days perhaps. Maybe a few years. Husband, I would do anything to spend that much time with you."

Husband spit into the dirt at the side of the cooking fire to indicate his unconditional surrender. Who could not admire Cripple above all other women?

"*I* will carry the machete, and I will carry you," he said.

"Husband," Cripple said softly, "you will not have to carry me but a short way. At my place of employment there is a box on wheels that is used to transport wood from the chopping block to kitchen, or perhaps to the storage hut. I can easily fit inside that box, Husband. Believe me, for I have tried."

Husband laughed deeply. "I believe that you have, Cripple, and I shall be happy to give you and our little skunk a ride in this box on wheels."

In the Tshiluba language, the planet Venus is called the moon's wife. She rises faithfully as soon as the day is done to greet her husband. After spending some alone time together, they are joined by their children, the stars. Soon after that they part, for the moon is a restless husband and cannot stand to be kept in one place.

Cripple's twisted body had refused to give her a full night's sleep since the day it was wrenched from her mother's amniotic fluid. Thus it was that she knew the hour of the moon's rising and bedding on the night in question. Amanda Brown, however, claimed to be able to sleep like a baby, although Cripple would have been happy to tell her that babies don't necessarily sleep well, and that sometimes they can squall for no reason and keep one up all night.

Although Amanda didn't believe in fate, she did believe in God, and that He worked in mysterious ways, but she would never have thought that He'd use her bladder as a means. She normally woke between three forty-five and four in the morning, thanks to a large glass of milk before going to bed, but tonight she'd had three club sodas over at the OP's and was up at three thirty.

Amanda was a heavy sleeper, which meant that most mornings she would hardly even remember having gotten up, unless a toad or a snake got in her way to the toilet. This morning, however, the second her eyelids parted, they popped open wide as the memory of Pierre and the kiss that night before banished all thoughts of sleep.

Or wait; was that just a dream? Because if it wasn't, then that stuff about the man and the crocodile had to be real as well. But it was too horrible to have been real! Oh God, Amanda felt the need to be sick. She rushed into the bathroom, and threw herself on the floor in the classic drunk's position, arms around the toilet bowl. Try as she might to retch, nothing came up.

When she was satisfied that she could keep her stomach under control, she used the toilet for its original conception, but even then she felt reluctant to leave the room. Something unusual was happening outside the window; she could feel it in her bones.

She turned off the light and slowly peeked between a pair of heavy lined curtains. That old saying about it being darkest just before dawn was certainly right on the money; at least this side of the house was deep in shadows. In the mango grove the spaces between trees showed up as black. Although the turbulent falls appeared white at all times of the night, she could see only a sliver of them from this window.

You could hate the falls for all their treachery, for the constant noise they made, and for their seasonal threat to precariously perched structures such as the Missionary Rest House, but without them Belle Vue would have no electricity. They were its life force, its heartbeat. But as she peered between the curtains Amanda felt drawn to the blackness of the mango grove instead; it was as if a powerful force of energy was pulling at her from somewhere down amongst those trees.

Amanda dressed hastily, but still appropriately for the outdoors. The night watchman, Kind Person, was more often than not asleep on the job, but she surely did not want to be seen by anyone in her nightdress and bathrobe. So skirt, blouse, bobby socks, and oxfords, it was, complete with the brassier which had been unsuccessfully worn by the real Ugly Eyes the preceding day.

Although Amanda carried a large box-shaped flashlight with a powerful beam, she did not turn it on until she reached the edge of the cultivated lawn and was actually about to step beneath the first tree. She'd walked quickly and quietly, keeping to the shadows, like Tonto on *The Lone Ranger* television show. Her heart pounded as the circle of bright light revealed first one tree trunk and then another, and then finally it shone upon three abject, terrified human beings crouched around her wheelbarrow.

Seeing them gave Amanda quite a fright, but apparently they got a good scare as well. Cripple beat her arms against her husband and then fell to the ground moaning.

"Oh Mamu Ugly Eyes, do you not know that you look exactly like that white woman's ghost?"

"Cripple," Amanda said, whilst trying to appear cool, "which white woman's ghost do you refer to? And how is it that you know this?"

"The OP's wife, *Mamu*; the woman went over the falls in the truck when it was the second month of August. It is said that she roams the cliffs on this side of the river late at night calling out for her body, and that she is particularly loathsome."

Amanda was at first dumbfounded, but Cripple's husband stepped forward as if to shield his wife. "*Mamu*, please forgive my wife for her foolish words. She is an intelligent woman, as you know, *Mamu*, but quite often she steps on her tongue."

"There has been no offense taken, Cripple's husband. Since the OP's wife has been under the falls for two months now, I am quite certain that she is indeed loathsome to look upon. If it is true that I bear a resemblance to her, then my appearance has greatly improved since I arrived in Belle Vue."

Both husband and wife stared at her openmouthed for a second or two and then convulsed with laughter.

"Shhh!" Amanda held a warning finger to her lips.

"*Mamu*," sniggered Cripple, "those words were but said in jest. You are not as loathsome as that."

"And you are less hideous than the rear end of a jackal. Now come, we have not a minute to lose."

Cripple's husband, whose reputation was that of failed witch doctor, stepped in front of his small, misshapen wife. "*Mamu*, what is it that you wish us to do?"

"Why, to do whatever it is that you had planned before I showed up. By the looks of things, I would say that the three of you are planning a trip. If so, then we must hurry and get out of Belle Vue before the sun rises."

"*Mamu*," Ugly Eyes said, speaking for the first time, "why is it that you help me, a Mushilele? I am but a savage, the daughter of a headhunter. Surely I am beneath your consideration."

"Ugly Eyes, do not insult my intelligence like that. If I will stoop to befriend these two worthless Baluba, then why would I not do the same for you? Now, let us move and not talk. When we reach your village, then we can sit and talk like old women—like Cripple. Do you understand?"

"Yes, *Mamu*. And I promise that when we reach my village I will not let anyone take your head."

"Thank you," Amanda said, both surprised and touched by the kind words. "I am moved by those words."

NINETEEN

The OP also spent a sleepless night. How could something like this possibly be happening? It was a bloody nightmare, to borrow from his English friends. The *scheme*, if that's what you wanted to call it—he preferred the word *plan*—was supposed to have happened thirteen years ago. It should only have taken a few days, then the whole thing would be over, and both whiney wife and ill-suited female child would be shipped back to Belgium.

He'd been approached by post, by an anonymous source, suggesting what seemed to be a rather easy way for him to kill two birds with one stone. Mastermind had been very thorough in researching the OP's situation. The Mastermind knew that the OP was not the baby's father, that the OP loved playing cards in the evening but lost on a regular basis, and that the OP had fewer morals than a bitch in heat. The Mastermind seemed well acquainted with the *baba* whom Heilewid had employed as their child's full-time nanny. Well enough, that is, to get her on board with the plan, before even he had been recruited.

Nannies came cheap in the Belgian Congo—real cheap. One could be hired for thirty francs a day, which was far less than an American dollar. The *babas* were usually more than happy to farm out their own children to relatives and live full-time inside the white man's sturdy house, sleeping on the floor next to their little pink charges. But that particular nanny, Francine—yes, she had an African name, but it wasn't wise to encourage its use—Heilewid had done the hiring herself. She'd heard of Francine through Charlotte, the wife of a former Belgian employee of his.

But the plan had failed! The baby's perambulator had been found empty next to the gravel pit, with a goddamned Bashilele arrow piercing the bonnet. After that, the OP hadn't heard a peep out of the Mastermind. Not one letter or telegram. Not one message delivered on foot or by cyclist. That's why now, after all these years, and the almost miraculous—the OP had no use for religion and bonafied miracles—return of the girl to whom Heilewid had given birth, the OP had been able to come up with a plan of his own.

It was similar to the Mastermind's plan; actually, it was identical to the Mastermind's plan minus the Mastermind. The girl would go missing, *again*, ransom would be demanded, and the Consortium would be conned into paying a king's ransom in uncut diamonds. Most of the details were yet to be worked out, but now—the whole thing was off! And all because the Mastermind decided to surface all these years later, as if lying in wait for the day when Heilewid's daughter would turn up. It was unbelieveable! What cheek!

So what was there to do now? Should the OP work his butt off for the next two years, until the Congo became independent, and the mines became nationalized and he got thrown out? Should he retire now, even though he was nowhere near the top of his game, if only because the mines had been showing a loss ever since he'd opened a new facility in a box canyon twenty miles to the south? Should he accept a lateral position that had been offered to him in South Africa, even though that country's take on apartheid disgusted him even more than what he saw implemented here? Plus, he doubted that South Africa could ever function as a free and independent country, given its racial history. Just imagine the kind of man it would take to be able to untangle that bunch of hurts!

On that warm, sticky October night in 1958, the OP sat alone on his terrace and nursed his fifth Johnnie Walker Black. Any minute now he would start to feel the heat in his chest, the mild warning that enough was enough. Then, since having one for the road was just some silly invented idea, he would have two more quick drinks before setting out for the gravel pits. There he would lie in wait and be the element of surprise. *Then* who would be the Mastermind?

Madame Cabochon loved secrets, and one of her secrets was that she enjoyed herself. Oh not in the obvious hands-on sort of way, but just lying back on her pillows, with her fabulous hair spilling about in molten waves, her alabaster skin gleaming white even in the darkest hours just before dawn. Sometimes she would wake up and hold a mother-of-pearl mirror above her and sigh with satisfaction, while Francois, snoring away next to her, bleated like a goat being led to the slaughter.

This night, Madame Cabochon found that due to the stimulation of the OP's party, not to mention the powerful, and therefore sexy, OP, sleep had to be chased into the bottom of a half-filled bourbon bottle. Once there, it was fitful; she could hardly tell when her dreams started and stopped, and then started again, or when even more troublesome daydreams began. At one point she began to dream that she was being burned at the stake. That's when she woke up and discovered that her dream was but a pale imitation of life.

In his house—really a villa, as were all the Belgian residences in Bell Vue—Pierre Jardin slept soundly. He invariably did. Sleep was the one thing that blocked out unpleasant memories: his mother's death when he was just eleven, the beatings he occasionally received from his father, the unsympathetic nuns and abusive teachers at boarding school, and some really nasty thing he'd seen in his line of work. Sleep obliterated everything for seven or eight hours. Sometimes, if he was lucky, on his day off he was able to sleep even more.

When Pierre woke up in the darkest part of that morning, he wasn't sure if he was dreaming. It felt as if Sister John the Beloved was whipping the soft skin at the backs of his knees with the plastic tubing that came from the aerator of the classroom aquarium. That had become an almost daily ritual, just like morning mass. After catechism came math, French, geography, science, and then Pierre's whipping.

The reasons for Pierre's daily whippings varied, ranging from incomplete assignments to accusations of spitball throwing, but the aftereffects were always the same: Pierre's legs felt like they were on fire, while Sister John the Beloved's face seemed to glow beatifically. She began to refer to Pierre as her "little cabbage" and at Christmas gave him a real Timex watch, which his father later confiscated. When he returned to school for the next term he learned that Sister John the Beloved had been transferred.

But tonight—tonight the stinging sensation moved rapidly until it reached Pierre's crotch. At that point he realized that it was not a dream. He reached for the lamp switch beside his bed.

"*Mon Dieu!*" he cried. His bed was crawling with driver ants. He leaped to the floor. It was an automatic response. However, what was normally a cool concrete floor now crunched under the weight of his feet. There were so many of the wretched creatures that the ones that escaped being squished clambered aboard immediately and enmeshed themselves in his hairy legs. It was impossible to dislodge them as fast as they climbed on, and anyway, no matter what one did, their ugly, brutish heads still stayed behind embedded in one's flesh.

Pierre had gone to bed naked; he was a firm believer in giving the "boys" some air. But the boys were on fire now; it was excruciating pain. Unbearable pain. Worse than anything Sister John the Beloved could ever dream up. He raced to the bathroom and turned the knob that switched on the lights. It was roiling with ants but he ignored them long enough to complete the task. He pushed them off as well as he could with this other hand and climbed into the claw-foot bathtub. There was no time to close the curtain before turning the shower knob to its hottest setting.

It took what seemed like hours for truly hot water to dribble from the mineral-encrusted showerhead, and even when it seemed hot enough to blister his skin, the little demons held tight. What's more, the buggers were now dropping on him from the ceiling of the bathroom like miniature kamikaze pilots, not only aware of their upcoming deaths, but actually anticipating them.

"*Merde!*" Pierre roared, and that was just the first of many invectives.

Captain Pierre Jardin was not a superstitious man, but at the peak of his desperation, when he was reduced to swearing, the lights went out. There was no warning flicker. Just inky darkness. And the constant bombardment of insects equipped with pinchers as sharp as swords and the fighting will of Spartacus, every one of them bent on his destruction.

There was nothing left for Pierre to do but grab a towel, feel for the closest flashlight, and flee the house.

The stumbling band of refugees had just crossed the bridge in the moonless predawn light and had turned right onto the road that would taken them to the gravel pit when Cripple bade them stop.

"Listen," she said, "do you not hear that?"

"I hear only the waterfalls," the white *mamu* said. Husband failed to understand how it was that a woman who could be so annoying could at the same time be so rich and so powerful.

"I hear the beating of my heart," he said. After all, Husband had been pushing both Cripple and the white *mamu* in the wheelbarrow. His wife, of course, was unable to walk that far, that fast. As for the white *mamu*—he had felt obliged to offer her the ride, and she had felt obliged to accept. In the old days it would have taken four men to carry her in a sedan chair. The young Ugly Eyes, being both a white and a Mushilele savage, was left to get by on her own pair of legs.

"*Tch*," said Cripple impatiently, "listen closely."

"It is the *luhumbe*," Ugly Eyes said.

"Yes, yes," the white *mamu* said. "That is the sound that Cripple heard at the place of the elephant." *Muaba wa kahumbu.*

"The place of the elephant?" Husband asked. There had been no time to talk to Cripple, to hear about her trip to the territory of the Bashilele, and the sacrifice of this great and generous elephant.

"*E*," Cripple said. "It was the *luhumbe* that drove the elephant out of the thickets and into the short grass so close to the white man's road. With my own eyes I could see that these most vicious of all ants had dared to climb into the elephant's trunk, its ears, and even its eyes. They drove it half mad so that it was an easy mark for the bullet that followed."

"We have a saying amongst my people," Ugly Eyes said. "The smaller the animal, the more dangerous it is."

"Unless it is a mamba," Husband said. "They are much larger than any ant, and far more lethal. I get many requests for amulets to ward off mamba bites, but to tell you frankly, it cannot be done. And yet, the little pouches of anti-mamba powder remain my best-selling potion."

"Husband!" Cripple said, for she was genuinely shocked. Never had she heard him make such an admission. Although Cripple had never put much stock in Husband's magical potions—how could she, when she knew him so intimately?—neither had she dismissed him as a complete charlatan. Was not Husband a man of integrity?

"Cripple," Husband said sharply, "we will speak more of this at a later time—but only if it is necessary."

"Indeed it is, Husband."

"*Tch.*"

Cripple's cheeks burned, for she felt shamed in front of the white *mamu* and Ugly Eyes, who was almost a white *mamu* herself.

"Look," the white *mamu* cried. "All the lights in Belle Vue have gone off! What does that mean?"

"It means we must hurry, *Mamu*," Cripple said pragmatically. She had no doubt but that the driver ants were somehow to be blamed for the sudden power failure. The details, however, were something that had to wait. For now, her only job was to get Ugly Eyes to the gravel pit and show her the aquatic path that would lead her back home.

TWENTY

Having grown up the daughter of a tugboat captain in Antwerp, Madame Cabochon was a woman of many fine and varied curses. These she hurled at Monsieur Cabochon, and not at the vicious intruders. After all, the ants were merely doing what they'd been created to do: eat. It was Monsieur Cabochon who'd talked her into moving to a bush town where such invasions by wildlife were commonplace.

Of course the curses hurt M. Cabochon's feelings; he was only human, was he not? Oh how he hated his wife, but at the same time, he cherished her beauty. During his many years in Africa, M. Cabochon had observed many species of animals that were deadly, and thus deserved to be hated, but nonetheless were really quite attractive. He particularly admired the big cats. He'd once stalked a lioness with such skill that he'd gotten close enough to smell her breath. *C'est vrais*, even in that moment he'd been reminded of Madame Cabochon.

At any rate, now that he was an old colonial hand, the first thing M. Cabochon did was rip off his wife's negligee and the bedclothes. She beat him about the head and shoulders as he did this, and clawed his face and bare arms with her long red fingernails (what exquisite instruments of torture they were!) but it was a job that needed doing. The next thing that M. Cabochon did was run to the kitchen, from whence he momentarily returned bearing a large canister of wheat flour. Enduring all manner of bodily pain to his person, he pushed their monstrous bed into the middle of the room and sprinkled a barrier of flour around its perimeter.

Apparently these insidious tiny creatures, capable of felling even a mighty elephant under the right conditions, cannot, or will not, cross such a barrier. The theory is that the fine flour plugs up their breathing apparatus. The curious thing is that one would expect to find thousands of flailing and dying ants along the perimeter of this sort, as opposed to the dozens that one does find. But as Monsieur Cabochon was soon to discover, those that didn't perish in the vanguard merely turned around and headed for the walls. Soon they were dropping from the ceiling like the black sleet of a November's day in Brussels.

"*Mon Dieu*, Madame Cabochon shrieked, "we are going to die! And it is your fault, you imbecile with turds for brains!"

Monsieur Cabochon did not respond but ran from the room again. He pulled a well-used folding cot from the storage shed and set it up on the south terrace, which seemed to be the only place in all of the Belgian Congo that was free of the damn ants. At least that much was good.

Then he raced back into the house and scooped up his hysterical wife and carried her to her new canvas bed. By this time she was writhing in agony and most of what she said made no sense, so he gave himself permission to ignore the words that did.

"Why did you leave me alone, you sniveling coward?"

He'd forgotten to fetch a kerosene lantern, and since he was trying desperately to pick the ants off her exquisite body before they did any more damage, he had to hold the flashlight in his mouth. A few torturous, gagging sounds escaped his mouth, but apparently they were just enough to further inflame her rage.

"You fool! You imbecile, Maurice! Papa was right about you! Take those handcuffs off me, right now!"

Monsieur Cabochon's heart sank. Who the hell was this Maurice that he should come to mind when his wife was in the throes of delirium? Furthermore, the sounds he now heard at the edge of the lawn confirmed his wife's earlier accusation; he did have turds for brains.

Being the Great White Hunter that he fancied himself to be, M. Cabochon had insisted that they live in the house closest to the bush on the south side of town, where the land lay undisturbed for tens of kilometers, almost to the Angola border. The proximity to nature allowed M. Cabochon to hunt for either francolins or guinea whenever he heard them calling, and there were a number of occasions when they obliged him by coming right onto his front lawn to feed in the early-morning or late-afternoon hours. The same thing applied to antelope—just not quite as often.

One day, even, a troop of baboons, hunting for grasshoppers, made it as far as the rear of the house, where they stole half of the laundry hanging out to dry. Although the damn monkeys dropped the clothes before disappearing into the tall *tshisuku*, the houseboys nearly burst their guts laughing, and almost overnight an urban legend developed amongst the white children that there existed a troop of baboons thereabouts that dressed in human clothes.

This is to say that the Cabochon residence may as well have been built in a game reserve. Monsieur Cabochon was properly terrified, but not surprised, when a pack of laughing hyenas came loping out of the high grass and headed straight for the cot. Madame Cabochon, on the other hand, was, mercifully, protected by her delirium.

"Why, it's my friends, Papa! Why didn't you tell me you were throwing me an eighteenth birthday party? And I'm not wearing so much as a touch of rouge."

What? Only her eighteenth birthday party? Was that all Madame Cabochon was raving about? Well, Monsieur Cabochon hadn't even met her until she was twenty-six! Pff! Then that was nothing; he could forgive that. But first he needed to defend her against the hyenas, which had begun to circle the cot, prancing and nipping at the air, just centimeters away from Madame Cabochon's once lovely limbs.

And then too, for the first time Monsieur Cabochon became acutely aware of the hundreds of bites he'd suffered during the savage driver-ant attack; indeed the ants were all still clinging to him.

Mrs. Gorman had never felt so much alone. Although to her credit she'd managed to put on a good show after the servants had been dismissed for the night, and the girls had been picked up by the handsome Belgian police captain and taken across the river to the OP's party. If only she knew Mr. Gorman's whereabouts. She'd had to lie at dinner, to make up some story about him deciding to pay an impromptu visit to the village because the Lord had laid it on his heart to pray with so-and-so there. They bought her story, of course, because it was bald-faced and outrageous, but couched in familiar language.

Mrs. Gorman had managed to get a ride back early from the party whereupon she immediately began a thorough search of the Missionary Rest House property. She knew it was only a silly notion, but she began with Amanda's room anyway. Then on to Dorcas's room, the other empty guest rooms, her daughter's room, the pantry, and then the outbuilding with the woodshed where the strange white girl and her savage father were quartered. How odd, Mrs. Gorman thought, that there should be a mattress on the floor but no sheets, no blanket, and not a speck of clothing. There was not one piece of evidence in that stifling little room to indicate that someone was living there. Had Amanda moved the girl inside, into white quarters, without telling anyone?

Mrs. Gorman shivered at the thought. What an awful thing to have done—if indeed that was the case. Just because the young woman had a white skin did not mean that she was civilized.

What if she rose up in the night and murdered them in their beds? And where was her father to stay? Surely in the village somewhere, because if Amanda even thought to bring him under the same roof—now what was *that*? Mrs. Gorman whirled, and seeing nothing, stepped quickly outside.

There it was again; the same sound. An anguished cry—not unlike Mr. Gorman sounded last year when he received the telegram informing him of his mother's passing into Glory. In fact, so similar was the cry that Mrs. Gorman's pulse raced with excitement at the discovery, although her heart sank with the foreknowledge that the details were not going to be entirely pleasant. Keeping that in mind she followed the familiar sounds around the corner of the outbuilding.

Sure enough, there, seated on the platform used by Protruding Navel to hold the washtub when he scrubbed clothes, was Mr. Gorman. Even without the aid of a flashlight Mrs. Gorman recognized him immediately by the way he held his body, for years of close observation and intimacy had etched every subtle variation of his shape and movement into her mind.

She called loudly to him, both to be heard above the noise of the falls and so as not to startle him when she got too close. He immediately choked back his sobs but would not look up.

"Mr. Gorman," she said, unable to refrain from scolding him, "I have been worried sick in regards to your whereabouts."

"It is my soul that you should worry about, Mrs. Gorman," he said, "for today I killed a man."

The OP enjoyed driving drunk. He took pleasure in every close encounter with a tree, or boulder, because the encounters were just that—*close*. There was no one on the road at that hour of the night, and no animals either, except for nightjars and jackals—both creatures that he hated.

He detested the former because they seemed to explode into your windshield and could startle you off the road, and he couldn't abide the latter because it was a jackal that had caught and eaten his favorite cat, an orange male tabby named Monsieur Bon Chance. Whenever he had the opportunity, the OP drove with his lights off at night, and then turned them on at the last second in order to blind his victim.

Of course one never entirely goes unobserved, so gossip had come back to him. He knew there were citizens of Belle Vue (white, of course) who thought he was as heartless as a Nazi storm trooper. Others approved of his behavior. Some even made jokes, substituting Africans for the nightjars and jackals.

That night, after seven Johnnie Walker Blacks, the OP would make his way to the gravel pits. He was too drunk to hit one jackal, and too off-course for the nightjars to collide with him, but a couple of times he almost tipped over after running up on the dirt embankments that flanked the unpaved roads. As he neared the pits he had to slow considerably—well, for a drunk who barely gave a damn, that is—because the road cut through deep forest and here the embankments sprouted trees.

As he rounded the last curve and saw the largest gravel pit lying just ahead, an antelope leaped over the hood of the car—no, it wasn't an antelope! It was something else altogether; perhaps it was a chimpanzee, although these apes weren't supposed to be found this far south.

Hell, whatever the creature was, it passed so close to the OP's open window that he was able to smell it; it smelled of death, of a jackal corpse that had been rotting in the sun for two weeks. And strangely, because the OP didn't have a religious bone in his body, it smelled of evil and fear.

Perhaps if he hadn't had that extra Johnnie Walker Black for the road, Monsieur OP might have been able to remain calm enough to stop the car before it went into the pit. Unfortunately he could not. Also, most unfortunate was the fact that the car entered the pit at its deep end, where its depth exceeded five meters.

Of course the car did not sink immediately, and the OP did

try to escape and would have swum to safety had not the strap of his gun holster gotten caught on the handle of the car door. When his car filled with water a minute later—*if* he'd been able to tell you—the OP would have said that he felt as if someone was pushing down on his shoulders. The feeling was both terrifying and comforting.

As the water filled his lungs and at last he lost the battle to breathe, the OP suddenly felt—well, he felt *nothing*! No fear, no panic, no pain—just awesome, peaceful, nothing.

"Monsieur OP," someone said.

"*Oui?*" He didn't even feel as if he needed to turn and face the speaker, because the speaker seemed to be everywhere.

Mastermind also arrived at the gravel pits much earlier than the appointed hour, but immediately Mastermind knew this was a grave mistake. Even though Mastermind did not believe in ghosts, there was an energy connected to the place so pervasively evil that one could hardly breathe. Surely one could not sit and calmly plan the next stage of a very complex operation in an atmosphere like this. Mastermind was contemplating leaving, and then return-ing an hour later, but then along came the OP's car, and it drove straight into the pond.

The Mastermind could see everything, from beginning to end, but really, there was nothing that could be done for the poor man. The car only stayed afloat for a minute—maybe less. It looked like Monsieur OP was struggling to get out, but what was Mastermind to do? Mastermind couldn't swim. Not one stroke! There really was nothing to do but watch the gravel pit claim yet another life.

This man-made scar upon the face of the earth had become a living thing; it was a watery monster that demanded to be fed. Mankind had created it out of his avarice, and now it was feed-ing on man's flesh and blood. So far as Mastermind was aware, the gravel pits had claimed only European lives—Belgian lives at that—which was fitting, proving that there was justice under the sun after all.

Although Mastermind believed it was totally inappropriate to do so, she smiled.

TWENTY-ONE

Mrs. Gorman prayed that her words would henceforth be gentler. She even laid a hand on Mr. Gorman's shoulder; it was an act alien to their relationship, unless it was one of their scheduled days of intimacy. However, the aforementioned days never fell in October.

If her brazen action shocked her husband, he certainly didn't show it. "I killed a man," he said again.

"We are all guilty of murder in our hearts, Mr. Gorman. Why, just last week, I found myself getting so irritated at Pastor Mukedi-Paul that I wanted to—well, I didn't of course. I only imagined something dreadful, like him stepping into quicksand on his way back home to his village. But as we both know—"

"Shut up!"

"I beg your pardon?" Even though he could at times be an arrogant and pompous man, Mr. Gorman was never downright mean. That had been Papa.

"I said shut up! You don't know what you're talking about. I really killed a man. A *real* flesh-and-blood man."

Mrs. Gorman sat abruptly, and with some force, on the hard-packed earth next to the washstand. Either she was married to a murderer, and that was going to take a bit of adjustment, or she was married to a crazy man; that too would be rather taxing. If only they had returned to the United States as scheduled. If only they had not delayed their return by one week so that they might view the headhunter's bizarre white daughter.

It had most certainly not been worth it. But how was Mrs. Gorman to know that she would find herself so attracted to the sight of mostly bared male flesh again—that is, white male flesh—at the club swimming pool? Well, really, she ought to have known. After all, didn't she teach the African children in Sunday school that *Satana* lurked in the most pleasurable places, just waiting to pounce on those who let their guards down?

"Please explain yourself, Mr. Gorman. But first, should we have a word of prayer?"

"I have done nothing but pray for these last many hours, Mrs. Gorman, yet nothing has changed in my situation. Alas, the man has not revived—nor did I expect him to—but neither does the burden of sin feel lifted from my soul. I am lower than a worm, Mrs. Gorman. I am no longer worthy of continuing on as a seeker of souls. This morning I took it upon myself to confront the Mushilele headhunter."

"Why, husband?"

"Because I believed it sinful—a filthy thing—for a savage like him to be rearing a beautiful young white girl like that. Did you know that he spoke Tshiluba?"

"No! But I thought he could only speak their gibberish—whatever it is."

"Bushilele."

"Yes. Mr. Gorman, what did you mean by saying that he *spoke* Tshiluba? Where is he now?"

"That is who I killed, Mrs. Gorman. The headhunter and I—well, I saw that he was armed, and I believed that he was going to kill me with his knife. So I put some of that good old U.S.A. Marine training into play and we wrestled, and I overpowered him, and I pushed him off the cliff. God help me, I pushed him off the cliff!" He grabbed her hand and pulled her from the ground and half carried her to the exact spot where he'd stood when he'd given the Mushilele headhunter the fatal shove.

For a moment Mrs. Gorman was unsure of her own future, so intense did her husband sound. She prayed that God would forgive her sins, she thought of Peaches one last time, she thought of her mother, and she thought of butter-pecan ice cream.

"I watched him fall," Mr. Gorman said. "I watched him bounce from rock to rock, and then at the bottom a crocodile grabbed him. It was worse than anything I saw in the war, because this man had done nothing to deserve it. But I realized that only when it was too late."

Mrs. Gorman pulled loose from her husband's grip and took several steps back from the precipice. "Tell me," she said. "Would you have been so upset with this man if his daughter had turned out to be fat and ugly?"

"Hells bells!" Mr. Gorman roared. "What kind of question is that?"

"A good one," Mrs. Gorman said, and then she turned and walked away.

"Stop, Husband," Cripple whispered in a terrified voice. "I see the ghost of a white woman."

Husband stopped the wheelbarrow so abruptly that Cripple and Amanda were dumped out onto the road. Lucky for them it had a layer of soft damp sand that cushioned their impact. Nonetheless, Husband recognized that for Cripple it was an opportunity to express her fear of the spirit world in a way that wouldn't embarrass herself in front of the *mamu*.

First she made quite the show of groaning while the *mamu* got up and brushed herself off. "Husband," she then moaned, "perhaps you will find it in your heart to have mercy and bring your machete down upon my poor twisted neck."

"Not while a spark of breath remains in you, little one," Husband said. "For how then will our son yet live? Who will breathe for him? The worms in the ground? Would you have the cockroaches feed our baby boy until he is old enough to rise from the grave, himself a ghost? What then shall I name him? *Mukishi*—Ghost, now that is a fine, original name, is it not?"

Cripple jumped to her feet and commenced to hop about like a baby bird in a crowded nest vying to be fed. *"Aiyee!* We will *not* name that which grows within me Ghost! To do so will curse both it and me! Then we will surely die, Husband."

"Cripple, stop!" the white *mamu* begged. "Do I understand correctly? Are you with belly?"

"Eyo," Husband said proudly. "So powerful is my *lubola*—penis, that even this one jumps with happiness like a gazelle in the Song of *Solomo.*"

"Ah, so although you are a witch doctor by profession, you know the Christian Bible?"

"Tch," Husband said, deeply offended. *"Mamu,* I am a Christian—a true Christian. I am a Roman Catholic. Perhaps the Holy Fathers do not teach us as many stories from the Bible as the Protestant missionaries teach their students. But do you not agree that the Bible contains many vicious stories that are unsuitable for human ears?"

"Well, I—"

"Look!" Cripple cried. "The ghost; she comes closer!"

Husband paid heed for the first time, and what he saw made his knees go weak and his heart pound. The ghost had two enormous round eyes that glowed in the dark and it was bearing down on them faster than he could think.

"That is not a ghost," the *mamu* said slowly. "Listen! What do you hear?"

"I hear *you, Mamu,"* Cripple said. "But then, who is there in all of this forest who can *not* hear you? At least your accent has improved a little bit since your arrival. Honestly, *Mamu,* in the beginning I thought you were speaking to me in *Chinois*." Then Cripple laughed—like a monkey!

"Wife," Husband said, deeply embarrassed, "have you ever heard *Chinois* spoken?"

"Stop it!" *Mamu* ordered. So like a white, eh? "That is a car that we hear. Those are the lights of a car that we see! It comes to us now, so we must move to the side of the road!"

Dorcas Middleton had observed quite a bit in the last hour from her post beside the largest gravel pit. She'd come very early, like Jesus had come to Gethsemane to pray on the night of his betrayal and arrest. Dorcas, however, had come on a much different mission. She'd come to pray, yes—that much *was* like Jesus, but mostly, she'd come early so as not to be outfoxed by that wily Monsieur OP.

Instead, she'd had the horrifying, yet strangely gratifying, experience of watching the greedy, womanizing Operations Manager driving drunk, go off the road, straight over the bank and into the deepest end of the pond. Then she saw him struggle to get out and flail about as he screamed for help.

Dorcas knew for a fact that the OP's soul was not saved from damnation—he'd told her that he didn't believe in that "Protestant stuff"—so clearly, he was headed straight for hell. On that account, Dorcas felt justified in believing that she saw a clawlike red hand pulling him back into his car, and that's what was holding him back. That hand, of course, belonged to Satan. The Devil. The Prince of Darkness. Emperor of the Gravel Pits.

Even if she hadn't seen a giant red claw, but just spots in front of her tired seventy-nine-year-old eyes, what difference did that truly make? Dorcas Middleton had never learned to swim. In her day, proper middle-class girls did not parade around in bathing costumes in mixed company, just as they did not ride bicycles—well, there was another reason for the latter. Girls who rode bicycles might prove not to be virgins on their wedding night.

Dorcas shuddered at the thought of someone touching her there. Or anywhere, for that matter. And *especially* a man. She'd given the matter a lot of thought over the years, and was grateful that the Lord had led her to the mission field, where the opportunities for her to get married had been slim to none. After all, how could she explain—well, she couldn't. She couldn't explain it to herself, except to say that those feelings were from the Devil. He was certainly persistent, wasn't He, this Prince of Darkness?

He'd first come creeping into her mind when her cousin Florence Rebecca stayed over the night of supposedly the worst snowstorm ever. Both girls were thirteen, but Florence had developed far faster than Dorcas, a fact that both fascinated and inflamed the poor girl. Neither of the girls mentioned their disparate development, but from that night on, Satan was Dorcas's constant companion.

No matter how many times she whispered "get behind me, Satan," the tempter slithered right back into her mind at the slightest provocation. Once, in a misguided attempt to purge herself of these thoughts, Dorcas asked to be stationed at a mission that was being established on the fringe of Bashilele territory. Her request was based on the fact that the Bashilele women who were not yet Christian—the missionaries took the liberty of calling them heathens—wore only loincloths, which they made from the fibers of raphia palm leaves. In a traditional Bashilele village, or sometimes even at church on the mission, it was possible to see hundreds of bare breasts of all sizes and shapes, bouncing and bobbling about (the church breasts were more sedate, to be sure).

If Dorcas could train herself to be immune to the attraction of so much flesh to meet the eye, then maybe she could keep simple thoughts locked out of her mind when there was no visual stimulation. Unfortunately, after only three months she asked to be reposted. She felt like she'd been living in Sodom and Gomorrah—although she was the only one thinking that way. The other missionaries were quite happy with their posting and confused by Dorcas's request. Much to Dorcas's great relief—and Satan's disappointment—the Mission Board complied.

Although every now and then when Dorcas would meet another single missionary lady for the first time, she would wonder why that woman was single. Was it because men were not exactly that woman's particular cup of tea—so to speak? Sometimes she was sure she detected something about the other woman that wasn't quite—well, "feminine." Of course, she never asked the woman for personal details; nor did she ever act on her thoughts— not once in fifty-four years. And although Dorcas had never, ever committed a single sexual act in all of her seventy-nine years, in the eyes of the Lord she was guilty of it too many times to count.

But yes, yes, she'd watched as Monsieur OP had drowned, and she'd prayed that at the last minute he'd repented in his heart for being a Catholic and was now well on his way to heaven. That was the best she could do. It was only a few minutes after he'd died, and the last ripples had settled on the pond, that a leopardess and two half-grown cubs padded silently out of the forest to the water's edge. There they lined up along an accessible stretch of bank and drank noisily. At that hour the almost rhythmic slurping produced by their wide tongues was the only sound audible to Dorcas. Their thirst slaked, the cubs engaged in some rough-and-tumble play until the mother cuffed one of them to signal it was time to retreat back into the shrinking shadows.

It was time for Dorcas to leave as well. Her plan had been thwarted by her arch nemesis: Johnnie. Johnnie Walker Black. He seemed to have a lot of friends among the Belgians, along with his friend and partial namesake, Johnnie Walker Red. The OP was supposed to have brought her some of his back stash of diamonds. It wouldn't have been as much as the original plan had called for, but something was better than nothing. One should always be grateful for something, and give God the glory, for He was the Ultimate Giver—"from whom all blessings flow." From whom everything flowed, right?

For that reason Dorcas was feeling utterly calm when she saw the next hurdle the Lord saw fit to set in her way. This was before she'd even left the gravel pits behind. Caught in the head beams of her car were Amanda Brown, two Africans, and most important, the Belgian girl whose life she had ruined by the abduction so many years ago. Dorcas drove slowly forward as she prayed for strength; then finding none forthcoming she forced herself to stop and got out of the car.

"*Muoyo wenu*," she said. Life to you.

"*Eh, muoyo webe*," the cluster of four said.

"What are you doing here?" Dorcas asked.

"This girl," Amanda Brown said, gesturing to the child, who should have gone by the name Danielle. "She desires only to go home. The stream that feeds these diamond-bearing gravel pits—uh—many, many miles from here this same stream passes through the valley behind her village. Theoretically, at least, it is possible for her to follow this stream and end up at home. I mean, it's been done once before."

"Then I am sure that it can be done again. Just now—*mene mene*—a leopard with her cubs came to drink at this pool. She would be glad to accompany the girl—at least part of the way. Then too they say that this valley, which may look like paradise to us Europeans, has one of the highest concentrations of black mambas in just about all of the Congo. And let me remind you that the mamba—*nyoka wa ntoka*—is one of the deadliest snakes there is."

"With respect, old woman," the Mushilele girl said, "I will not be made afraid by the likes of you. I will do what I must do."

"*Bimpe*," Dorcas said, with a smile. Good. "And so you must. In that case, if you dare to ride in my machine, I will drive you back to your village as far as the path will take us. Leopards and snakes will not be a problem, I assure you."

The girl had the courage to look her straight in the eyes. "The beast that belches and moves without legs does not frighten me; it scares only the little children and old women—such as you!"

Dorcas cackled with delight; they were a few precious seconds of blessed relief. "Well said, well said. Ah, how many will be coming with us?"

"I will," Amanda Brown said.

Dorcas swallowed. Speaking of snakes in Paradise; there was no need for the young American from South Carolina to ride along, now was there? But since Amanda Brown had been involved in the so-called rescue effort of the child whom Dorcas had abducted, then how could Dorcas refuse her?

"Anyone else?" Dorcas asked.

"My wife and I will return to our home," the African man said. Without wasting another word he turned and began pushing the wheelbarrow containing the housekeeper named Cripple.

Dorcas Middleton, a.k.a. the Mastermind, had never intended that any of the ransom money be used on her; her needs were simple—like those of a nun. No, the diamonds were to be converted into cash, which would be used for the Lord's work on the mission station of *Lubomo*. This was the mission station to which she had been temporarily assigned, and the one which was adjacent to Bashilele territory.

The plight of Bashilele girls had weighed heavy on Dorcas's heart. They were often betrothed before birth, as locally polygamy had reduced the availability of eligible girls. It had even given rise to the noxious custom of polyandry, whereby some women were obliged to take on more than one mate. Imagine that! So Dorcas felt called on by God to create a girls' boarding school where these child brides might take refuge and learn their ABCs, as well as their Bibles, instead of what it was like to give birth at age twelve or thirteen, when their pelvises had not yet obtained their full size.

To do this she needed money that the Mission Board claimed not to have—however, she knew that they would agree to the school if she were somehow able to finance it. (Perhaps Dorcas was an heiress and had conveniently neglected to mention that fact when she'd signed up to be a missionary or perhaps a favorite aunt had recently passed.)

After many years of faithful service to the Lord, God in His wisdom introduced her to the OP and his evil ways, and showed her the plan for taking back what was really the Africans' all along! And that's how she knew it was God and not the Devil speaking to her this time; because everything about the plan was *good*, just as God was good.

The diamonds belonged to the Africans, and it was the drunken Monsieur OP who was doing the stealing. God's plan for returning the profits to the natives was so very simple. Briefly, it went like this: she had given the OP's governess, Last Born Child, a gift of money—a retirement gift, if you will—in exchange for a small favor. In return, Last Born Child would deliver the OP's baby safely to the gravel pits, where Dorcas Middleton's houseboy would drive by to pick them both up.

The Gormans were, at the time, on furlough to America, leaving Dorcas alone on the mission station of *Mpata*. She envisioned keeping the infant girl no more than three or four days—after all, the Belle Vue vault was already bursting with diamonds. So not only would she get the ransom, but she would miraculously "find" the child on her doorstep and perhaps be the beneficiary of a reward as well. As for Last Born Child, she'd already observed so much deviant and abhorrent behavior on the part of Monsieur OP that she couldn't wait to get out of that house. There was no need to worry about her double-crossing Dorcas.

The Bashilele girls would be spared the horrors of child-marriage. A well-stocked clinic would be established along with the girls' school, saving an untold number of lives. The Africans would get back what was theirs to begin with.

No crime would have been committed; no sin would have been committed. At last Dorcas Middletown would be able to retire from the rigors of the Belgian Congo missionary field in peace.

The Gormans left the Missionary Rest House before first light. It was their assumption that both Dorcas Middleton and Amanda Brown were in their respective rooms sleeping off the effects of the party. After all, the noise had been loud enough to wake the dead up on the hill in the white cemetery. Gawd, if they knew what time Peaches had snuck back to her room, they'd have had a cow. Anyway, it was awfully rude of them to wake her up that early, before even the roosters up in the village had begun making their racket.

Now if they would just shut up and let her go back to sleep in the backseat. Mr. Gorman was confident that the quickest way to get back to the United States was through the city of Luluaburg. It was a large enough city to merit daily flights on Sabena Airlines to the capital city of Leopoldville. If memory served him right, he said, prattling on and on, and *on*, there were also daily flights to Elizabethville—still in the Belgian Congo—but there were twice-weekly flights to Johannesburg, South Africa, as well as to Salisbury, in Southern Rhodesia. Anyway, Mr. Gorman was going to make arrangements for someone at the Luluaburg mission to drive the car back to *Mpata* for him.

All that stuff was just yakkety-yak-yak except for the mention of Southern Rhodesia and Salisbury. Peaches Gorman had heard—from kids at her boarding school who had been lucky enough to go there—that Southern Rhodesia was practically like America. The whites all spoke English, as did almost all the blacks, there were lots of shops in Salisbury, and best of all, they had television. Oh, and the official religion was Protestant, not Catholic—not that Peaches much cared one way or another. But then again, there was no point really, in going all ape shit over a boy if your parents were just going to make you break up on account of some stupid religious customs made up by men in skirts.

Or on second thought, maybe there was a point after all: maybe there was a kick to be had in watching the old folks go all ape shit. Hmm, that was worth thinking about later, when her brain was sharper.

Oh phooey, look at the night watchman. He was asleep and didn't move one muscle when they drove by only an inch from his nose.

"Honk, Daddy," Peaches said. "Honk, please! Scare the pants off that old drunk! No wait; that might not be a pretty sight."

"Hush," Mrs. Gorman said. "Why I declare! I never raised you to talk like that."

"You didn't exactly raise me, Mama. You sent me off to boarding school when I was just seven years old. Remember?"

"But dear, I had no choice. Not if I was going to set about doing the Lord's work."

"Aren't *I* part of the Lord's work?"

"*Peaches*," Mr. Gorman roared. "Don't be a smart-mouth with your mother! If I have to, I'll pull over to the side of the road and perform a Proverbs 23:13 on you."

Peaches kept her teenage mouth shut for less than ten seconds; then it took on a life of its own and the words just *had* to come out. They truly did, or else she was going to burst, or perhaps die from a horrible internal itch that was worse than a million African chigger bites, which were, of themselves, a million zillion times worse than the ones in America.

"What's that stupid old verse say?" she said.

"That does it," Mr. Gorman snarled, but he didn't do anything drastic. He didn't even slow down. He had never intended to do so. Peaches Louise was the most spoiled child in all of Africa, and if she had lived in America, she would have been the most spoiled child in that country too, and she knew it.

"It says: 'Do not withhold correction from a child, for if you beat him with a rod, he will not die. You shall beat him with a rod, and deliver his soul from hell.'"

"That's just mean," Peaches said. "I thought the Bible was supposed to be a good book; about love and that kind of stuff."

"It is," Mr. Gorman said. "Don't you ever read it?"

"I'll have to agree with Peaches on this one," Mrs. Gorman said. "There are a lot of things in the Book of Proverbs that give me the willies."

"Woman!" Mr. Gorman thundered. "I turn your attention now to Proverbs 25:24: 'It is better to dwell in a corner of a house-top than a house shared with a contentious woman.' In my case, better make that two contentious women."

"Mr. Gorman," said Mrs. Gorman, "need I remind you that you are currently in a vulnerable position?"

Much to Peaches' utter astonishment, Mr. Gorman burst into tears. His shoulders shook and he started sputtering things about being sorry.

It was so embarrassing that Peaches wanted to die, except that there wasn't anyone around to see it except a man pushing his wife in a wheelbarrow. (At that moment they happened to be pass-ing the turnoff to Belle Vue's fabled gravel pits, with its storied ghosts.)

Now wait just one Alabama minute, as Grandma Gorman would say. Wasn't that woman in the wheelbarrow the same one who worked at the Missionary Rest House? Yes, for sure it was *Tshijeku*—Cripple.

One thing that set Peaches apart from her parents was that Peaches did not grow up thinking that all black people looked alike. It was probably safe to say that she had seen more black people in her short life than many much older black people in America had seen, or would ever see. Not only did she recognize individual traits, but she could often spot tribal similarities be-tween groups of related clans.

So when Peaches Gorman thought she saw Cripple in the dawn's early light, she was undoubtedly right. However, she saw no reason to tell her parents this rather interesting tidbit of infor-mation. Absolutely no reason at all.

And then something even more interesting happened, and because her parents were so embarrassing and so very mean, she certainly wouldn't tell them about this. Although you would think that they would notice that there was a car waiting at the turnoff to the gravel pit, and that there were three people inside. After all, it wasn't like the Congo was overrun with cars, especially once you got out of town.

Now if they had been as attuned to their surroundings as they were always hollering at her to be, then they would have seen the old lady, Aunt Dorcas, the kind of cool young one, Aunt Amanda, and the really strange Mushilele, Ugly Eyes. They would have also seen that about two Alabama minutes after they passed the turnoff, Aunt Dorcas—she was the driver—turned on to the Luluaburg/Belle Vue Road and appeared to be following them. Now how cool was that?

Peaches giggled softly while Mr. Gorman blubbered in the front seat and Mrs. Gorman alternated between words of comfort for her husband and prayers of strength for herself. What had begun as a long boring trip with two of the dullest people you could ever hope to meet on planet Earth had suddenly gotten a lot more interesting. Who cared anymore about Southern Rhodesia?

TWENTY-TWO

Monsieur Capitain," the houseboy said, gasping for breath. "You must come to see this!"

The man had been tapping on Pierre's window like a lunatic woodpecker. He was breathless, not from running so much as from laughing—laughing drunk. Every now and then the brazen fellow actually lost his balance and fell down in the bushes. Of course that set him off even more.

Finally, having ascertained that the houseboy was merely annoying rather than threatening, Pierre flung open the windows of his bedroom. "Go away," he growled in French. "I could arrest you for drunkenness, you know."

"But *Capitain*," the houseboy protested, "I am not drunk. I am merely amused beyond belief!"

"*Pardon?*"

"*Capitain*, I cannot to explain in this French. You must come and see."

"Do you speak Tshiluba?" Pierre asked in Tshiluba.

"*Eyo*. That is the language of my mother. But I cannot explain in Tshiluba either. Truly, truly. This is something that the eyes must see for themselves."

After firing off a string of invectives in a multitude of languages and dialects, Pierre pulled on his work khakis and a pair of shoes, and then vaulted out the window. This stunt of athleticism apparently delighted the houseboy to no end.

"Monsieur Capitain," he said in awe, "I have heard that you are not like the other *Bula Matadi*."

"In what way?"

"You are like a real person, *Capitain*."

Pierre couldn't help but smile. "Thank you."

"They say that you were born in the Congo and that you speak Tshiluba. Is that true?"

"Yes, I was born in Luluaburg."

"And do you speak Tshiluba?"

"What is your name?"

"*Musangu*."

"Listen to me well, Birthmark, what is the language that I am speaking now?"

Birthmark slapped his thighs with mirth. "*Capitain*, do you not see? You even have a sense of humor, unlike the white man!"

"What is it that you find humorous now, Birthmark?"

"*Capitain*, just now you started speaking in Tshiluba, but pretended that you did so all along."

"No, Birthmark, I truly was speaking in Tshiluba all along."

"*Aiyee*, Monsieur Capitain, so well do you speak, that I did not hear. On that account, when the revolution comes, I will not kill you, for truly you are one of us."

For the first time since meeting him, Pierre sensed that Birthmark was deadly serious.

"Thank you," Pierre said. "Now, is there not something you wish to show me?"

"*E, Capitain*. Come."

Birthmark started off at a trot toward the pretentiously named Boulevard des Allies, and then turned left along the boulevard, until just before it merged with the thick *tshisuku* and brush at the southern end of town. At that hour the almost unbroken canopy of dark green mango leaves overhead gave one the impression of being in a tunnel—that is to say, a tunnel with a dirt floor, and one which had hundreds of squeaking fruit bats returning to roost high in its rafters.

Pierre prided himself on being in shape, but he was no match for Birthmark. If, after the revolution, Birthmark reneged on his promise and decided to come after Monsieur Capitain, he was going to catch him, at this rate. He was huffing and puffing, and sweating like a Flemish whore when they arrived at the Cabochon residence.

"This is the home of my master," said Birthmark. "I will have no problem killing him."

"*Attention!*" Pierre barked in French. "You are speaking to a policeman."

"So?" said Birthmark with a grin and a shrug. "It will be our country then, will it not?" He lapsed back into his native tongue. "The *Bula Matadi* will be ours to do with as we please. Some we will put to work for us, as we have worked for them—as slaves in the past—and some we will kill—as they have killed so many of us. But as for this woman, and her enormous breasts and child-bearing hips, she will be mine. Now come and see what I have brought you to see. It is very, very humorous."

He switched on a flashlight and led Pierre through a hibiscus hedge and behind the outbuildings to the side yard that bordered on the wilderness. There, supine upon a mattress, and as intertwined as two copulating snakes, lay the stark naked forms of the Cabochons. Their alabaster skin was dotted with angry red welts, many of which had heads of driver ants still attached to them. Beside the mattress, on the short lawn grass, lay a rifle, a double-barreled shotgun, and two empty bottles of Johnnie Walker Black.

It was a scene straight out of one of his worst nightmares. *Mon Dieu*, he thought, what a waste! Two lives—just because of some damn ants. And that lovely body; it was a sin surely to look a second longer, but her right breast was splayed in his direction, her nipple erect in the cool morning air. And what was that tuft of hair peeking out from beneath Monsieur's leg? No! Madame Cabochon was not a natural redhead; she was barely even a brunette anymore. The graying sands of time were catching up with her.

Next, still acting *Police Capitain*, mind you, Pierre gave Monsieur Cabochon a cursory glance. The man was lying on his side with one leg and arm over his wife. His flaccid buttocks were concave, while his shriveled member was so short that it appeared to have gotten lost somewhere in his impressive black bush. Birthmark caught Pierre's eye and he burst into knowing laughter. "Monsieur Capitain," he said, when he could finally speak. "I have always wanted to know what a *Bula Matadi* looked like beneath his clothes. Do all white men have a *lubola* as short as this?"

Pierre was both amused and annoyed. "These people are dead, Birthmark. Do you want their spirits to follow you home?"

"But Monsieur Capitain, they are not dead; they are only drunk. See?" Birthmark poked at the outstretched hand of Madame Cabochon with what passed for a shoe. Madame Cabochon opened one eye, closed it, and then let out a belch that literally sent into flight a pair of purple plantain eaters that had spent the night in a breadfruit tree on the south edge of the lawn. Pierre found that he was so relieved that his mirth knew no bounds. He pounded the ground, he laughed so hard. In fact, between the pair of them—that is to say, Birthmark and Pierre—their rude behavior was at last responsible for rousing the soused couple and getting them into the house and possibly into some clothes.

When the door slammed behind them, Pierre turned to Birthmark in a more serious vein. "Friend," he said, "why is that you reported to work so early today?"

"It was the time I always come in, Monsieur Capitain. I must have the first cup of coffee ready for Monsieur Cabochon by five."

"In the *morning*?"

"Truly, truly."

"But that is ridiculous!"

"Monsieur Capitain, you are free to say that; I am not. That is, if I wish to keep my job."

"I see." Pierre turned to go. There were so many other people he needed to check on, things that he needed to get done today. "Birthmark," he said, "you'd better get started on that coffee. *Tuite suit.* No more looking at the white man's foolishness."

"*E.*"

"And just so you know; if you were ever to visit Belgium, no one would kill you—out of vengeance, I mean."

"They would have no reason to, monsieur."

TWENTY-THREE

There was so much Dorcas Middleton needed to confess, she didn't know where to begin. Amanda had insisted on sitting in the back, along with the OP's daughter, because Dorcas's panel truck had only two seats in front. That was when Dorcas pulled out the card of age and rank of senior missionary and practically ground them into the gravel under her high-heeled oxfords.

Now, with a sullen Amanda up front, she had to choose each word carefully. Her task, as she saw it, was not to exonerate herself—oh no, she was far too old to worry about her physical self. Her task was to see, now that there was no hope that the Bashilele could benefit from the OP and his diamond mine, that at least his daughter could.

"Amanda, I have committed a grievous sin."

"So have I," the girl said.

Oh my; that wasn't at all what Dorcas had been expecting. She couldn't help it if she choked on a few words and snorted—all of them unladylike sounds associated with women who have been living alone for too long.

Amanda ignored Dorcas's strange utterances. "I was involved in a drunken-driving accident that claimed the lives of eleven people," she said. "Was yours as grievous a sin as that? Every day I wonder what these people would be doing if they were still alive, because I knew them all—except for two, who were from out of town.

"These two were a middle-aged couple from Vermont that had just gotten married and had driven to the South on their honeymoon. They'd taken the small back roads because they thought they would be more scenic. They just didn't take into account a couple of cars full of drunken teenagers playing leapfrog with their cars up and down the hills of western York County."

Dorcas prayed for clear speech. "Amanda, if I understand the Bible correctly, there is no one sin greater than another. But the good news is that *all* sins can be forgiven—well, that is, all sins but that of rejecting God."

"What was your sin, Dorcas?"

The old woman resumed speaking again in a clear, strong voice. "The girl in the backseat—the girl you know as Ugly Eyes—I knew her as Danielle. *Before* she was abducted. I was invited to her christening. All the whites in the sector were invited to her christening in the Belle Vue Roman Catholic Church, and of course, that included all the Protestant missionaries.

"But this particular group of Protestants is a stiff-necked bunch and none of them would go—well, except for me. Thus began a friendship of sorts between myself and a number of the Belgians, the baby's mother in particular. You see, Heilewid was a very high-strung woman—neurotic even—very unsure of herself. She was in need of a good nanny—a *baba*—and had heard that the best *babas* were trained at Protestant mission schools, and could I recommend any. That's when Satan first put the plot in my mind."

Amanda turned, suddenly all ears. "What plot?"

"The plot to ease the plight of Bashilele girls—the ones who don't want to get married before they are physically developed."

"Please, go on; I'm afraid I don't understand."

"I needed money to do so. A great deal of money. So I kidnapped the daughter of the OP—the Consortium's OP. But something went terribly wrong, wouldn't you know, and the child went missing, even though no harm was to come to her."

Dorcas stopped there because she knew that Amanda was a very bright young woman, bright enough in fact to fill in the blanks. She didn't have long to wait.

"All this is because of you?" Amanda hissed.

"Yes, all this is because of me. And it gets even worse."

"It can't possibly." Amanda put her hands to her ears, but didn't cover them tightly. "I can't believe I'm hearing this. I can't believe a missionary is telling me this."

"Not that it makes any difference—because sin is sin—but I thought that the money that the Consortium was stealing from the natives might as well go to a good cause. The whole thing— my kidnapping plot—was supposed to last less than a week. More like three days."

Amanda pointed to Ugly Eyes in the backseat, acknowledging her presence for the first time. "And now this girl has to pay the price."

"Yes, she must pay the price." *And so must I,* Dorcas thought. *The girl is young; she has a fighter's spirit. She has it in her to survive, no matter what. But I am old; I will turn eighty next month on American Thanksgiving Day. However, I do not expect to celebrate, for what I have done will pull me down to my grave. The price that I will pay for having listened to Satan and concocting such a foolish plan, the price is my life. I feel it in my bones; I feel it in my soul. Redemption will only come with death.*

"Why do you take her back?"

"Because she wills it. She is like a flower that has been up-rooted and is wilting for lack of water. Amanda, you know it, and I know it; she is as African as your housekeeper, Cripple."

They rode in silence then until they reached the dirt path that led to Ugly Eyes' secluded village. Much to Dorcas's great surprise, before stepping out of the truck to say good-bye to her friends, Amanda laid her hand gently on Dorcas's arm.

"What you did was wrong," she said. "I'm not saying it wasn't. But if I had to choose between growing up as the OP's daughter and having this girl's father as my daddy, I think that I might pick the latter. Just as long as I didn't have to eat too many icky things."

"Or get married when you were ten," Dorcas said. Oh, why couldn't she leave well enough alone? But Amanda laughed— although perhaps nervously.

Then, after a moment of uncomfortable silence, for nobody had made a move to disembark, not even Ugly Eyes, Amanda removed her hand from Dorcas's arm, and then leaning away from her, cocked her head.

"What are you going to do next?" Amanda asked.

Dorcas knew exactly what she meant. "I plan to drive straight to Luluaburg and turn myself in to the provincial authorities there. I was hoping that you would come along so that you could drive the car back."

"Yes, yes, of course. But why not turn yourself in to Pierre?"

"I've known Pierre since he too was a baby, and I am ashamed to face him just now. Please, Amanda, allow an old lady this one piece of vanity."

"You bet," Amanda said, and she sounded every bit as sad as Dorcas felt. "Who am I to judge?"

Dorcas had driven as far as she could. From there the only way to reach the Bashilele village was to walk. Amanda couldn't help but feel relieved when the younger Ugly Eyes, the *real* Ugly Eyes, refused to allow them to journey with her farther.

It wasn't just the prospect of returning in the blazing sun, or being rewarded with aching muscles; she had the health of an octogenarian to be concerned about. All right, so there was more to it than that. Amanda shuddered every time she remembered the less-than-stellar reception she'd received her first time to the village. Now to return without the girl's father and with the girl herself very much changed—why, she would be nothing more than a thief returning damaged goods, and with half of them missing.

"We laugh and we cry," Ugly Eyes said to Dorcas. Thank you.

"Mmm," Dorcas grunted. She shook hands stiffly with the girl and then climbed back in her truck.

"Perhaps we will see each other again," Amanda said. Her eyes, which were fixed on an acacia tree halfway to the purple horizon, had begun to puddle."

Ugly Eyes said nothing for a long time and then: "When you see my father, please tell him where I am."

"Yes, of course."

Ugly Eyes coughed softly. It was the African's way of letting the European know that they had to get a move on. It was time to go.

"*Yaya bimpe,*" Amanda said. Go well.

"*Shala bimpe.*" Stay well.

You see? Amanda thought. The girl didn't really resent her. Someday soon, maybe very soon, like when independence came to the colony and the black population began to extract retribution against the whites—well, she'd think about that later. Like Scarlett O'Hara, she'd think about it tomorrow.

TWENTY-FOUR

Excuse me, madame," Detective Fermat said to Dorcas Middleton. "I mean this as kindly as possible, but has the sun cooked your brain?"

"That is very rude, monsieur," Amanda interjected. "This woman is eighty years old, for heaven's sake. Show her some respect!"

Since arriving in Luluaburg, almost three hours ago, Dorcas and Amanda had been put through the wringer—and now this! Yes, Amanda didn't have to be a part of this; she certainly could have dropped the elderly missionary off at the police headquarters and then driven off, but that was not in her nature. Well, she wished to heck it was now.

For starters, no one believed that an American missionary woman, acting alone, had kidnapped the baby in the famous Belle Vue kidnapping case. They couldn't even get past the outer lobby for the first hour. They couldn't even get behind the door marked *Les Blancs*. Whites.

Finally they were directed to an English-speaking detective, one who'd been educated at Cambridge, no less, but he was an insensitive idiot. Well, he'd underestimated Amanda Brown.

Maybe she lacked power, but she was chock full of persistence, and someday, somehow, she would make sure that he was going to get what he deserved.

"You see, mademoiselle," Detective Fermat said, turning to look directly at Amanda, as if he could read her thoughts, "in the old days, when people of Miss Middleton's generation—be they missionaries, government, or business, first arrived in the Belgian Congo, they were told that they simply must keep a pith helmet on their heads at all times. Only mad dogs and Englishmen went around bareheaded in the noonday sun, it was said. A tale was circulated of one man who challenged this edict and almost instantaneously dropped dead of heatstroke.

"But now I see that neither you, nor Miss Middleton, are wearing any type of head covering. So tell me, Miss Brown, has the sun cooled by a number of degrees, or have your brains cooked as well? That would certainly explain such a preposterous story."

"*Preposterous?*"

"Miss Brown, look here, even if you are telling the truth—I mean, what is the point in having the old gal confess?"

"*Because I'm guilty*," Dorcas said through clenched teeth. She'd been sitting quietly throughout Amanda's exchange with the detective. Her hands were folded in her lap and tears were coursing down the deep creases in her cheeks.

"Aha, so now you speak! Well then, answer my question, Miss Middleton. Have you been faithfully wearing your pith helmet every time you step outside, particularly between the hours of ten in the morning and four in the afternoon?"

"No, sir, I have not. But I have lived in the Congo so many years that—"

"That's just it, isn't it? You have lived in the Congo *too* many years. This type of dementia is very common amongst members of the Caucasian race who have lived too long in equatorial lands, especially those who have not bothered to cover their heads.

Madame, I cannot take your confession seriously. I will, however, make reference to your visit in my notes. In the meantime, I suggest that you see a doctor for treatment."

"Treatment?" Dorcas cried. "For what?"

"My dear, for heat-induced dementia." Detective Fermat turned to Amanda. "Perhaps I should be speaking to you."

"This is outrageous," Amanda said, her voice rising a full octave.

Detective Fermat cocked his head, a sad smile appeared briefly on a face lined by cares far more important than the bizarre tale spun by two crazy American missionaries. "What would you have me do?" he said. "Shall I call in a magistrate? Shall I arrange for a trial and send this old woman to prison for the rest of her life? No? Oh, that's right, because here, in the Belgian Congo, we hang kidnappers."

"I—I—well, I originally came just to give her comfort," Mademoiselle Amanda Brown said. She began to cry.

"That's what I thought," Detective Fermat said. It was absolutely impossible for an American missionary to even contemplate kidnapping the infant daughter of an important Belgian company official like the Operations Manager of the Consortium Mining Company of Belle Vue. Therefore, these women were utterly confused, did not belong in his office, and were both wasting his valuable time. "Please see yourselves out," he said tiredly.

"Yes sir," Amanda said. It was difficult to say who was crying harder at this point: Mademoiselle Brown, or Mademoiselle Middleton.

"Just one last detail, Mademoiselle Brown."

"Yes," Mademoiselle Brown blubbered.

"Captain Pierre Jardin of Belle Vue called in via shortwave radio this morning."

The young woman blushed. "*Oui?*"

"He was worried about you. He said there was no one at the

missionary residence except a man with an enlarged navel"—
the detective glanced down at his scribbles on a piece of yellow
paper—"and he spoke to a crippled woman. At any rate, he had a
hunch that you might be headed here, so I wasn't exactly unpre-
pared."

"Pierre *knows*? I don't see how—"

"Mademoiselle, this is a man you may wish to keep—if you
know what I mean."

"She does, and she will," Mademoiselle Middleton said. She
didn't sound the least bit addled then.

The sun was warm on Ugly Eyes' back as she topped the last rise.
Ahead lay her village, just as she remembered it, as if nothing out
of the ordinary had happened in the last few days. Of course for
the village, nothing untoward *had* happened. Roosters crowed,
hens clucked, goats bleated, smoke rose from cook fires, babies
cried, and women laughed. Women *laughed*.

The laughter of women as they set about doing their daily
chores. Next to her mother, *that* is what Ugly Eyes had missed the
most about village life. White people were so serious, their mouths
perpetually pulled down at the corners, their foreheads so quick
to pucker. Ugly Eyes did not know of a single village woman who
bore a vertical crease between her eyes, yet almost every woman at
the party the night before had at least the beginnings of one.

Although she had not so much as closed her eyes the night
before, the sight of her village filled her with new energy and her
feet became light and swift like that of a gazelle. As she neared
the first houses children ran out to greet her and follow along,
as did their dogs, and soon, there was a great pack, composed of
dozens of young, strong legs pounding the smooth packed earth,
practically in unison.

"What is it?" this woman or that would ask in a startled voice.

"It is only Ugly Eyes, the Headhunter's Daughter. She returns
by herself."

"Is he dead?" someone asked.

"He is dead," another answered.

And so by the time Ugly Eyes wound her way around the spiral and into the heart of the village, where her parents' hut stood, Mother had heard the word that Father was dead. The message had rung true to her heart, but she waited until she saw her daughter before dropping to the ground in order that they might express their grief together.

"Wait!" Ugly Eyes pulled at her mother's arms. "Mother, from whom did you hear this news?"

Mother rose to her knees. She wished to bury her face in her daughter's familiar scent, but it was no longer there. Instead, her daughter had no smell; at best she smelled like springwater.

"Listen, the cry goes up throughout the village; your father is dead."

"That is because I have returned alone. These people know nothing."

"*Eyo*, but my heart knows. News of your father's death was carried by the unseen spirits that accompanied you. At first it was a whisper so soft that I could not be sure of what was said, but now I hear the spirits clearly, and they are shouting your father's name alongside the voices of our people."

"*Aiyee*," Ugly Eyes cried. "This cannot be so!"

"But it is so, my daughter. For why else would you leave the village of the white man and return here without your father?"

"I do not know, Mother. Truly, I do not know! There was an opportunity which presented itself, and Father could not be found—"

Mother remained kneeling and clasped her odorless, weeping daughter tightly to her bosom. "Listen to me," she said, "for this is a matter of great importance."

"*E*."

"Yesterday the slave chief ordered the village to move, but I would not, because I feared that your father might have difficulty in finding us. On my account Iron Sliver would not leave, and soon another would not leave, and then another, and then so on, until it was decided by the village council that we would all remain here waiting for word from either you or your father. After all, the manioc has already been planted, and the game is plentiful, now that rains have come and the new grass sprouts forth."

"How did the slave chief react when the people disobeyed his order?" Ugly Eyes said.

"Let us just say that he is no longer our chief."

Ugly Eyes grunted softly.

"Your father was selected as our chief. It is to be a hereditary position."

"But Mother, that means—"

"Yes, Ugly Eyes, you have discerned the matter correctly. Both the witch doctor and the wise woman predicted that you would return someday, and who better to lead our people than someone who knows the mind of the enemy? Besides, child, is it not true that there is a segment of the Bakuba people that is led by a queen? And she is a very great leader, I have heard."

"But I am, as you have just said, a child. I cannot lead anyone!"

"You show promise in that statement, Ugly Eyes. It is something that most members of the council have already observed for themselves. They have already said that in a case such as this they will lead on your behalf until such a time that you feel comfortable enough to rule. Then you will step in and your name will be changed from Ugly Eyes to *Nfumu Mukashi*—Woman Queen."

"Mother, I do not want this; I want only that Father should return!"

"*E.*" Mother pulled gently away from her daughter's embrace. "Ugly Eyes, it is time to listen to the spirits that brought news of your father's death. Will you not join me in the mourning rituals?"

"No, Mother, I will not. I do not believe that my father is dead; I will stand and wait for his return."

Ugly Eyes waited for a very long time.

AFTERWORD

On September 21 (which is my birthday), but in the year 1757, my eight times grandfather, Joseph Hochstetler, along with his father and one brother, were taken captive by a band of Delaware Indians during the height of the French and Indian War. This occurred in Berks County, Pennsylvania.

Two days earlier the Amish family had looked out of their cabin to see a raiding party of Indians in full war paint standing near their bake oven. The two boys, ages ten and twelve, immediately begged their father to allow them to defend themselves with their hunting guns. But the family patriarch refused his permission; the Amish are pacifists and believe that there is no justification for taking a human life—not even in defense of one's own life.

The Delaware began their attack by shooting flaming arrows at the cabin. It soon caught on fire and the Hochstetler family took refuge in the cellar. As it was autumn, the cellar had just been stocked with barrels of apple cider, so as the cabin burned to the ground over their heads, the family splashed the juice on the ceiling in order to keep the thick wood planks from burning all the way through and collapsing on them.

The family waited patiently until the ashes above them had

cooled and they were sure the raiding party was gone. Then, one by one, they climbed out of a small cellar window. Unfortunately for them a young warrior known as Tom Lions had remained behind to gather ripe peaches from around the family's fruit trees. When Tom saw the family emerge he called out to the others, who then descended upon the family and began the massacre.

That morning my many times great aunt (only two years old!) was tomahawked and scalped, and my many times great uncle (a boy about eight) was likewise tomahawked and scalped. Their mother, the patriarch's wife, was apparently especially disliked by this particular band of Delaware. She was fat, and had gotten stuck in the cellar window. Instead of being tomahawked, which was an honorable way of dying; she was stabbed through the heart and then scalped.

The patriarch and his two older sons were taken captive. My ancestor, Joseph, was ten years old at the time. His father had advised him to stuff his pockets with fallen peaches as there was no telling when they would have their next meal. After a long march they arrived at the large village presided over by an important chief. Immediately the Hochstetlers presented him with the fruit Joseph had carried with him.

The chief was so impressed by the gesture that, instead of turning the captives over to be tortured in the traditional manner by the squaws, he decreed that their lives should all be spared. My ancestor Joseph was subsequently separated from his father and brother and taken to a different village. There a ceremony was conducted wherein Joseph was led down to a river by three Indian women and then plunged underwater. He was then held underwater while they vigorously rubbed his body, symbolically washing away his white blood. Later, in the council house, with all the Indians dressed and painted to the hilt, the chief delivered a formal speech of adoption.

In *Descendants of Jacob Hochstetler* (Joseph's Father), by Harvey Hostetler, which is a genealogical compendium of my ancestors and relations, there is an account of what was most certainly a similar adoption speech. It was delivered to James Smith, also of Pennsylvania, who was captured in the year 1755. It can be found on page 35 of the Hostetler book. It is, in part, as follows:

> My son, you are now flesh of our flesh, and bone of our bone. By the ceremony which was performed this day, every drop of white blood was washed out of your veins . . . you have nothing to fear; we are now under the same obligations to love, support, and defend you, that we are to love and defend one another. Therefore you are to consider yourself as one of our people.

Now that he was a full-blooded Delaware Indian—and no longer an Amish boy of Swiss ancestry—Joseph was given to an Indian family to raise. He lived with his new family for nine years, growing to love his new parents and his new siblings. When at last Joseph was returned to his original family, he was nineteen years old. By then he spoke only the Delaware language, having forgotten all of his native German, except for a few words of the Lord's Prayer.

Like many released captives Joseph did not want to go back home. He saw himself as an Indian, and home was with his tribe. In fact, for hundreds of captives that were released at the close of the French and Indian War, reunion with their birth families was a very painful process, one that involved many tears. It was recorded that their Indian families cried as well, begging them to come and visit whenever they had the chance. And they did.

For the rest of his life my eight times grandfather, Joseph Hochstetler, lived between two worlds. Whenever he could, it was written, he hunted and played sports with his Indian friends. You see, one is not just the color of one's skin; one is also the color of one's heart.

A⁺

AUTHOR
INSIGHTS,
EXTRAS &
MORE...

FROM
TAMAR
MYERS
AND
AVON A

The Author Answers Some of Your Questions

The interviewer is Devil's Advocate (D.A.).

D.A.: When and where were you born?

Author: I was born in 1948 in the Belgian Congo. The country is now called the Democratic Republic of the Congo—although it is anything but a true democracy. At any rate, it is one of the largest countries in Africa and straddles the equator right in the heart of the continent.

D.A.: Is it true, as you claim, that you were raised with a tribe of head-hunters? That seems to be so preposterous as to be a gimmick to sell your books.

Author: It is indeed true. After my parents had been in the Congo for eighteen years—having arrived in 1932—they were asked if they would be the first of their affiliation to establish a mission station among the Bashilele tribe. At that time the Bashilele were known as fierce warriors who didn't take kindly to outsiders. Their coming-of-age custom for boys—think Bar Mitzvah—was to kill a man from another tribe. That man's skull became the boy's wine mug.

D.A.: Well then, how did you and your family survive?

Author: First of all, we didn't violate any of their sacred taboos. Sadly, the previous missionary, who was of a different faith, immediately began to chop down the villagers' sacred tree, The Tree of Life. His head became the witch doctor's drinking cup.

D.A.: Oh my! It must have been really strange growing up with these people. What was it like? How did you feel about it as a child?

Author: It wasn't strange at all; it was normal for me! Strange was coming to America. Strange was seeing the Midwestern countryside chopped up by fences—fences everywhere you looked. And pavement!

D.A.: What kind of house did you live in? What sorts of foods did you eat?

Author: I was born in a brick house on an established mission station. When my parents accepted the challenge to work among the headhunters I was two years old. My three sisters were five, seven, and sixteen, respectively, going up the ladder. We all lived at first in a house made of palm leaf stems (probably *Raphia hookeri*) and palm leaf thatch of the same species. This was the same material that the local people used when they built their huts.

At any rate, our house soon became a live-in buffet for millions of termites. It got to the point that just by pressing the walls one could get the entire house to commence shuddering as the insects "sprang to life." Later my father built a concrete block house with a corrugated iron roof and we felt like we were living in a palace.

For food we relied heavily on canned goods that were shipped up by sea from South Africa, then by riverboat up the Congo River and its tributary, the Kasai, and lastly, carried overland by truck. Beef arrived by special bicycle messenger overland through the forest and the beef often wore a shimmer of green, so Mother cooked it until it resembled black shoe leather—but it is a taste I still enjoy. Occasionally we ate game, such as antelope, wild boar, guinea, and francolin. Once my mother even served us "hamburgers" made from an elephant's trunk. She cooked these in a pressure cooker before pan-frying them to make them brown like real burgers. At boarding school—more on that later—we ate a lot of buffalo meat and hippopotamus meat.

D.A.: What did the Bashilele people eat? And tells us how they lived.

Author: The local people ate a very limited diet. They relied heavily on the manioc plant which was imported to Africa from Brazil centuries earlier. All parts of the plant are poisonous (they contain strychnine). The roots, which form the bulk of their diet, must be soaked in running water for three days. They are then dried in the sun and pounded into flour. The flour is subsequently stirred into boiling water until it forms a very stiff mush that is molded into a ball. When it is served, the person eating it tears off a piece and shapes it into a scoop using his thumb and forefinger. They he scoops up a palm oil gravy that may or may not contain some bit of protein, and the boiled leaves of the manioc plant (they must be boiled and drained twice to rid them of the strychnine).

The Bashilele men were renowned hunters. They hunted with bows and arrows. The bows were tightly strung and six feet tall. The arrowheads, made of hand-smelted steel and mounted on lightweight palm-wood shafts, came in a variety of shapes and sizes; each style had a different purpose. There were arrowheads for shooting down the giant locusts that flew like birds across the savannah skies to arrowheads meant to lodge deep into the hide of very large antelope, like kudu. Even an arrowhead this size could not bring such a large animal down immediately, but it could cause it to bleed considerably, allowing the Bashilele, along with their barkless dogs, the basenji, to chase the prey until it had "bled out." But when game was scarce the tribe relied on alternate sources of protein such as grasshoppers, grubs, bird eggs, snakes, etc.

D.A.: You mentioned boarding school in the book. Is that how you received your education?

Author: Yes. I was homeschooled for grades one and two. From third grade on, I was sent to a boarding school two days' drive away. Sixty-five kids attended the school altogether—all of them white, and most, but not all of them, American. About ten children lived on my "route." The two-day trip in a panel truck along a dirt track included three ferry crossings, one of which was always quite an adventure. You see, the Loange River was in Bapende territory, and the Bapende in years past had been cannibals. The people still filed all of their teeth to points and wore their hair in elaborate mud cones decorated with porcupine quills.

The Loange ferry consisted of dugout canoes lashed together and then straddled by a wooden platform. The ferrymen with their pointed teeth and mud cones would pole their way across this very wide muddy brown river and greet us with the chant: "*Tende mah-ye, tende mah-ye-he, wo-tende-mah-ye.*" Getting the truck onto the ferry was always exciting to watch, and we got to see it several times in one afternoon because there were huge underwater sandbars in the river that necessitated lightening the ferry load. Here the truck had to drive through the water and we children had to wade. To add to the excitement, the river was home to hippopotamuses and crocodiles. The latter could sneak up on us without our knowledge and snatch us in their powerful jaws. We successfully avoided that by holding hands and shouting, to make it seem as if we were one large animal instead of ten small frightened children.

D.A.: Were there any other dangers you faced during this period?

Author: Yes. In many cases the Belgians had treated the Congolese cruelly, so a lot of resentment had built up against whites in general. This was especially so if you were unknown to the locals. As the time for independence drew near, the Africans grew bolder and their behavior became—well, perhaps "combative" is the word. Here is one event I will never forget:

We were making the two-day trek back from boarding school and had stopped for a picnic in a clearing surrounded by elephant grass. Of course we didn't have ice and thus no way to keep perishables, so when we traveled, we usually ate sandwiches of canned Spam. On this day no sooner did we settle in to eat, then suddenly out of the elephant grass poured about a dozen African boys, all begging for the empty Spam tin. They spoke in a language we did not know, but it was very clear what they wanted.

You see, at that time, in their society, a tin can was an extremely useful commodity. It could be used as a small cooking pot, turned into a cutting instrument, shaped as an arrowhead, or even fashioned into jewelry. I had even seen a Spam tin given new life as a pair of dentures. At any rate, my mother gave me the job of deciding which of the boys would be the lucky one to receive this treasure. Unfortunately, although I had a very generous eleven-year-old heart, I also thought with an eleven-year-old's brain. I thought the fairest thing would be if I tossed the can up in the air and let them scramble for it.

Well, they scrambled for it! However, in the ensuing melee one of the boys received a laceration on his scalp from the sharp edge of the Spam can. Although the wound was shallow, it bled profusely. Then before we could offer him first aid, several angry young men emerged from the elephant grass and strode over to us. Although language was a problem, they spoke some French, and my mother spoke a smidgen of it. We understood enough to know that they were demanding an enormous sum of money on the boy's behalf—but refusing first-aid care—and that if we didn't pay it, they were going to take me as a hostage. Forty thousand francs was about eight hundred dollars, which is about ten thousand dollars in today's money. Since my parents only made a thousand dollars a year, there was no way that my mother would have had that much cash on her.

Quietly, but firmly, my mother and the male driver ordered the ten missionary children back into the panel truck. Meanwhile the young men grew angrier and their threats more violent. If we fled, they said, we would be met by a roadblock—they would send a signal by drums to the next village—and instead of just being held captive, I would be taken off the truck and killed. But flee, we did. And when we approached the next village, I was instructed to lie flat on the floor of the truck, while the driver pressed the pedal to the metal. It was something we would repeat for the next several villages until we were well into another tribe's territory. We did not encounter any roadblocks that day, but needless to say, on subsequent trips to and from boarding school, we skipped that clearing in the elephant grass when it came to choosing a picnic location.

D.A.: Goodness gracious! What else? Do tell!

Author: Well, just a few months later the chief of the Bashilele village nearest where we lived appeared on our front verandah during our noon meal. We were used to be being observed while we ate—we had the funny habits, after all—but usually the observers were women and children, not a chief and his warriors. So my father went out to see what this man wanted.

D.A.: And?

Author: The chief said that when independence came he was going to move into our house. He was also going to take us girls as his wives.

D.A.: So what did your father tell him in response?

Author: He told the chief that he wasn't going to get his daughters and that he better get off our porch. So the chief left, but not before threatening to burn us out of the house.

D.A.: Did that ever happen?

Author: No. We left the Congo for America for a year-long furlough just one month before Independence Day. However, we were one of the very first white families to return to the interior of the country. By then many whites had been killed, tortured, and raped. It was a very difficult time to grow up—especially since now there was a tribal war waging between the Baluba and Lulua tribes and we found ourselves caught smack-dab in the middle.

D.A.: We'll get to that in a moment, but I want to backtrack a bit and ask you about boarding school in the Belgian Congo when you were younger. Would you please describe that?

Author: My sisters will hate my answer because I'm a more negative, less forgiving person. Well, to begin with, like I said before, there were sixty-five children and one set of houseparents—at least for my first two years. The only way to maintain discipline in that kind of situation—or so they thought—was to beat us for even minor infractions. For instance, my first morning there, as part of an initiation process, I was yanked out of bed by some high school students before the six-thirty gong had sounded, which was against the rules. Following classes that afternoon I was soundly beaten. Another time in sixth grade the school principal beat me with a mahogany cane until he was out of breath—paused to rest—and then resumed beating me. This was just because I did not understand long division and had not completed my math homework.

Sure, there were good times, like playing "lion and sheep" on Friday nights. The thrill of this game was heightened by the fact that the school was located in real lion territory and employed a hunter, named Samson, whose job it was to keep track of how close lions were to the campus. On days when lions were within a couple of miles, our activities were restricted. Anyway, one day when real life got to be too much I told the housefather I'd had enough of his cruelty and was going to run off into the forest. He told me to go ahead and to get a sandwich from the kitchen first—which I did. I'd gone less than a quarter of a mile from the campus when I heard a lion roar and came hightailing it back. When I reported the lion to the housefather he merely laughed. It's possible that he'd known about it all along.

The school followed an extremely conservative Protestant theology. As a child I lived in constant fear of hellfire and damnation and being left behind. We were forever confessing to sins we couldn't possibly have committed and yearning for our mansions in the sky. Our dorm was built at the very top of a steep hill, and when viewed from below the clouds seemed to sweep over it. One day a friend and I were playing below the dorm when a cloud appeared to land on just the other side of it. My little friend and I were positive that this was the Second Coming and that the cloud held none other than Jesus himself. We raced up the hill, our lungs bursting, lest we miss the big event and be left behind. Imagine then both our disappointment and relief to discover that this had been simply an optical illusion.

D.A.: Okay, now you're straying into dangerous territory of another kind, Tamar. You know that you're going to get some flak for this. Maybe it's time to skip ahead to the tribal war.

Author: I couldn't agree more. Indeed, I'm sure it was my own fault that I allowed tales of eternal torture to haunt me in the third grade. Now a word about the civil war: one possibly good side-effect of colonial rule (others will hotly dispute this viewpoint) is that it put a lid on tribal warfare. The Baluba and Lulua peoples were linguistic cousins who had, at times, lived peacefully with each other and often intermarried. The war actually began before independence, but erupted with renewed vigor afterward. In the end hundreds of thousands of people died on both sides.

At any rate, the site for my fictional town of Belle Vue was the real city of Tshikapa. It was, and still is, famous for its diamonds. After independence the Belgians fled, leaving a ghost town of sprawling villas on the hills above the Kasai and Tshikapa Rivers. We leased one of these villas. At that time the Baluba tribe was predominately situated on one side of the Kasai River, and Lulua tribe on the other—well, that is they were so after a refugee exchange. Then machine-gun fortifications were installed along the hilltop above our villa and across the river at a lower elevation.

The gunners were aiming at each other, not us, but unfortunately our house got right in the way. When shooting commenced we had to crawl around on our hands and knees. Then one night my parents came into my bedroom with news that the opposing tribe was expected to breach defenses and make it across the bridge that night. As we were ensconced with the enemy—well, let's just say that my mansion in the sky was dusting off its welcome mat again.

"But," Daddy said, "there's that nook there above your bedroom door, where we store the suitcases. Stay in your room, and don't come out, no matter what you hear. Just climb into that nook and pull that big suitcase in front of you. Your mommy and I might be killed, but if you survive maybe you can slip down to the river unseen. Just follow the river south. Then keep going until you reach Angola."

D.A.: And?

Author: Well, obviously I survived.

D.A.: *Yes, but did they—I mean, what happened that night? Don't leave us hanging!*

Author: I honestly can't remember the rest of the night. We weren't attacked; I know that much. But later our African neighbors were—they at least had their car burned in their driveway. Then I never saw them again. I have a lot of memory gaps of that period. Forty-six years later I still listen for the sound of footsteps under my window; I listen for men coming to hack me into pieces with machetes.

D.A.: *Now you've done it again; you've forced me to change subjects. You haven't talked much about animals. Did you have many animal experiences?*

Author: Not really. My part of Africa was a mixture of savannah and forest, situated along the southern edge of the Congo rainforest. It was forests in the valleys where there were streams, and tall grass on the hills and plains. There were no open grazing lands capable of supporting large herds like in East Africa. Most of the animals I saw were either on my dinner plate or staring into the headlights of our panel truck at night.

One night my uncle (a mere lad in his twenties and fueled by testosterone) purposely ran over a leopard in the road and then tossed it in the back of the truck where we three children were sitting. The leopard was dead, but every time we hit a bump its giant paw would jiggle, causing us to shriek in abject terror. My uncle was thoroughly amused. Oh, lest I forget, my father was bitten by a deadly green mamba—and yes, he survived.

D.A.: *Tamar, before we wrap this conversation up, is there anything else you'd like to share about the headhunters? Did you get a chance to learn any of their customs?*

Author: My father was a man of many interests, including anthropology. From the time he arrived in the Belgian Congo he began taking and keeping notes. He also wrote to his mother in the States on a regular basis. My grandmother saved the letters. When she died the letters were returned to my father and now I am their keeper. Most of my knowledge comes either directly from him or his writing. Very little of it is firsthand because I was a child at the time, and even though I had close *Mushilele* friends, topics I am about to discuss are not ones children normally talk about with their friends.

D.A.: Such as? I mean, should we be warning sensitive readers that they may wish to set your book down at this point?

Author: Absolutely. If they have queasy stomachs or have trouble remembering that this was the situation in the first half of the twentieth century in traditional tribal culture of this *one* tribe, then they should stop reading now. By the way, I have no idea how things stand now. I'm not even going to guess.

D.A.: Okay then, I think that's enough of a warning. What unusual custom pops into your mind first?

Author: Burial customs—actually, they involve burial except for one. And that's polyandry. Did you know that the Bashilele are one of the few polyandrous societies in the world?

D.A.: Uh—no, because I don't know what polyandry means. Please explain.

Author: Polyandry is when a woman has more than one husband.

D.A.: Ouch!

Author: My thoughts exactly. But it can be to her advantage. With multiple husbands she and her children are ensured of being supplied with food and shelter. And she gets to select the additional husbands—just not the first one; that's her father's choice.

D.A.: So how did this unusual custom come about?

Author: It's a response to polygamy. When all the available young women are taken, what are the young men supposed to do? Sharing a wife keeps them from stealing another man's wife or engaging in bloody battles for the right to breed. But when a young girl does come of age and can be purchased by one of the husbands in a polyandrous relationship, he may disengage from that relationship and start his own new family. It is really a rather clever social construct when you think about it.

D.A.: If you say so. I'm afraid many readers with a traditional view of marriage are going to find the concept offensive.

Author: I only "report the news." Besides, isn't *our* system of marriage, divorce, and remarriage a form of *serial* polyandry?

D.A.: Now you've really gone too far. Please, let's move on to burial.

Author: (Sigh.) Let's begin with an ordinary death. Let's say Grandpa dies from choking on his manioc mush. Grandpa has grandchildren and other kinfolk in a number of scattered villages, and getting them all together for the funeral will take weeks, not days. Plus, food will need to be collected for the feasting and dancing that are part of the celebration. The total amount of time needed might be as much as three months. This is the tropics we are talking about, so what is the family supposed to do with Grandpa in the meantime?

Ah, the answer is simple. Every Mushilele hut contained a smoking rack, centered over the fire pit. As the family cooked their meals on rainy days, or warmed themselves on chilly nights, they would also be preserving fish, game, herbs, or whatever. Now it's time to move over food and put up Grandpa. Keep the fire going. Of course Grandpa will be oozing juices and fat, which will drip down into the cooking pot. By the way, that is not cannibalism; it is simply passing Grandpa's good qualities on to the next generation.

Hey, you haven't started to judge, have you? Because I can say plenty about silk-lined, bronze caskets with puffy pillows in this country, while across from the cemetery children go to bed hungry.

D.A.: Truce, shall we?

Author: Hmm. All right, but you won't be happy because I'm going to talk about twins.

D.A.: Twins?

Author: Yes—and here is where sensitive readers *must* stop reading. What I'm about to say will be really hard for most Westerners to absorb.

D.A.: Proceed. We've been sufficiently warned—I think.

Author: You see, in many tribes in my area twins were considered taboo. After all, everyone knows that it is normal to have just one baby at a time. Therefore, when a second, or third, baby shows up, then the spirit world is obviously up to mischief. Unfortunately there is no way to tell which child is the authentic twin, and which one is really an evil spirit masquerading as a human twin. The solution then is to kill both babies, thus ensuring that the evil spirit can do the tribe no harm. This is done by shoving hot peppers up the babies' nostrils and burying them alive in an ant hill. This is not to hurt the children, mind you, but to torment the evil spirit. The suffering baby is collateral damage. It sounds terrible, I know, but we "civilized" people have done things equally terrible, and on a much larger scale.

D.A.: Are you getting political here? Because if you are, then this interview is over. Besides, we no longer use napalm—that was the Vietnam War.

Author: Good example, but relax. I'm just relating customs, and I only have one more. This one is about the chief and his wife. A Mushilele chief is quite often not a Mushilele by birth; he is usually a slave that was kidnapped or traded from another tribe. The reason for that was because when the tribe misbehaved—in the eyes of the Belgians, that is—it was often the chief who was punished instead of the entire tribe.

D.A.: Oh, I get it! If a foreigner was chief, it really didn't matter if he got punished.

Author: Exactly. But there were perks for being chief. You had real power, which led to riches, which led to lots of wives. And there were perks to being a chief's wife, like having your own hut, and not having to sleep with the old coot that often. However, there was one very, *very* major downside to being a Mushilele queen.

D.A.: Uh-oh. I'm afraid to ask. (Sigh.) Bring it on.

Author: When the chief died, his wives—all of them, be it just one, or even thirty—had to accompany him, *live*, to the next world. As you can imagine, the royal women were not happy about being buried alive with their husband, so they had both arms and both legs broken so that they could not dig their way out of the communal grave.

D.A.: Stop! I can't take any more of this—really.

Author: I understand. I did try to warn you, however. Maybe we can talk a little bit more when my next book comes out. I have a lot more I could talk about.

D.A.: Maybe. What is the title of your next book in the series?

Author: *The Cannibal's Confession.*

Photo by Penny Young

TAMAR MYERS was born and raised in the Belgian Congo (now just the Congo). Her parents were missionaries to a tribe which, at that time, were known as head-hunters and used human skulls for drinking cups. Hers was the first white family ever to peacefully coexist with the tribe.

Tamar grew up eating elephant, hippopotamus, and even monkey. She attended a boarding school that was two days away by truck, and sometimes it was necessary to wade through crocodile-infested waters to reach it. Other dangers she encountered as a child were cobras, deadly green mambas, and the voracious armies of driver ants that ate every animal (and human) that didn't get out of their way.

Today Tamar lives in the Carolinas with her American-born husband. She is the author of thirty-six novels (most of which are mysteries), a number of published short stories, and hundreds of articles on gardening.

Tamar Myers